Dedalus Europe
General Editor: Timoth

THE PRICE OF DREAMS

Patricia Highsmith,
the novel of her life

Margherita Giacobino

THE PRICE
OF
DREAMS

Patricia Highsmith,
the novel of her life

translated by Christine Donougher

Dedalus

Supported using public funding by
**ARTS COUNCIL
ENGLAND**

Published in the UK by Dedalus Limited
24-26, St Judith's Lane, Sawtry, Cambs, PE28 5XE
email: info@dedalusbooks.com
www.dedalusbooks.com

ISBN printed book 978 1 910213 95 7
ISBN ebook 978 1 912868 18 6

Dedalus is distributed in the USA & Canada by SCB Distributors
15608 South New Century Drive, Gardena, CA 90248
email: info@scbdistributors.com   web: www.scbdistributors.com

Dedalus is distributed in Australia by Peribo Pty Ltd.
58, Beaumont Road, Mount Kuring-gai, N.S.W. 2080
email: info@peribo.com.au

First published by Dedalus in 2020

Il prezzo del sogno © *2017 Mondadori libri S.p.A., Milano*
This translation has been made possible thanks to the mediation of r. vivien literary
agency - Padova, Italy

The right of Margherita Giacobino to be identified as the author and Christine
Donougher as the translator of this work has been asserted by them in accordance
with the Copyright, Designs and Patents Act, 1988.

Printed and bound in Great Britain by Clays Elcograf S.p.A
Typeset by Marie Lane

The Author

Margherita Giacobino, born in 1952, lives in Turin. She is a writer, journalist and translator. She has translated, among others, Emily Bronte, Gustave Flaubert, Margaret Atwood, Dorothy Allison and Audre Lorde.

She made her debut in 1993 with the novel *Un'Americana a Parigi* written under the pseudonym of Elinor Rigby. Her latest novel, *L'Età ridicola*, was published in 2018.

Her novel *Portrait of a Family with a Fat Daughter* was published in English by Dedalus in 2017, to great acclaim.

The Translator

Christine Donougher was born in England in 1954. She read English and French at Cambridge and after a career in publishing is now a freelance translator and editor.

Her translation of *The Book of Nights* won the 1992 Scott Moncrieff Translation Prize. Her translations from French for Dedalus are seven novels by Sylvie Germain: *The Book of Nights*, *Night of Amber*, *Days of Anger*, *The Book of Tobias*, *Invitation to a Journey*, *The Song of False Lovers* and *Magnus*, *Enigma* by Rezvani, *The Experience of the Night* by Marcel Bealu, *Le Calvaire* by Octave Mirbeau, *Tales from the Saragossa Manuscript* by Jan Potocki, *The Land of Darkness* by Daniel Arsand and *Paris Noir* by Jacques Yonnet. Her translations from Italian for Dedalus are *Senso (and other stories)* by Camillo Boito, *Sparrow (and other stories)* by Giovanni Verga, *The Price of Dreams* by Margherita Giacobino and *Cleopatra goes to Prison* by Claudia Durastanti.

to Claudia

to Claudia

If I took life seriously,
I would have killed myself long ago.

What wakes her is the apprehension of death, pouncing on her like a predator, crushing her thin bones on the bed, forcing itself into her eyes, her mouth. Death has been with her for a while, but now it is right here, breathing in her face.

Then, with one leap across the room, it returns to crouch in the shadows.

This is not the first time she has experienced this: all sensations have an intermittent rhythm. Even the fiercest pain, the darkest angst come and go in waves – otherwise we would probably be unable to bear them. The awareness of death closes in and draws away again, getting closer for a little longer each time, and the distance when it draws away ever lesser – until eventually there will be no more time and no more distance.

The intervals, when the wave withdraws, are life. What is left of it.

The patient wipes a hand across her face, or perhaps only thinks she does, there is no difference now between real gestures and only imagined ones.

She remembers: she is in hospital. They brought her here yesterday evening. The transfusion. She moves an arm, braces herself, scarcely manages to move her body on the mattress. She slowly turns her head towards the door under which a strip of pale light filters in. The raspy breathing that was the background to her sleep resumes, and it is her breathing, she listens to it, amazed at that alien sound that comes from her.

She remembers what she thought just before waking, or rather: it is not what she thought, it is what she clearly heard a voice say, so it is what she dreamt. For her, dreaming and thinking have always been two contiguous states of mind, inseparable from each other, even if often conflicting.

The voice in her head said: "Death has always been my profession."

Is that true? Was that her profession? To kill, to free herself of ghosts, to ward off the fear of death? Nonsense. Her profession was to write. To leave ajar the doors of reverie and capture the voices.

But writing, this continuous anxiety for which it is itself the only remedy, is a perpetual flight onwards, to the limit and beyond – and now the limit is here, the dark wall there is no way to get past.

Art is a dance with death. But an artist – is that what she is? Is that what she was?

Years ago she wrote a silly little ditty: "I dabble in all the arts and make a mess of each, I'm a person of many parts, with a goal beyond my reach."

That is exactly how it went. The joy of being able to say something true, however slight and silly. And immediately afterwards, having only just said it, the dissatisfaction. No, that won't do. Let's try again.

That has been her life. Death ought to be calmness, rest. But evidently it is not so, no rest at all, only the last surge before nothingness.

With death, you do not get bored.

Time goes quickly when you are together, death is a demanding companion. It absorbs you. It is never out of your thoughts. How can you think of anything else when death is there?

The last lover.

She has just turned seventy-four. There are people her age who keep fit, go to the gym, jog, all things that are not for her, too much effort to stay young, who are they trying to kid?

She has had a lot of love affairs during her life, a lot of friendships. People have said that she is a misanthrope, anti-social, but also that she is a good listener, that when she looks at you, you have the sense of being seen, seen within, swallowed up... now she looks on death without batting her eyelids, meeting death's slit-eyed feline gaze with her own.

It is a challenge, a declaration of love, a fight to the bitter end. Every breath costs her effort, the disparity between her and her adversary is overwhelming. Ridiculous.

And that is why, when the girl comes bursting into the room, switching on the light, pushing her rattling trolley – she stops dead in her tracks, shocked.

The patient's gaze is a mirror in which death is reflected, at half past six in the morning, eyes black, with no iris or pupil, nothing but black.

The girl briefly raises a hand to her throat, catching her breath. In a voice none the less full of life, she says: "Good morning! How are you feeling? I've brought you some breakfast."

The patient does not respond. Not a muscle moves in that blade-edged, thin, lined face contracted in a grimace of impotent rage. The girl hesitates, feels threatened, reproached, and even – absurdly, in the face of such a weak creature – scared. But she is a good nurse, with steady nerves and has already seen more than one patient die. She takes a deep breath and proficiently, decisively, brimming with the firm compassion of her youth, she advances towards the old lady, smiling.

The girl quickly gets used to the wrinkled face, to those fleshy and pendulous lips – as if they had not the strength any more to remain tightened – to the bags under the red-circled eyes. The old lady has a yellowish pallor, the colour of those who are anemic. With difficulty, she gulps down a bit of biscuit, drinks a few sips of tea. She is so light, the girl thinks, that instead of slipping the bedpan under the dry nest of her pelvis, she could pick her up in her arms and carry her to the bathroom. But she is afraid of breaking her.

The formidable old lady leaves herself entirely in the nurse's hands, this is not a surrender, it is an acknowledgement of reality.

Two doctors arrive. They feel her, observe her. Another transfusion. She knows it is pointless, she has had so many in recent months, now they are not enough any more.

However, the blood helps, especially in the absence of alcohol.

The fresh new blood gives energy and lucidity, like the first martini of the evening when she was young.

The doctors adopt a light playful tone, which is presumed to help the seriously ill. They check her pulse, ask her how she is.

"Reasonably well," she says. "I'm not in any discomfort, apart from the pain in my legs."

"Very good," the older of the two says jovially.

"I'm dying," she says.

"Don't say that! What gives you that idea?" the younger one scolds her.

"It's true," she says, suddenly infuriated by his stupidity and lack of respect for the truth. Her anger provokes a fit of coughing, she spits blood on the clean sheet.

Great agitation all around her. They change her, put her on a drip. The nurse has trouble getting the drip needle into her arm, the thin veins might rupture.

The old lady, who is no lady, would like to send them away, they are disturbing her. These are her last hours of life, why spend them amid this commotion? But she has not the strength to protest.

And anyway, what does it matter? Inside her, death is making a great deal of noise, pulsing with the blood in her veins, rasping in time with her breathing. Dilating and contracting, like the chambers of her heart.

How foolish, to think that death comes from the outside. It comes from within, from deep inside the body.

It entered her some time ago. Now they are inseparable.

They have been left alone together, the dying old woman and the girl. The nurse bends over her, adjusts the sheet, little routine gestures, not really necessary.

She asks her if she is cold. She is so thin.

The old lady does not reply. Then in a rasping voice, the fragile wraith, the shattered frame of what must have been the deep gravelly voice of a smoker, asks her what her name is.

"Maria."

"How old are you?"

"Twenty-five."

The hand, large and frail, with swollen knuckles and soft empty pads at the fingertips, makes a movement on the bed cover, signifying: "Sit here, stay with me for a while."

The girl sits down. She tells her story. She is the third of four children, lives in Ascona, beneath Monte Verità. A little apartment all of her own. She comes on the bus. She does not mind getting up early in the morning, on the contrary: it is a pleasure to walk through the empty streets before the town awakens.

She likes her job, and what else? Reading, travel. Marriage? Maybe some day… a wave of the hand. But travel first.

She speaks schoolgirl English. The patient listens, never taking those incredible eyes off her.

On impulse, not out of pity but out of some obscure attraction towards the woman in her nearness to death, the girl takes the cold and desiccated hand lying on the bed.

The patient lets her hold it for a few moments, then slowly withdraws it.

"Now try to get a little sleep, Miss Highsmith," the nurse says, walking away quietly in her soft-soled shoes.

"Call me Pat," says the patient in a surprisingly clear voice.

Highsmith, Patricia: nationality, American, resident in Tegna, Switzerland. Age, seventy-four. Height, five foot nine. Weight, six stone. Smoker. Drinker. In September 1993 underwent surgery in Locarno hospital for the removal from the large intestine of a polyp. Medical record: nose bleeds and haemorrhaging, nausea, immune deficiencies, removal of tumour from the right lung (London, 1986), loss of weight, frequent blood transfusions. Suspected metastases but chemotherapy not possible because of deleterious effects on other pathologies (aplastic anemia).

The girl closes the file. She dutifully writes down the doctor's prescriptions, the times when she will administer the medication, the examinations scheduled for tomorrow morning.

If there is one – a tomorrow morning – for the old lady. For Pat.

The girl's face is smooth-skinned, with hazel eyes like hers, and beautiful, the way young people are, as she herself was fifty years ago. Pat closes her eyes and for a moment a story begins: early morning in winter, patches of snow among the trees emanate a pale glimmer, the wet road is black and gleaming. A girl comes walking down the hill with her hands in her pockets, whistling. The bag she is carrying on her shoulder bumps against her hip. Someone is walking behind her, a harmless passer-by or someone who is following her, does the girl, Maria, know that life is dangerous, that you need to watch your back always? The dull rumble of the early-morning bus can be heard, lower down, round the bend. The girl starts to run.

The vision lasts only a moment, is lost in the indistinct blur of possible lives, of stories not yet told.

She closes her eyes. How long does a dream last? A

fraction of a second…

The clock is turned back. The girl within her, the one who sometimes appears in the fierce and furrowed face, surprising those speaking to her, rends the mask of old age and shines forth in the hospital room.

There is no one to see her, except death. The old lady, who is no lady, offers to her last lover the smooth-skinned luminous face of her tumultous twenty-five-year-old self, full of frustration and hope, of happiness and despair.

I

A toast!
To strange passions!

It is June 1946, America has won the war, America is the centre of the world and New York the beating heart of that vast and strange country that is hers. Pat wanders through the city in a state of almost terrifying euphoria. Around her, like a tangible reality, is the presence of the woman she met only a short while ago and who already means everything to her. Carol. The streets still resonate with the echo of her footsteps, the air in the summer twilight is imbued with her light fragrance, all the women who pass by are imperfect copies of her, oblique mirrors that momentarily afford a glimpse of that unique, perfect image.

Carol is New York and New York has meaning only because it is constructed around Carol and for Carol, it is her abode, the labyrinthine shell with the promise of her splendour round every corner.

Pat wanders the streets of the New York that she has known for years, where she was brought as a child, plucked from the protective presence of her grandmother and from the confines of the domestic spaces of the small town in Texas where she was born. The city that has never become her own, the exciting and frightening metropolis she loves and hates, which will never offer her a place where she might feel safe, a home where she might leave her fears and anxieties at the threshold, a temple where she might celebrate the only rite capable of purifying and elevating her, the rite of productive work.

But in that late afternoon in June, New York has reached the apogee of its beauty, the peak in which opposites join together in harmonious embrace, day and night, pain and joy, cruelty and tenderness, the city is her very self, and she a small thing contained within it, they are a single resplendent mystery, and the key to that mystery is Carol.

If God is the unity of the cosmos, the greater harmony of the elements that from our narrow point of view we see only as war and chaos, the sole thought capable of raising us out of the misery of our fragmented existence – then Carol is God.

This is what Pat thinks, wordlessly, with her head upturned to the sky and pervaded by silent explosions of jubilance as she wanders through New York at sunset. And as happens to her in the very best moments, in those unrepeatable instants of beatitude, time disintegrates and she holds within all her selves at every age, she is a child, an adolescent, a girl and also the woman that she will be, a writer, in command of her life and of a profession. An artist. Capable of creating something out of nothing, of giving form to that which previously did not exist.

This would be a terrifying thought were it not that she knew that whatever is created is always very far from the hoped-for perfection. It is only continual failure that makes the divine act of creation endurable.

She saunters along the pavements of New York, beneath the sunset-red clouds, and the energy within her superabounds, the future opens up before her, limitless.

Today, every single day of her life shines clean and bright, as though recently washed, redeemed by the dawning light of her new love.

There have been days of passion, rage and hate.

Mary, her beautiful and impossible mother, loved and feared, who gave so little of herself, who had married her stepfather Stanley just to have a man to argue with, it seemed.

How she had hated him as a child! In her little room, in the evenings that went on too long, in the apartment that was too small and cramped to allow her the comfort of solitude, forced to listen to raised voices, the incessant accusations and threats, her sole consolation and entertainment was to imagine the possible deaths of her stepfather, in a providential accident or at the hand of a ruthless assassin.

Die, Stanley – you are the first of my characters, killing you is my writing exercise in the evening. One night a stranger, infuriated by his domestic unhappiness, will run into you in the street on your way home, and without thinking, driven by an irresistible impulse, he will grab you by the collar, give you a pounding, leave your lifeless body in a dark alleyway and go on his way feeling better…

Poor old Stanley. He was like one of those dummies used to simulate car crashes: he died a hundred times and did not even know it.

Useful fantasies. Nothing in life goes to waste.

As, for example, when she dashes off with scrupulous diligence one story after another for Mushroom Man, the name she gives, because of the bizarre hat he wears, to the hero of one of the series of comic strips for which she writes storylines. Stories that will later be illustrated, often hurriedly, by another assembly line worker like herself, and that will appear sprinkled with interjections such as "Argh!", "Sob!" and "Crash!", which sometimes still make her laugh and at other times fill her with a desolate boredom.

But work is work. The superhero flattens his adversaries with a single blow, immolates the bad guys with a mere glance, throws himself off New York's tallest skyscraper and does not go crashing to the ground. Just like someone who is love-struck. The superhero is vulgar, grotesque, often stupid. The love-struck person is vulnerable, at once happy and desperate, almost always stupid. Both are human in the extreme and superhuman. Jumping off the tallest skyscraper, the love-struck will not end up splattered on the ground either, but will fall directly, eternally, into the arms of the beloved.

Also of great usefulness has been what she read as a child, the book by that psychiatrist Karl Menninger, who under the title *The Human Mind* collected true stories of kleptomaniacs, pyromaniacs, psychopaths of all kinds. People who believe they are someone else, or think they are being spied on by Russian secret agents, a spurned lover who cannot accept rejection and barricades himself in a world of his own, a man who assumes the identity of another and steals his life, a falsifier who invents the thing he falsifies… it was all there, even if she did not yet know it.

But on some days in June, in New York, it is easy to think of life, of the future, as a host of ideas still in embryo, in bud. *Keim*, that German word adopted by her in honour of the origins of a father practically unknown to her. The germ, the seed, the kernel of the story. The fertile idea from which one day, if the ground is suitable, if the weather is encouraging, if it is sufficiently nurtured, a story will grow.

A writing space begins to extend behind her, around her. The only true reality, the only real truth in this world where the true and the real are at war with each other. The seedbed of her mind.

The time will come when she will no longer need to write for comic strips, when she will escape the treadmill. And she will dedicate herself solely to cultivating the countless germs of ideas that she has gathered and put aside.

In New York one day, when she was twelve years old, when she was not entirely a child any more but nor was she quite old enough to cotton on to the tricks of adults, Mary told her that she had got divorced from Stanley. The two of them were to go back to Texas to stay with her grandmother Willie Mae.

With what fervent trust, with what gratitude, she had gone with her mother, although it was of course a wrench to move away from the city it had taken her years to settle down in, to leave behind such hard-won friendships when at last they had stopped making fun of her accent and her Texan ways. However, for Mary, *with* Mary, she would have gone to the North Pole, barefoot, in the middle of winter.

But after only a few days Stanley had rejoined them, or

rather, he had rejoined his wife. He and Mary shut themselves away in the bedroom to talk.

She, shut out, excluded, dismayed, despairing.

A few hours later Mary left, returned to New York with him, leaving her there.

No explanation, not a word, nothing. Only the anguish and the slow, crushing certainty of betrayal. How grotesque it all was, her mother had made her believe the two of them were escaping to go back to their Texan paradise, to her grandmother's house where they would live together for ever without her stepfather, and instead it turned out to be a ploy to get rid of her, the unwanted encumbrance, and return to New York with that man.

For Mary, *she* was the intruder, not Stanley!

From paradise, the childhood home was transformed into limbo.

The silent stern love of Willie Mae was no longer enough for her, she no longer enjoyed playing with the little black kids in the alley behind the house.

Abandonment taught her an important and terrible lesson about life.

Mary had lied to her. She should have expected it, knowing what her mother was like. Even a cruel truth would have been better than a lie that in any case was bound to be exposed. But Mary lied constantly, often for no reason, without even admitting it to herself.

Mary the self-centred, the bully, the lunatic. You never know what to expect of her. Gentleness and fury, seduction and betrayal. She is a dangerous woman, her mother. Loving her means walking on shifting sands, on the rim of a volcano.

This is what she has learned about love, ever since babyhood.

But today, a summer's day in her twenty-fifth year, Pat can forgive her, can accept her coldness and her fickleness, because every event in her own life is taking on new meaning. She has survived, she is strong, and for this she can thank her mother, because with her it is a question of be strong or die. Over time she has even got used to Stanley, has come to sympathise with him, to see him in his true light as redoubtable Mary's chosen victim.

Abandonment, rage, the constant terrifying sense of inadequacy, her forbidden and concealed sexual desires: everything made sense, having served to make her what she is and what she will become.

All the pain has been redeemed now that Carol lights up the skies of New York.

The secret that others regard as her doom pulsates within her, radiating life and warmth.

There was that day when she saw the two little girls.

They were sitting on the steps in front of a doorway, close together, conspiratorially. The sound of her footsteps had surprised them. An abruptly interrupted gesture as she came by – a hand withdrawn, the hem of a chequered dress hastily pulled down over the knees – was the sign that something had happened between them, something secret and mysterious and illicit.

Pat had hurried past them. Only after a few steps had she turned round to steal one last image of the two little figures in front of the doorway. She carried away with her a vision of those guilty, radiant, wondering eyes. She was certain the two little girls would have remembered, maybe for ever, that moment when discovery and pleasure, mystery and guilt, were combined in a single heartbeat. The same had happened to her as a child, at certain moments that she recalls even today; hidden convulsions of the heart.

Those two were like her, as she was then and as she was now: a child frightened by her own audacity, torn between flight and defiance. Committed to the terrifying beauty of forbidden desire.

But how wonderful that desire now seemed to her and she knew for certain it was worth the price of fear and guilt.

Those two little figures sitting close together were as though fused into a single being, emblem of a fulfilment beyond words.

The day it appears in *Vanity Fair* – the story of which she is so proud, the only thing of real value to have come from her pen so far.

It is entitled "The Heroine" and it has taken her years to get it published. She has been told that it is strange, no one knows how to define it. That her protagonist is mad and unlikeable.

"The Heroine" is the story of a young girl who is alone in the world, the orphaned child of a mother with psychological problems, and she too if truth be told is a bit bizarre, but then not so different from many others, someone who, if you met her in the street, you might mistake for normal, someone who has learned to hide her little tics, but don't pretty much all of us do the same? The girl is taken on as a governess by a wealthy family. Her employers are kind, the children are lovely, polite, well behaved and affectionate. They all like her, they make her feel one of the family, they treat her with every kindness. An ideal situation, a dream come true. Impossible not to feel love and gratitude. Impossible not to want to give back something in exchange. But what? She has nothing, they have everything. Her love is boundless, she would like to offer them life, salvation, then she would be loved for ever, and never be at risk of losing them. If something terrible happened, some catastrophe, she would do everything to save them… this too is a common desire: who has not fantasised about saving a woman in danger or distinguishing oneself by some noble act? So that people can say, "Look, that's the guy or the girl who did that heroic deed, look how self-effacing they are, what a good-natured and modest person!" But since nothing happens and the opportunity does not arise of its own accord, the girl herself sets fire to the house so as to be able to rescue the occupants – or perish with them, as the ending, which her friends have described as "disconcerting", perhaps suggests.

"But of course there are precedents," she retorted in reply to a drunken editor one evening at a bar in Manhattan, she too in her cups. "In *Jane Eyre* Rochester's wife sets fire to the house, she's insane, certainly, but she surely will have loved Rochester before going mad, and perhaps loves him still, and no one can tell us what the motive for her action was, maybe she…" And there she stopped, because she felt the sweaty hand of the editor on her neck and realised the guy was much more interested in going to bed with the young writer than listening to her literary theories.

She managed to escape from him only because he was

really *too* drunk, and for months the story lay on her desk, like wreckage washed up by the waves. Then she plucked up courage again and sent it to other magazines. And now at last there it is, on the page, her story, her name, hot off the press. For the first time she has the feeling of having done something good. A sense of justification, such as a mother might feel when she has brought a child into the world, although looking at her married friends with children she has serious doubts about that, and her own mother seems to give the lie to this view.

No, what is created by the effort of writing is something different from giving birth: a story is a child only in the sense that you have to bring it into the world and help it to walk alone, but unlike a human being it does not betray you or let you down, it continues to be part of you. It proclaims to all: now look here, the modest existence of the woman who wrote me is meaningful, has its own significance, precisely because she has created me and I exist, a sliver of truth maybe invisible to most people, but precious to anyone who sees it glint and stoops to glean it.

And today, as sunset turns to dusk in the sky above New York, she knows that she will write again, she will always write. That is her true path, the only one possible. Drawing, music are only private passions, minor talents that will not take her anywhere. Writing is her destiny. She will carve out time for herself, from days that are overburdened with hack writing, she will write at night when the doors of reverie stand ajar, she will be organised, full of energy and determination. She will create something fine. She will write by the light of her new love for Carol.

Carol will be her own violation of the rule she has imposed on herself: never to write about women.

To inhabit a body that is not hers, an incorporeal body, that of a man, made of words, big hands, shirt sleeves, cigarettes, long strides in the dark.

Everything that a woman cannot be or do. Not because she lacks the capability, but because it not allowed.

Carol certainly is not the first – at twenty-five Pat is a veteran, having lived through a good number of passionate attachments and break-ups, and crumpled a good few sheets – but Carol is the crowning glory of this period of her life, the triumph and zenith of her headstrong awkward youth. Carol is a revelation. The Ideal Woman, the Absolute.

One day, years later, she will see the Victory of Samothrace in the Louvre, a winged figure of perfect proportions caught in mid-stride, in a strong and graceful pose. Nike. An eternal model carved in stone, she who guides you from the prow of a thousand ships, who inspires you on the field of battle, Nike the bold, the joyful, the fearless.

On more than one occasion she will tell journalists that the virtue she most admires in women is courage, and in men, gentleness.

Why? But that's obvious, she will reply impatiently: women are physically weaker, less free to act, to take the initiative, while men are stronger by nature and accustomed to having the upper hand. A courageous woman, a gentle man: two more complete human beings. What is virtue if not the bright phantasm wrestling with the dark demon?

At the Louvre she will stop in front of the Nike as before the portrait of a long-lost love, with cynical nostalgia. Half-closing her eyes, she will picture the movements – the very breathing – of her own personal Nike from New Jersey, the loved and lost Mrs Caroline Seymour Clark.

What is more, the Victory of Samothrace is headless, and Carol too was prone to losing hers.

Carol is Virginia, Kathryn, Lil, Anne, Ginnie, Lyne and others besides, Carol is one and many, she is all the beautiful, elegant, reckless, daredevil and self-destructive women who shine like diamonds in New York display cases, who drink too much, who drive too fast, who try to fly with their wings of stone.

When she saw her, she was leaning against a door frame in Rosalind's drawing room. The room was full of people, artists, art dealers, beautiful women and rich men, young talents anxious to be noticed and girls like herself, in their twenties, starting out in the world, still fresh and bright-eyed, in their thirties, having already lost their shine in the effort of forging their way every day through the anonymous crowd threatening to swallow them up.

And suddenly everyone else has faded into the background, the voices have become a distant murmur, and there remains before her only the woman leaning against the door frame, across the room.

She is wearing a green dress that sets off her mahogany-coloured, short, wavy hair, in one hand she holds a cigarette that every now and again she brings to her lips with a nervous and absent-minded gesture, the other hand resting as though forgotten on the back of an armchair. Long white fingers, an emerald ring. She has eyes that are so clear they seem to burn with pure colourless light. She is talking to another woman whose face Pat cannot see. Nor, of course, can she hear what they are saying amid the chatter in the room, but in that conversation – whispered, nonchalant, intermittent – she recognises the unmistakeable signs of a secret language with which she is now familiar. Then the woman in the green dress laughs, a brief, full-throated, slightly husky laugh, a sound that Pat would like to hear again and again. Now the woman looks round and lets her gaze wander over the small gathering, as if she has sensed Pat's attention and is seeking her out. And all of a sudden she is near to Pat, coming across the room, and she passes by, almost brushing against her, their eyes meet for a moment and Pat feels overwhelmed with an intense uneasy pleasure, as if a velvet paw had caressed her in the dark.

In Rosalind's elegant drawing room, nothing else exists for her now, apart from the exquisite torment of observing the unknown woman and knowing that she herself is being observed in return. Until the lady of the house comes up to her, enveloped in the scent of her discreet and expensive perfume and in the radiance conferred on her by a couple of martinis, and with her extraordinary intuition steers Pat towards the group of people surrounding the woman with mahogany hair and introduces her to Mrs Caroline Seymour Clark, who extends a soft and slender hand and says, "They usually call me Carol."

Rosalind, her fairy godmother. Ever since Pat, aged just eighteen, happened to set foot in her art gallery, which she had dared to enter with a couple of fellow university students, naive and ignorant like herself, her life had changed.

Initially Pat was ridiculously intimidated by Rosalind, she seemed a kind of sophisticated and elegant goddess, whose every word, every gesture Pat soaked up, treasuring every bit of information about her that was given. Gradually they became friends, although friends is perhaps not the right word, Pat is naturally a little in love with her, how could she not be? Rosalind is forty, and the most interesting woman she has ever met, she has taste and experience and seems to be the repository of the measure of all things. Be it a painting, or a dinner, or a love affair, or a work appointment, Rosalind is acquainted with its secret, she knows what the right thing to do is.

At first Pat courted her with timid, dogged devotion. Which Rosalind graciously accepted as an almost inevitable tribute to her fascination, but conceding nothing. She has a stable relationship with another woman and a few other liaisons on the side. When Pat realised there was no hope for her, she tormented herself for a while, drank too much, talked too much, made scenes, behaved like a child that wants to be scolded. Then she consoled herself with other women, and indeed she certainly had no lack of lovers – "You fall in love every other day, it's ridiculous," Rosalind tells her, "you should calm down and take yourself and your work more seriously." But basically perhaps Pat is still convinced that only Rosalind can save her – despite all the women she has met and loved and with whom she has dissipated her nights and her days.

Save her from what? Her mother's disapproval. Total failure. Herself. The terrible anxiety of not being good enough. Of being for ever an outsider in this society she would like to be a part of, in which she would like to be appreciated and loved. While Rosalind is right at the centre of it like a queen bee in the hive.

But now, at the very moment when the lady of the house is introducing her to Carol, the scales of desire subtly and significantly shift and Pat realises that although Rosalind is and will always be her fairy godmother – or at least will be for as long as their very different personalities manage to tolerate each other – what she feels for her is not, and never has been, true desire. Because desire suddenly ignites around this woman with eyes the colour of light, who is completely different from Rosalind.

As she wanders the now almost dark streets of New York, recalling Carol's vaguely sardonic gaze focused on her, her white neck thrown back when she drinks and when she laughs, the brusque, almost fierce gesture with which she pulled on a glove before leaving – Pat feels that with this woman the skies above the city grow loftier and the people become smaller.

The people she considered so important until a few hours ago now seem to her remote, engaged in activities that do not interest her, and even her own success, the struggle for existence, sending out her stories, hoping to meet someone who might put in a good word for her at a prestigious magazine, all this falls away from her, relieving her of a burden, making her feel light, free.

Carol is freedom, with her the confines of the city expand,

New York becomes infinite and untamed, it extends the impalpable web of its unrest over the whole great continent of America.

"It's not been easy for her," says Rosalind, drinking her black sugarless coffee and nibbling the one sandwich she allows herself for lunch, because she is on a diet. They are in a cafeteria in Manhattan, outside on the pavement the women passers-by wear coloured dresses with short sleeves, their hair gleaming in the sunlight, and the men take off their jackets and dangle them on one finger over their shoulders. Pat is sober, so wonderfully sober it makes her head spin.

"She's divorced," says Rosalind, "he was rich, obviously she is too. Her people are the Seymours, the ones in the aviation industry. There was a trial. She had a girlfriend and it seems the husband had her followed by a private detective while they were somewhere in Maine, and he tried to blackmail her, either she agreed to forget about the divorce, and of course the girlfriend, or she would never see her daughter again. She didn't agree. Carol's like that, a rebel, intractable, and he accused her of you-know-what in front of the judges, obviously it wasn't a public scandal but word got around, these things always do, and they took away the child from her, she doesn't even get to see her any more. Now she devotes herself to the aircraft, apparently she's got her pilot's licence."

Their first date. Carol drives fast but Pat is not afraid, she has absolute trust in her, her hands on the steering wheel are sure and steady, they make her heart flutter with joy.

Why not die like this? That would be the best way, she thinks, drunk with happiness, pushing her hair off her face to no avail because the wind immediately blows it back again, while her better judgement tells her they will not die, not now.

The car roof is down, their light scarves are flapping in the wind, and in order to talk to each other they have to shout, so they exchange only a few words. Carol is not the talkative type. When she is not concentrating on driving she becomes immersed in thoughts that make her knit her brow. Or else Pat catches her studying her intently, almost as if Carol had suddenly become aware of her presence and was asking herself questions about her.

Pat feels befuddled in her admiration, she wants more than anything to please Carol but she is unsure about her every gesture and her every word, as if the last years spent at Rosalind's academy were nothing more than a thin veneer that is coming away, leaving her exposed in her foolishness and naivety, in her painful exclusion from every social group and milieu.

But then Carol turns and offers an outstretched hand to help her. They have left the car on the side of the road and are climbing up a dune along the shore, the sky is low and cloudy with bursts of sunshine. Carol's high heels sink into the sand but she walks on briskly without ever losing her balance. They stand side by side, gazing at the sea in silence and Pat is filled with the sudden exhilarating certainty that Carol likes her.

In an unassuming little kiosk run by an old man wearing a sailor shirt they have a strong bitter coffee, one of the best ever in her life. And behind that kiosk Carol kisses her for the first time, as though on an unexpected and irresistible impulse, without worrying whether anyone might come along.

A moment after they have stopped kissing a family

appears, father, mother and children, emerging from the path along the sand dune, heading towards the kiosk. Carol greets them gaily, keeping her arm around Pat's waist, and with total self-confidence exchanges a few friendly words with the newcomers. Only Pat detects in her voice the reckless euphoria of risk-taking. She is proud of her.

They run down the dune, holding hands and laughing.

On their return to the city Carol grows sullen, one of her sudden mood changes that Pat will learn to get used to. This will not be too hard for her after what she has been through with her mother.

They will not spend that evening together, Carol is invited somewhere.

But now they know there will be other evenings, other nights.

They see each other irregularly, without fixed times or days. Carol has commitments, she has commitments – although even at the cost of running into trouble over work, she is nearly always ready to put hers off, if it means meeting up. But she is not complaining. The uncertainty increases the tension, every day holds out the magical possibility of seeing her, every day contains expectation and hope that extend, dwindling, until evening, and contract painfully within her breast if during the course of the day she does not receive a telephone call, or a telegram – and then at night, at a certain point, start to grow again before she goes to sleep, or in her sleep, when her desires and expectations bring on the dawn of another day in which they will surely see each other.

Pat does not want any other life, she cannot even imagine it.

This is how the girls and the woman around her live. They have clandestine love affairs, almost always short-lived, they are usually promiscuous. They meet in bars or better still in private houses where everything takes place in a discreet and sheltered way, where you know at first glance how things stand and who you are dealing with. You know that you are among people who are – well, like you, from that point of view.

They are independent women, who work as designers, models, secretaries, journalists, people who belong to a sparkling and exclusive world, or move on the fringes of it. Some are rich, others – like Pat – hide their poverty as best they can. But all of them know the meaning of the messages that are exchanged: looks, gestures, allusions, phrases that are not explicit but revealing.

Pat knows that, if she wants, she need never go home alone.

Sometimes it is exciting, at other times it is even too easy. It leaves you with a vague sense of disgust, like a hangover. Then there are the rivalries, the jealousies, the wretchedness of the *les girls'* world, a closed universe in which sex and dalliance are common currency, but beware of forming any deep attachments because it is forbidden to cross the boundary, to let things filter into the other world, the one outside, the real world, among colleagues, friends and family, neighbours, respectable people.

After a while some get married, change their life, disappear. They are spoken of in an undertone, as if they were people who had died and ended up in the paradise, or hell, of normality.

It is not unusual for these married women to rejoin the

milieu after a few years, returning to haunt the places they have known and which they cannot do without.

This is certainly what Carol did, even before the divorce.

Yes, there are some stable couples. Pat knows one couple who even live together, but they are the exception, they have money, they can afford to buy two adjoining apartments, they have no family to answer to, nor any need to work.

For those like her, who do not enjoy these privileges, living together is impossible but they can take a different girl to bed every night, or have relations with three or four women at the same time, provided that everything remains hidden and nothing gets out. The secretiveness intensifies firstly the lust, and afterwards the sense of satiation and nausea. Here, you love avidly, hurriedly, knowing you will part the next morning and may ignore each other within a week if by chance you were to meet.

In a way this suits her very well, because she knows how demanding a stable relationship would be, how much time and energy it would take away from work. But the drawback is knowing that it is not permissible to display your love with head held high, in the light of day. Obviously under these circumstances relationships are destined to be short-lived, because everything that keeps two people together for any length of time is forbidden to them.

It is the common view – and the novels that are sold in the railway stations and drugstores are convinced of it – that *queers*, *perverts, les girls* are not capable of any lasting and healthy relationship or true love. Even when they are in love they hate each other because they hate themselves. Ambivalence and contempt are the hallmark of their sentimental lives, and betrayal, if not violence and sadism, are the order of the day among them.

And what if all this was nonsense? But this nonsense is in the air we breathe. No one dares to contradict it out loud. Not even Pat contradicts it. Apart from anything else, it replicates exactly the same message she gets from her mother. This is what her mother makes her feel when she wants to punish her: different, ashamed, warped. Depressed and inept. Inadequate.

The truth must be kept hidden, always. You must always be ready to repudiate yourself, to pretend. In these circumstances who would not despise herself?

Other than an artist, or a criminal. A counterfeiter, who makes a profession of faking and thereby taking revenge.

But there is another side to her love for women, her love for Carol. A side that is wonderful, dazzling, divine.

Light and shadow, contempt and wonder, courage and shame. She lives a secret life, as an outlaw. Opprobrium is the price that has to be paid for her splendid freedom. As separation is the price of her meetings with Carol.

There are also, it is true, working-class women – but this is another world – who set up home together, in some suburb or other, confronting the world's hostility and disapproval every day. Pat has seen them, women of this kind, in certain bars where on one or two nights a week different social strata take the risk of mixing with each other. In these couples there is always one of the two who acts as a man, and this type of wo-man inspires her with revulsion and fear. Often they are violent and belligerent, they are coarse in their ways and bullnecked.

Not that she is very feminine herself, in fact she likes to

dress in a sporty and comfortable if not entirely masculine style and her mother has nagged her ever since her adolescence about her scruffy clothes and her awkwardness. But those women, who pose as men in such a literal way! She knows that she has masculine qualities, a spirit of adventure, determination, tenacity – if she only has faith in herself to meet the challenge the world presents to every one of us – but these qualities she will put to use in her work, not in her choice of shirt or the way her hair is cut. And certainly not in the way she walks, or picks a fight brandishing a beer bottle!

Years and years later, when she is mistaken for a man by a waiter or a beggar in the street, she will recall, not without wryness and curiosity, having seen certain women at that time in the bars of New York, and she will wonder how much she now ressembles them. Do they still exist? What has become of them? The world has changed in the meantime and when on a trip to the States she goes back to look for one of those bars, she will find a place full of uninhibited young black women who arouse in her once again, although in a different way, unease and fear.

An alternative to the life she leads does exist, and it is the one available to every woman, a door she too could pass through, if she wanted.

Marriage.

Whether rich or poor, happy or unhappy, marriage in all its forms is hellish. Or, in the best of cases, a bore.

(Yet think about it: once you go through that door, how many others will then open to you? You need not be afraid any more of being an outcast, of being jeered and censured, everything will fall into place automatically, you will be a married woman, a married writer, you will be set right.)

The young married women she knows do nothing but devote themselves to household chores, preparing meals and looking after children. Some work to support their husband financially while he pursues his studies. Many seem to have changed character, they have become slovenly and totally lacking in ambition, or domineering, domestic tyrants to whom the husbands subjugate themselves with more or less good grace, seeking consolation in their friends, in beer, in other women.

But worst of all are the so-called successful marriages, those in which the young couple are united in saving and setting up home together, and the spark of passion, if it ever existed, has given way to discussions about buying a dresser on an instalment plan.

Marriage is the end of the story. After that, for a woman, there can be nothing else.

Sometimes, when Carol is asleep, one hand lying carelessly on the sheets, Pat, while gazing at the russet reflections in her hair, catches herself imagining a big country house, a garden with lilac bushes, Carol's favourite, and then she appears, her Carol, coming down the path, her cheeks gilded by the setting sun and walking with her, still unsteady on its feet, a child who looks like her. Mother and child wave happily, smiling, impatient: to someone arriving, someone they have been waiting for, and that someone is Pat herself.

She faithfully records these fantasies in her notebook.

Honesty is the most important thing, especially in observing yourself. Do not be afraid even of banality.

Yet she knows, in the very same moment that she surrenders herself to it, that the American dream is false.

Occasionally it seems to her that the world in which she lives – the city of New York itself – is false, feigned. It does not exist in reality. It is a collective dream. Shimmering, stifling, hung round her neck.

The only thing that truly exists is Carol.

And also the books she reads, Gide, Camus, Kierkegaard, Kafka and Dostoevsky, who at this time is her favourite. Only some authors give her the necessary breath of air, with them she feels her chest and her mind expand. What she likes most of all about Dostoevsky is the constant overt attraction the characters feel towards sin, the forbidden. Transcending the so-called moral values imposed by society, man knows in his heart of hearts that he has need of something else, something just as vital as food and water.

To set his own rules, and submit to them – or transgress them: one thing invites the other, inevitably. What are good and evil, lawful and unlawful, if not conventions? We are born with the capacity to kill no less than the capacity to protect, to hate as well as to love.

And Carol, with her mood swings, with her now benign, now cruel power, seems to be the proof of it.

There are moments when she radiates a superhuman confidence, like the time she took Pat flying with her.

Going for a drive, on the face of it as on previous days

to nowhere in particular – Carol with a cigarette clamped between her teeth while she rummages on top of the dashboard in search of her sunglasses and who seems by chance to take one turning rather than another – yet at a certain point Pat realises there is a particular destination.

After an abrupt turn they stop alongside a hangar on the edge of a grassy strip. "Go on, get out," Carol tells her. "I want you to meet someone important."

"Here he is," she says, her eyes sparking with pride, but also with childlike mischievousness as she observes Pat's reaction.

"He" is Richie III, a small light aircraft, grey with broad red stripes on the wings. A man in overalls, his hands dirty with grease, emerges from the hangar and comes towards them, greeting Carol respectfully. She addresses him in a friendly way – Carol can be pleasant and considerate with strangers just as she can be rude or distant with those she loves – they talk for a few minutes, and Pat is left out, excluded from a conversation she does not understand and cannot even hear very well because of an engine running in the hangar, which drowns out their voices. Then Carol says to her in the most casual way possible, "Well, are you coming or not?" And a moment later she is inside the plane and all Pat can do is follow her, putting on the leather helmet the man holds out to her as he helps her up the steep boarding ladder.

The plane rolls down the runway, takes off and climbs through the air as though diving upwards in jerks that leave her with her heart in her mouth, gripping the seat, white with terror, and for a moment she is convinced that Carol has brought her here to die together, not such a ridiculous or far-fetched idea, considering the life they live.

But Carol seems extremely calm and perfectly in control of the situation. Well defined and inspiring, her profile is silhouetted against the pale sky, the great expanses of green and the ocean in the distance. The plane climbs, its flight becomes more stable and steady, now it is gliding through the air like a bird with outspread wings. Pat's heart regains its regular rhythm, slowly calms down. As in the car, the idea of dying no longer frightens her, on the contrary: in that moment, suspended hundreds of feet above the ground, she and Carol alone in the fragile metal cockpit, she contemplates death with equanimity, seeing it as a logical and marvellous outcome. What better ending than to die in the arms of the woman you love?

Then Carol lands the plane expertly on the runway, and shortly afterwards they are having a drink before dinner in a restaurant by the sea. Two martinis for her, a few straight whiskies for Carol, who holds her liquor extraordinarily well – until the moment she collapses. And that moment, as Pat well knows, always arrives sooner or later.

Until dinner it has been a perfect day. The flight – silent and filled with emotion – still holds them together, with their movements in synchrony, as if they had just taken part in some secret ceremony. It will be an intimate and quiet meal, thinks Pat. Almost a solemn affair.

Until a couple of friends of Carol's ex-husband come in and sit down on the far side of the vast, almost empty dining room. The two are so far away it is quite conceivable they simply have not seen Carol, but Pat knows this is not so, they have definitely seen her and chosen to ignore her. Under

Carol's persistent stare the woman moves her chair slightly so as to turn her back on them. Carol starts laughing and is more amusing than ever. Deaf to Pat's attempts to change the subject, she recounts, one after another, incidents from her married life, both ghastly and comic.

Later, in their room, while Carol is undressing – and Pat, already in bed, observes in silence her graceful body, full of promise, which will soon be under the sheets beside her – all of a sudden comes the unexpected but no less inevitable explosion. With a gesture that might seem inadvertent Carol knocks a chair to the ground, then continues hurling other objects, a bag, an ashtray. Pat rushes to restrain her, she is no longer new to these outbursts of rage, but this time Carol does not just break free, she gives Pat a violent clout, with more to follow but for Pat hitting her back. Carol falls to the floor and remains there, dazed, with her head in her hands. There is the sound of footsteps in the corridor, somone knocks at the door, asks what is happening, is there a problem? Do the ladies need anything? The words offer help but the voice is a call to order, threatening the retribution of the Law.

Pat forces herself to take a deep breath and replies no, they don't need anything, they are sorry for the disturbance. She waits until she hears the footsteps move away. Her voice trembles. Her hands shake. Now Carol is calm, sitting on the ground half-dressed, with tears running between her fingers. When she uncovers her face, Pat's heart lurches in a much more violent and alarming way than in the plane a few hours ago, because for a moment the person in front of her is not Carol but a woman she has never seen before, a frightful, drunken, mad woman.

There is no love in which, at a certain point, violence does not inevitably insinuate itself.

This is not an unfamiliar idea to Pat.

She will write it in her diary. She must return to it, it is a topic that fascinates her.

The diaries: black notebooks, identical in size and format, ruled with blue lines. There will be a great many during her life. Diaries and work notebooks, with a subtle dividing line between them that sometimes becomes invisible because life and writing converge, overlap, feed off each other.

Writing, even before it becomes a profession, is a necessity, a therapy, a tool, a habit. Writing is the mirror in which she continually, obsessively seeks herself out and frees herself from her own self.

From Pat's diary

August '47, Cherry Grove
3 o'clock in the morning

What a relief it would be to kill her!

Knowing *that woman* is asleep a few feet away from me in the room across the corridor… My footsteps silent on the wooden flooring, on the thick rug beside the bed. My hands tightening round her neck, pressing a cushion down on her face, with all their strength.

Or perhaps a ligature of some kind would be quicker and more deadly. The belt of my silk nightgown is strong enough to stop *that woman*'s breathing for ever.

Another whisky won't help me at all to sleep, nothing, nothing will save me from these thoughts tonight. Nothing except the thought of violence can give me any comfort.

Carol has not said a word to me, she has not once sought me out, not even with her eyes. I would probably have forgiven her everything, the scenes, the anguish of these past months, all the heartache past and future, if only she had deigned to make the first move, if she had told me *that woman* is just another mistake, another attempt to hurt me. Now she is toying with me, with herself. She is in a fury, filled with that terrible spitefulness of hers. Intent on the need to punish me and to punish herself.

Or else she has simply had enough and there is no room for me now, I do not exist any more.

From the moment I arrived here two days ago Lil and Alice have been keeping an eye on me, curious and secretive and worried. They would like me to reveal all, that is obvious, but to talk about Carol with them – or with anyone else right now – is the last thing I can do.

I learned of Carol's probable arrival yesterday. It was Alice who told me, she was embarrassed and guarded, she apologised: they couldn't not invite her. Fine, I say. It's your house, you can invite whoever you like. My heart had lurched, but I was determined not to let anything betray my emotion. I could have taken the train and returned to NY, and perhaps I should have done. But no, because deep down I harboured the hope that Carol was coming for me, because she knew that I was here – L and A would certainly have told her.

Today, at the cocktail hour, while some woman from Baltimore called Ethel – I think she writes for a fashion magazine – tries to engage me in a conversation that does not interest me, I suddenly smell *her* perfume and my legs tremble. She is here, on the verandah, wearing a plain, simple, sleeveless dress that shows off her slender figure, her hair just a little longer (it is almost a month since I last saw her), the perfection of her face, which I know so well, marred by a shadow that is like some premonition of mortality (or merely the traces of a hangover).

She, Carol, is a step away from me, if I stretch out my arm I can touch her. I wish I could sink through the floor, be instantly consumed by flames, reduced to ashes.

I want to throw myself at her and hug her so tightly she would not be able to breathe. To crush her ribs against mine until they fused and became one, bone against bone, our hearts like two birds emprisoned in twin cages welded together so they could never be united or apart from each other.

I should have left immediately. Before *that other woman* appeared, the jumped-up vulgarian Carol brought with her. And who is now resting a proprietory hand on her arm. Carol throws back her head and laughs, her shrill laughter causing me physical pain, a knife-blade in my side. She avoids my gaze, and when I do momentarily catch her glance a gleam of cruelty and madness appears in her eyes.

Carol can live her life, as far as I am concerned. I cannot, and do not want, to keep her tied to me exclusively. Carol is an untamed creature, too much of a rebel for anyone to think they could restrict her, keep her confined to a single relationship, a single love affair. It would be like hobbling a magnificent race horse. How could I not admit to myself that part of her allure is her changeability? Her feminine fickleness, the compelling and irresistible charm of her demands, of her mood changes, of her sudden fits of boredom.

But why choose that parody of a woman? Mrs Sidney Franklin calls herself, very appropriately, Sid, she moves like a man (something she could well be were it not for her breasts and squeaky voice) and she dresses like a suburban thug. She is somebody in cinema, a big shot, so they say, but I have never seen her name in any film credits. However unlikely it may seem, she must have a husband or an ex-husband in Hollywood. Perhaps in her world – a world full of *freaks* and *queers* – no one takes any notice of her, but here, among us, she really stands out, and certainly not in any flattering sense. She seems to be going out of her way to be the embodiment of the most squalid and at the same time most banal image of perversity.

That Carol can bear – but what I am saying? – can accept with good grace that pudgy hand with its beringed fingers and squared fingernails resting on her arm, like the hand of some importunate vaudeville suitor, makes me see red.

Carol, it's not possible that we have come to this. I loved you, I love you, as one loves the Absolute. As one loves God. You were for me the sole certainty, the sole ideal. I knew, I know, that I would never truly attain you, never possess you. It was enough to get close to you, to touch the hem of your skirt, to adore you. I didn't ask to wake up in the morning next to you, I would have been happy with the warm memory of your lips on mine, of your voice in my ear.

I would be happy with so little. I would feed on memories for days, weeks, months if need be. I would look forward to the next date the way a thirsty person looks forward to water, the way a sick person looks forward to a cure. I would accept anything from you, including your betrayals, as long as they did not belittle you in my eyes.

I might even manage to overcome those terrible moments when alcohol turns you into a stranger who terrifies me – perhaps we would overcome them together, if only you allowed me to be close to you, to help you. If you didn't go into a rage and send me packing, if you didn't direct all your fury against me.

Obviously, it is not easy to accept her anger without hating it, and in a certain way hating her as well. Her terrible drunkenness, her anger, her anxiety, her impatience. Her hopeless battle against the world and the power it has over her. Despite her bravado and the icy gleam in her steely eyes, Mrs Caroline Seymour Clark has not at all escaped the judgement and disapproval of her family and her ex-husband.

And the daughter she has lost is a wound that does not heal. At first I believed her when she said she had dealt with the issue coldly, that basically the child was more attached to her father, that with him she would grow up feeling secure, loved and protected in the world that was hers by right. But out of the depths of her bouts of drunkenness a different truth emerged, when shaking and no longer capable of standing upright un-aided, she would ask herself in a tortured voice, "What will they tell her about me? What will they say to my daughter?"

Carol never talks about it but Alice says that at the divorce trial, her weekend in Maine with Julie, the woman with whom she was having a relationship at the time, was discussed in detail. Apparently the detective booked the room next to theirs in a motel near Bangor and planted a microphone in the wall to record their conversations.

Imagine: men, with hostile and judgemental faces,

strangers, ransacking your private life, rummaging, with their rough heavy hands, in your most inviolable emotions and dirtying them for ever, and in the end passing sentence on you with prurient contempt, without suspecting even for a moment that what they are destroying is a human life of just as much value as their own.

That is what homosexuals are: targets, marked out as guilty. Anyone can shoot at them. They have to be wary, live in hiding. Conceal their emotions so as not to betray themselves. But the secrecy, the shame, ends up undermining their sense of identity. Then they give way to lack of confidence, depression, and they become what others have wanted to see them as: weaklings, losers. And the first thing to be affected by that will be their love life and their sexual life: who is going to love a loser, a weakling?

Who is going to love you, Carol, if you degrade yourself by choosing as your partner a woman inferior to you in every respect?

If only Carol had a real interest, a strong passion, capable of sustaining her. If she painted, or collected paintings, or at least did up old country houses to resell. Art, beauty, or even just a real job to believe in, could save her. But Carol has never wanted to work, and will never need to, and as for art, she regards it as boring, like everything that has to be taken seriously and requires a cultivation of taste. Carol is a philistine, a sublime philistine, who does not need to struggle and suffer to approach beauty because she herself *is* beauty. But this will not sustain her for much longer, it is not enough any more.

The homosexual cannot seek an accord with the laws and conventions of society, which are denied to them for ever. From childhood we all memorise the common language of emotions and feelings – a language to which the property of reflecting natural law is fallaciously attributed – but some of us do not recognise ourselves in it, and feel we are strangers, outsiders forced to speak a language that is not ours and in which there are no words to express the things we hold most dear.

And then we fall in love, and suddenly everything seems to make sense: like all those in love, we are stirred by a landscape, elated by a musical phrase, a particular shade of colour makes us feel nostalgic. Like everyone else, we dream of a little white house with a garden around it, and a beautiful woman waiting for us at the door, smiling, and – why not? – a couple of fair-haired children running to meet us. For a moment we think we are at one with the world, that we have finally learned the language of the many. Except for one small detail.

We are very quickly obliged to recognise that it is not like this, that this language will never express our inner truth, that the most vital part of us is left outside, more alien than ever, in open conflict. The common man thinks he lives according to the laws of nature because he mistakes his own conventions for natural law; the homosexual on the other hand is conscious of being at odds with these conventions, which have nothing to do either with his or her impulses or with natural law. Homosexuals are forced to live out their desires and passions mostly in the imagination as these are not reflected in the society around them. So they live in a state of contradiction and tension, on the lookout for the dangers and ambushes they must continually face, from within themselves as much as from without. They live as strangers, as outlaws under a false name.

But they are closer to the truth than the man who believes himself to be normal, in accord with the natural order (which *does not exist*).

They are quick-change performers, counterfeiters, individuals with no identity because a single identity is not enough for them, will never be enough. They are artists. The best ideas, the most lofty inspirations are born of frenzy and tension, certainly not of satisfaction and satiety.

But perhaps all this is just inconsequential chatter to distract myself from the impulse that is keeping me awake and my muscles contracted, like a cramp. The impulse to go cross the corridor and open the door of the bedroom where *she* and *that woman* are sleeping together.

It would be so easy. No one would hear me, they are all sound asleep.

The belt of my nightgown is soft and flexible but sturdy, wound round my fingers closed in a fist.

I imagine the furrow it would dig into the bullneck of *that woman*. I see her congested face, the staring eyes that seem to be popping out of their sockets, the lolling tongue, enormous, obscene.

My hands ache from the strain.

If I don't do it, it is only because of the certainty that I would be discovered immediately. I would have no escape. And I am too afraid of the law to risk losing the only precious thing I possess, my freedom. But if there were a way, a way of killing without being discovered... if I could do it without leaving any trace, remaining in obscurity, beyond suspicion. If someone were to do it in my place: a killer, a hired assassin – no, that would mean exposing myself to blackmail. Yet there must be some means, it is inconceivable that an urge so strong, so overwhelming should be totally impossible to act upon. If I could swap one crime for another, like the characters in the novel I have had in mind now for almost two years. But to whom could I propose such a swap?

Women are too pusillanimous. It would have to be a man, obviously. Women do not kill: they scream, nag, torment, criticise, provoke, belittle – but they do not kill, usually. And think of the humiliation, the shame, if I were to go over there myself with the best of intentions and not succeed in carrying out my purpose, through physical incapacity, pure and simple, and the whole thing were to degenerate into a cat fight! A disgusting scene from "the sleazy circles of vice". How dreadful.

You see, Carol, what you have brought me to? This evening I would kill for you. I would commit any vile act, any crime. There is no moral code I would not transgress, that I have not already transgressed, at least in thought, since I fell in love with you.

And besides, what are moral codes, if not the law of the strongest to which the weakest submit?

August '47, New York

A horrible dream. I am with Carol in some place in the country, a log cabin like that little restaurant in Pine Creek last summer. And everything is as it was then, Carol is wearing a light-coloured semi-transparent shirt and round her neck she has the blue scarf I gave her. She is radiant, more beautiful than ever.

We are sitting at table, having evidently finished our lunch, and I am overcome with the strongest desire mixed with apprehension: where shall we go now? Will we be together this evening? I want to put my arms around her right there and then, to bury my face in her neck, to inhale the scent of her hair.

The anxiety within me grows rapidly. I know that everything depends on her, I know that I am waiting for her to speak, for a *yes* or *no* from her that will decide my fate.

She does not look at me, does not reply, although she seems to know what state I am in.

I say her name, *Carol*.

And then her gaze fastens on me.

All of sudden I am terrorstricken. I realise that this place which before was intimate and comfortable and bright with early-afternoon light, is now vast, in darkness. The shadows thicken, it is night, and there is no one around us, only dark countryside in which the cry of an owl can be heard.

Carol's face then undergoes a hideous transformation. Her gaze turns nasty, her mouth cruel. She laughs at me, at the pain she is about to inflict on me. Her eyes are cold and glittering like ice, and there is the gleam of deception in them.

She is no less beautiful than she has always been, yet she is horrible. More frightful than death.

I wake up in a cold sweat, my teeth chattering.

September '47, NY

Slept until late, got up with a headache. Rose turned up at two with a bunch of flowers from her garden and a jar of homemade peach jam. She is so good to me, poor Rose. I would have preferred a bottle of gin, however.

In bed she is sweet, soft. She cheers me up.

I am beginning to recover.

I am ashamed of my life, so dissipated, so pointless. Rose urges me not to be hard on myself, she tells me that what I have written so far is decidedly good (I have let her read the first three chapters of the novel).

When she left I felt much better. Wrote six pages. Then I listened to some music (Mozart, who always has the power to lift my spirits) and I got immersed in *The Seducer's Diary* by Kierkegaard. Obsessional, cerebral, contrived. I like it.

December '47, NY

Eight pages. I have not been out of the house.

I am beginning to get over Carol.

Yet I feel that she will always be my ideal woman. Precisely because I never knew her or possessed her, I never penetrated her mystery.

Her beauty, her courage, her dare-devilry. The supreme insouciance of her best moments.

What will remain with me for ever: her way of smoking, holding the cigarette between her lips, puffing smoke, rapt in thought, staring into space. Her quizzical look. The warm scent rising from her neckline. Her eyes glittering with anger. Her voice when it hardens, when it breaks, when it becomes husky. The curve of her hips. Her crossed legs. The lobe of her ear with a small pearl in it. Her closed eyes, the moan of pleasure. The white heat of her nearness.

Never abandon me, Nike. I don't mind suffering if that is the price of happiness. I don't mind fighting the very devil if the devil has your eyes. Bless my ambitions and passions, my loves and my hatreds, and preserve me always from peace of mind and peace of the senses. Amen.

II

I have an avid desire to live so many lives.
I want to be so many people before I die.

The post-Carol period is the now inevitable transition to adulthood. Years of struggling against herself. Of highs and lows, anxieties and uncertainties, work and dissipation, enthusiasm and despair. Pat still earns her living by churning out stories of sometimes amusing, more or less idiotic superheroes capable of meeting impossible challenges and almost all living a double life, endowed with an alter ego who is "normal" and beyond suspicion.

But now she is freelance, she no longer spends her mornings in a huge room thick with blue smoke and smelling of brillantine, among masculine colleagues who treat her with a more or less polite wariness or test her willingness to go out with them. She now writes at home, with neat piles of paper on her desk, alongside other piles that are her stories, her first novel, which as with almost all writers is not the first because it was preceded by another that has now been jettisoned, and in any case who can say whether this will actually be the first, that it will become a fully formed creature, capable of making its own way?

Writing, this apparently innocuous and pointless activity, requires great courage. You have to believe in words, believe that these signs on the page have such meaning, are of such importance, that it justifies dedicating to them the best part of a whole lifetime's energy.

Women of her age, in suburban kitchens, with their new electrical household appliances, or in offices in the city, are already veterans of a relentless battle for which they have been trained as loyal soldiers by their mothers: the impossible conquest of happiness. Wafts of the widespread despair called affluence keep them in a state of perpetual wooziness. They dream, they change their hairstyle, they cheat on their husbands.

Pat writes. Continually.

To convince herself, to train herself, to hone the instruments of her trade.

To survive.

Encounters, observations on the books she is reading, dreams, gossip, ideas for short stories and novels, obscene limericks, nasty thoughts, poetry. Writing is all-consuming.

In black notebooks she draws columns, diagrams. Charts on comparative sexuality: available woman and unavailable women. Those who are good in bed, those you can talk to. Graphs showing the impossibility of fulfilment, tables of failed love affairs. Classified by age, height, colour of hair and complexion, attainability and actual attainment, quality of sex, length of the affair, reasons for the break-up, mutual faults and failings – her lovers are laid out in an orderly and objective fashion on Cartesian axes, assaulted on all sides by a chaotic jumble of crossings-out, underlinings and revisions.

Writing is the Ariadne's thread of her personal labyrinth, from which she actually has no wish to find a way out, because by now she knows that exploring it is the most thrilling thing that could ever happen to her in her life.

Like her comic-strip heroes, she too has a secret identity and a double life: writing.

The heroes of the novel she is working on are two men one honest and law-abiding and the other wayward and immoral, indissolubly united by the attraction of opposites and by a pact obliging them to kill for each other.

It is natural, only to be expected, that the protagonists of her stories should be men. Her alter ego is a vaguely asexual male, a man who – unlike her – is well disposed towards women. At least until he kills them.

Besides, all the great writers have men as their protagonists, women are secondary characters at most: the object of desire, the loving mother, the pallid sister, things that do not interest her.

The action, the conflict, the moral dilemma are, as much in the artist's imagination as in the public's, masculine prerogatives. Her heroes must stride through the world, as she, Pat, would like to, the tall gawky girl in jeans, whose large capable hands wield with equal competence the clothes iron and the hammer. Pat who wanders the city on her own, who perches on a bar stool staring into space, or rather with her gaze fixed upon her ghosts, until a friend arrives and distracts her; Pat who goes home in the small hours, her head full of words, on her skin the still warm scent of a woman she is in love with or chasing after.

Pat who feels oppressed by time and space. How to make

the very most of her day in a disciplined pursuance of fruitful activity? Certainly not by sinking – as happens to her all too often, nearly all the time – into the vortex of darkness, alcohol, words, erotic pursuit that when successful soon leads to a sense of satiety and when unsuccessful takes its toll on the nerves, through what is initially delightful and then thwarted expectation.

Only work is of any signficance, wholesome, moral. Only work can save her.

However, the work by which she earns a living is work she despises.

She knows she is good at what she does, and diligence affords her a certain pleasure – fulfilling her assignments, earning money by tapping on the keys of her typewriter, seeing the tidy pile of sheets of paper growing. But the result of her mercenary activity, those crudely drawn comic books bought for a few cents from newspaper kiosks, is something she will never be able to take pride in and won't take her far.

It is imprisonment, nothing more or less… being a typist.

When she goes across the city to deliver her stories to the publisher, she sees around her thousands of people whose daily life is nothing but routine and repetitive work, individuals who may have some talent, but they have lost sight of it or given up on it, and are dragging out a miserable existence of deadlines, children, paydays, office managers… a prison life, totally under external control, the mere thought of which makes her shudder.

She dreams of a life at a comfortable pace, with no timetable, no constraints or obligations, such as only an artist may lead, a life in which work would not be a chore but a pleasure, a luxury, a clean-burning fire. A life that would be a work of art in itself.

However, perhaps she already suspects a truth that the other Pat – the one who will reread her diaries in ten, twenty, thirty years' time, leafing through and annotating the pages in a quest to find herself in this evermore circuitous labyrinth – could impart to her with cold lucidity, without batting an eyelid: that she is not and never will be capable of living the way she dreams of living.

She will always be tormented by the need to do more and to do better, to produce, to prove herself, while struggling against boredom, depression, self-doubt and the sense of inadequacy.

Just like millions of other Americans, she will always be a prisoner of work, no more nor less so than the swollen-footed sales assistants of the big department stores, the office workers who pour out of the subway stations heading for desks that are all alike, the door-to-door salesmen who drag round heavy suitcases redolent of cheap hotels and stale cigarette smoke, or the seamstresses who emerge from their workshops in the evening, hunched and weary-eyed.

The only real big difference there will be between them and her is that the work she wears herself out doing, with painstaking application to her craft, and ever dissatisfied with the results, is writing, which like every form of creation – however imperfect – is a transformation, something in the nature of a chemical process, which produces a heady distillation.

True, there is angst and stress, there is servitude and

failure. There is the dismal experience of fruitless striving, but if you persevere, if you overcome the limitations of your own stupidity – the miracle occurs.

Writing becomes pure joy, it makes your mind scintillate, it stimulates your muscles. It gives you an appetite, it makes you sleep well. It is a vital fluid.

Writing is a drug.

That is why anyone who has become habituated to it cannot stop – not because of the fame and the money, things that Pat, still in her twenties, has not yet attained and often despairs of – but because of the rush in your head, in your whole body.

A bit like flying, weightlessly, above all else. Or like the kick of energy, of lucidity, of power that alcohol gives you in the best moments of a binge – before you realise that your legs cannot support you, that words elude you, and tomorrow you will feel like death.

But writing does not have those unpleasant side effects.

Or like dreaming, when, at the moment of waking, you are able to prolong the dream experience and to guide the story towards the desired conclusion, but all this only for an instant, before daytime rationality destroys the delicate photosensitive texture of the sleep-woven plot.

Writing is the prolongation of those exquisite moments, beyond the confines of time and space.

To reach the state conducive to this miracle it is necessary to go through preparatory stages and imperfect circumstances, to overcome obstacles. Silence is required, a clear mind, the certain knowledge that you have hours at your disposal, a typewriter that works, a supply of blank paper and coffee, no pest who comes knocking at your door.

On top of which, you need to have slept well although not necessarily for a long time, suffered the travails of love to an extent that is stimulating but not debilitating, and to have enough experience of human imperfection to throw yourself audaciously into a new adventure, but not so much that you lose faith in yourself and are prompted to give up working and to go in search of adventures of a different kind in some bar or other.

With every day that passes New York is proving itself to be the least suitable place for writing. New York is full of worldly distractions and obligations, of opportunities and temptations. There is always someone inviting you out for a drink, there is always a glittering evening that turns into a jaded and lacklustre dawn. You need to be in so many different places, to meet the people who matter, to be casual and in the swim of things and *cool*, and Pat is not, never quite enough, there is within her something inadequate and guilty to be kept hidden, like a ladder in a stocking or evidence of a recently committed crime.

To anyone who does not know her well, Pat is an outgoing girl who can hold her liquor and take a joke, and nearly everyone likes her, even if she is a bit weird. But what would they say if they had any inkling of the rages, the yearnings, the crazed longings and the abiding obsessions churning inside her?

Her personality deep down is an abyss of unspeakabe emotions that she is constantly dissecting. No relation to the stereotype image of the extrovert young woman. For a start, there are her feelings towards her mother and family; then there is her pathological need to fall in love, and a sense of humour that others often find chilling. And obviously, the glue and the primer underlying everything, her homosexuality.

To be homosexual is to have a clandestine identity, to belong to a persecuted people or a secret society so reviled that its members, no matter how much they might want to approach each other, cannot do so without revulsion.

Homosexuality is a foreign accent that is heard murmured at the parties of smart sophisticated people but that in everyday life one has to be able to dissemble so as not to be exposed and condemned like soviet spies.

Homosexuality is the ever present subject, as she calls it in her notebooks, into which she unfailingly pours her life, her dreams and her way of thinking. Under the acronym NOEPS, Notes on Ever Present Subject, are secreted the preparatory jottings for the great encyclopedia of dual or multiple identity that the corpus of her novels is to constitute.

Pat is conscious of being an outlaw. On the wrong side of a law that is purely arbitrary, nothing but convention, serving a power that holds sway over individuals, obliterating their critical intelligence, promoting lies. People adapt or become complicit, because after all they have not a great deal to lose – but what if a person is incapable of adapting? If they do not want to lose the only thing they have, themselves?

They have no option but secrecy.

Pat does not want to lose herself or to renounce her most pleasurable emotions, which are also the most terrible, so for her there is no ecstasy without shame, no pride without fear, and the only truth lies in the minting of counterfeit coinage –

all of which is wonderfully inspiring for a writer but becoming too arduous to live.

New York is the capital of wasted time and angst, of fragmented identity and insomnia. She must get away from this city and perhaps even from America, the country of false promises.

America promises its children a new well-being; the war has banished the spectre of the depression and the post-war period is triumphantly heading towards a future that consists of detached houses, refrigerators and cars in which to go shopping at the supermarkets that are springing up around the dormitory towns like mushrooms.

But what is there for a woman in all of this? Nothing, apart from some snivelling brats, a new chrome-plated cooker and maybe some psychotherapy to understand what is eating her. Or to pass the time.

When Pat is depressed by her lack of success as a writer and feeling wretched about her impossible and culpable love affairs, she consoles herself with the thought that, if she were a wife and mother, she would be much worse off.

The wholesome and happy suburban family, the young couple who gaze into each other eyes, he strong and bold, she timorous and sweet, both proud of living in the land of opportunity and democracy – all this makes her want to vomit.

And not only because this is not and never can be her kind of happiness but because it is false.

The American people, so practical and cynical and un-complicated, eradicators of Indians and bison, builders of atomic bombs, have fashioned an ideal world that has no room for the living reality of the human spirit, which is ambiguous and dangerous, mysterious and unstable. American readers have no time for European novels with their irresolute and tormented protagonists. They prefer characters who are clean-living, honest and happy, in a word, normal. Normal up until the moment when, through excess of normality, they explode and kill their nearest and dearest, or their neighbours, as reported in the newspaper articles she has been collecting for years and in which she reads, not without some amusement, about another side of America, an America that is crazy and criminal.

Pat is beginning to wonder what chance she could possibly have of becoming a writer in a country like America.

A country whose dreams are, for her, nightmares.

Pat has nothing to do with American normality, and this is becoming ever more apparent. While as a young girl she took pains over her appearance and the way she dressed, with not always commendable results, now that she leads a freer and more solitary life she has less and less desire to waste time pretending to be what she is not. She is revealing herself. The hurried walk, the slightly too masculine shirt, the lock of hair too briskly flicked back when stressing a point in discussion. And these are only the external signs, the least important. Attitudes, tastes, ideas, there is not the smallest fraction of herself that does not express that irreducible deviance from the norm that is not permitted to the ordinary American citizen – to anyone, that is, who cannot claim to be an artist and therefore deviant by definition.

But is Pat an artist? Where are the fruits of her labour? The years are passing, she will soon be thirty, and what has she produced so far? For how much longer will she be interesting – and when will she become ridiculous, pathetic, a failure?

Her friends, especially the older ones, fascinating women in their forties, of whom Rosalind is the doyenne, and who will play such a major part in her life until she too is in her forties, are lavish with good advice.

In long conversations, which are nerve-wracking amorous sieges on her part and at the same time alcoholic marathons that could kill a horse, her friends tell her that a homosexual writer, whether a man or woman, rarely attains true greatness (indeed never in the case of women – no, Gertrude Stein does not count, she was an eccentric, not a great writer), which after all is the universality of human feeling, love between man and woman, reproductive sexuality, the sense of continuity through children, grandchildren and so on.

"Universal is what we all feel, but who are we?" asks Pat.

"The majority of people," her friend replies, "all of us, you too, if there weren't something not quite right about you…"

Needless to say, her friends, apart from Rosalind, are hetero, or at least that is their official profession of faith, even if they do not disdain to be courted by her, but rarely do they concede more than a kiss or a caress, round about three or four in the morning. They are normal women, in good standing with the world.

And while she sits at the other end of the table or of the sofa, with one part of her brain frantically trying to work out how to get closer, they tell her that she probably has some hormonal malfunction, no real woman whose hormones were in order would have big strong hands like hers, beautiful hands actually but too masculine, these days there are treatments available.

And what about that guy, the one she met at Yaddo, they ask, as she lies beside them in bed, worn out with desire and whisky, because it is almost dawn and they might as well invite her to sleep there, and luxuriate for a few hours in the nearness of her young and ardent body lying on the mattress, like Tantalus in the river in Hades.

Tantalus, so close to succulent fruits and fresh water, yet unable to eat and drink because fruit and water – her friend's bare shoulder, her hair lying on the pillow – perpetually elude his grasp, his pursed lips.

She was at Yaddo for two months, where she was allocated a big shady room looking out on the green expanse of a park. Her work went well despite partying with other residents in the evenings, perhaps because she did not have to put on a show of being normal for anyone there, it being a place of diversity, a realm of pure individuality, where everyone has the right and the duty to cultivate their own creative madness. Yaddo is a writers' colony, and those lucky enough to be able to stay there are exempted from the chores of everyday life, someone prepares their meals for them and cleans their room, nothing is required of guests other than what they have come into this world for: to write.

An oasis. A hundred pages of her novel.

Yes, that guy, she says, her mouth furred with smoke and anxiety. Ned is all right, she has great admiration for him because he has already had a book published, he has ideas and perseverance, he will get on. They see each other fairly regularly, they are engaged. Well, more or less. Maybe they will get married.

But that is wonderful, says the friend, turning towards her enthusiastically – and contact with that voluptuous body causes thrills of pleasure to pulse through Pat's side. Marry him, it is your great opportunity. Your treatment. There is nothing like marriage for making you understand certain things.

If she says so – after all she has been married two or three times – there is good reason to believe it.

And it may even turn out that, knowing her to be engaged, whoever is the friend of the moment grants her more than a kiss or a caress – because after all Pat is now safely launched on the comforting highway of normality and whatever happens between them is only a *divertissement* of no consequence.

Serving her as guide on her journey towards social acceptability is a Freudian, a certain female Dr Klein – no relation to the more illustrious Melanie, but the German name is already in itself almost a guarantee. If she really must pay, she might as well be getting the real thing at least, instead of some nasty *made in USA* imitation.

From Pat's diary

NY, November 1948

First session with Dr K. She is a woman of about forty-two or forty-three, a type that could be called "petite", hazel eyes, chestnut hair, an attractive voice, generally pleasant, perhaps a little too severely dressed, but obviously she has to maintain her position as a sober and respectable psychotherapist. Her consulting room is dark and solid, black leather armchairs, English hunting scenes on the walls, flounced yellow curtains being the only feminine touch. On the desk she has two framed photographs, one a wedding photo and the other of two smiling children, probably placed there to vouch for her impeccable normality.

She asks what has prompted me to come to her. I tell her that I am more or less engaged to a man who wants to marry me, and I would also like that, possibly, but I cannot make up my mind. In fact I am attracted to women, but naturally this constitutes a handicap for my social life and for my career – I am a writer, although I have not yet published anything apart from a few short stories – and so rationally I know that getting married to Ned is a good idea, but I cannot overcome my misgivings. What do I want of psychoanalysis? To allow me to marry without too many problems, that is all.

Dr Klein looks at me for a long moment.

"You say you're attracted to women. In what sense?"

"In *that* sense. That's to say, in every sense."

"You're sure of that?"

"I would say so."

"Have you had any emotional and sexual relations with women?"

"Yes, I have." (She spoke in the past tense, and I do not see any reason to correct her, in substance it makes no difference.)

"But now you are engaged."

"Exactly." (If she were not a psychoanalyst, I would say that she is dim-witted.)

"And what are your misgivings about marriage?"

"Firstly, sexual. I don't like going to bed with Ned. Every time I try, I hope things will go better, but they don't."

"Is he the first man with whom you have had sexual relations?"

"No, I've had sex with others, but there's not much difference."

"You do not manage to reach orgasm?"

"No, it wouldn't much matter to me about orgasm, the fact is" – do I really have to explain all this to this woman with her discreet lipstick and not a hair out of place, a ship in port anchored by the photos of her children – "I don't like the thing itself, it doesn't seem... it doesn't seem right to me."

"Right?" she repeats.

"I mean, not right for me. Wrong. Unnatural. It offends me. Physically. And not just physically."

Dr Klein studies her well-manicured nails, ten shiny little almonds at the end of her fingers, then she gives a faint smile. "You're very direct," she says.

"Well, I don't see any reason for beating around the bush. After all, I presume this session will be costing me a fair amount."

Doc Klein adopts a serious expression. "We'll have to start with your childhood," she says. "It's clear that you have a problem with men. This kind of thing usually has its origin in the early years of life, in the child-parent relationship. Tell me about your mother and your father..."

And I had to satisfy her and plunge my hands back into the old wasp's nest.

My father – who knows anything about my father?

"The first time I saw him I was twelve years old, and then we met again during my adolescence when, for him, I wasn't a little girl but a young woman, one he fancied to judge by the lingering kiss he gave me on my cheek and close to my mouth;

and, for me, he was a stranger, the person who had passed on to me the genes of a family of German immigrants. An interesting fellow, to be sure, but a father only in theory, and better that it stayed that way. It was my mother who wanted to marry him, she saw his photo in a photographer's shop window and decided to track him down and make him hers, and she succeeded, because Mary, my mother, is a woman who gets her way. Forceful? No, I used to think so, but that isn't the right word. I would say dogged and unscrupulous. A past-master at manipulation, a type of American woman more common than people think. They were married and separated before I was born, in fact I should not even have been born, she tried to abort me by drinking turpentine, but didn't succeed. Actually the turpentine must have done me good, because to this very day I like the smell – as a child I imagined becoming a painter because I was attracted by that good strong smell of solvents that painters use. What does not kill you makes you stronger. That's an old family saying, ha, ha."

Dr Klein does not laugh. After a moment's silence she suggests that my mother's attempt to abort is at the root of my resentment against her. I try to explain that this is absurd, I could never take exception to a woman who did not want a child, that's up to her, isn't it? In her position I would have done the same, a woman has the right to choose whether to have children or not to have them. Besides, at that time I, Pat, did not exist, what was in her womb was just a small shapeless blob, it wasn't *me*. The reasons I have for resenting my mother are quite different, dating to *after* my birth.

But Dr Klein looks at me and does not say anything. Obviously having studied the texts of Freud and Jung and other eminent European males, she now knows me better than I know myself.

NY, December 1948

Second day of work at Bloomingdale's. Only two days, and already I am engulfed in the unspeakable dreariness of a wage-earning job. After eight hours on your feet in the toy department, amid the continuous hubbub of customers coming and going and demanding your attention, the only thing you can think about when you get home is certainly not writing but having a long hot shower and collapsing into bed. It is systematic demoralisation, the scientific extinguishment of any creative impulse. Fortunately it will only go on for two weeks.

Ned turns up at seven o'clock with two steaks and starts cooking, even though I tell him I am not hungry. He adopts that attitude of affectionate protectiveness, of a fatherly husband, or perhaps of a mother, which irritates me so much. I pick at the steak and tell him no, he cannot stay the night. I am too tired even for "just lying side by side like two friends" and I tell him that friends usually lie in separate beds, and if they are in bed together they are not friends but something else.

He sulks, wheels out the fact that we have not been together for weeks, and so on... and I remind him that I am doing all this for him, that if I have taken a temporary job as a sales assistant it is only to pay for the extremely expensive therapy sessions with Doc Klein that are supposed to straighten out my psyche and turn me into what he wants, a wife. We discuss once again the fact that after getting married, each of us will be entitled to our own sphere of freedom, without any sexual or emotional obligation, and Ned comes out with the statement that husband and wife are a single unit, that being a couple implies a partial sacrifice of the rights of a single person, I tell him those were not the terms of the agreement, and we end up in the usual place: he loves me and I don't love him. And the reason that I don't love him is – guess what – because I am selfish and immature. I am not a real woman, generous and capable of thinking of others, but an insecure and self-absorbed girl, a narcissist who prefers to see herself reflected in another girl instead of engaging in a constructive challenge with a male. This is followed by a subtle allusion to the fact that this is precisely why I am not getting anywhere with my novel.

I tell him that in that case it is hard to see why he is wasting his time on such a loser, and he had better leave at once. I am enraged and hurt but try not to show it.

Ned looks at me and here once again is that metamorphosis against which I am defenceless. His face switches from anger to pathos, what looks suspiciously like a tear appears in his right eye, while the left gazes at me with the blind devotion of a rejected and importunate puppy. I allow him to stay.

And while I am with him I think of Rose, right here a week ago, and Liz, last spring in Cuernavaca, but that's no help because the idea of a woman's body, fragrant, seductive and desirable, makes the present situation even more intolerable to me. As usual, I end up feeling angry and humiliated – and how can I explain my anger to him? How can I tell him that I do not at all regard it as any right of his to desire me, or any duty of mine to lend myself to his desire?

All this anger – about the hours of wretchedness, the irresolvable thoughts, the sense of being right but not being

73

able to say so because no one would understand – suffocates me. I stay awake for a long time and in the morning I have a migraine. Ned makes coffee, he is affectionate, relaxed, happy. He thinks he has gained something, scored a point in his favour, so he can allow himself to be understanding of my bad mood.

But he is mistaken. And sooner or later he will have to come to terms with that.

NY, December 1948

In bed with chicken pox. Fortunately Ned is afraid of catching it and leaves me in peace.

Yesterday, at Bloomingdale's, halfway through a stressful morning, with waves of customers all in a rush besieging the toy counter, and me limping because one of my shoes hurts, and the clamour of voices so deafening it is impossible to hear your own thoughts inside your head – yesterday, suddenly, it happens.

A woman, tall, blonde, elegant, steps out of the elevator and looks around. For a moment the world stops dead in its tracks and a great silence falls. I know for sure that she has seen me, just as I have seen her, and she is coming straight towards me. As she approaches, one step after the other, unbuttoning her fur coat and revealing a dress of heavyweight silk, I hear only the beating of my heart and I think that what is happening is a miracle, a revelation, something that possesses me entirely. The unknown woman hesitates for a moment in front of the counter, then turns towards me.

She has eyes of green like mountain water when the ice melts. Her voice is deep and velvety, with a bit of edge to it, a hint of cynicism and disillusionment, it is kind, however, and so caressing that I feel my legs trembling and I instinctively cling to the counter.

There is in her tone of voice a subdued note of complicity, as though, despite not knowing each other, we share some secret. She wants a doll for her daughter. I show her the finest one. She asks if it can be delivered to her address before Christmas. I assure her, it will arrive in time. If I have to take it to her myself.

As she walks away, I clutch in my hands the little piece of paper with her name and address on it, it is a link that connects me with something new and wonderful, I shall not lose it.

In the meantime I have moved in with my mother because I have a high temperature. Her idea of nursing consists of reading out to me edifying extracts from a Christian Science textbook by Mary Baker Eddy, who herself maintains that you are not cured by medicines but only by raising your mind to God. I refused to listen. Fortunately, there was some aspirin in the house, dating back to the pre-Christian era.

NY, January 1949

Dr Klein does not understand. She is convinced that I have had visions, hallucinations perhaps brought on by fever.

What did the stranger at Bloomingdale's say to me? Nothing. What was written on the slip of paper? Nothing, apart from her name and address (her husband's name, actually).

And so what makes me think this encounter with a married woman buying a Christmas present for her daughter is so important, so fraught with signficance?

I deduce that Dr Klein knows nothing about the messages of desire that two women can exchange with a mere flutter of the eyelashes, in a language much more subtle than any between a man and a woman. She must at some time have exchanged similar messages – even though more crude and obvious – with a man! Or perhaps not, perhaps it is not something that truly respectable women do. Or rather, they forget they have done so as soon as they have landed their catch, because they no longer have any need of sexual wiles, they have already got what they want. Who knows whether Dr Klein is in love with the guy – already a little bald – who is in the wedding photograph with her, or whether she married him to prove to the world that she was a real woman?

In what sense, she asks me again, do I feel this encounter is important to me?

I don't know yet, I tell her – perhaps I shall send a note to Mrs Robert Senn, after all I know where she lives, and I will ask to see her again, or perhaps I will write a novel about her, about the two of us, a girl trying to find her way, and a woman who is at a turning point in her life and who has to show great courage.

In reality, both, the woman and the girl, have to be courageous if they are not to die. Or to marry Ned – did I really say that?

Perhaps not, or at least Doc Klein cannot have heard it because she did not react at all.

"Let's talk about your mother," she says.

"I'm beginning to be fed up with talking about my mother, there are other things to talk about in this world, aren't there?"

"You're trying to avoid the issue," Doc says insistently.

And we return to Mother. Who was everything to me in my early years – she and grandma. In reality it was grandma who took care of me, Grandma Willie Mae, I can feel her hands as though they were touching me now, that fine soft skin covered with little wrinkles. She smelled of biscuits and soap. She was the one who dressed me, and fed me. Calm, strict, down to earth, Grandma Willie Mae was a safe haven. I remember that as a little girl I sometimes took refuge in her arms as I have never done in those of my mother.

But my mother was the one for whom I waited anxiously in the evenings, when Mary was finally free from work and spent time with me – if she didn't have anything better to do.

And then along came Stanley, my stepfather, and there was almost no room for me any more, it was he that Mary wanted to please. And he with whom she started rowing almost immediately, and home became a place that resounded with arguments like an opera theatre with the obsessively repeated performance of some deafening work. There is a pattern, a score that arguments follow, like music, *andante*, *mosso*, *allegretto con furore*, after a while it becomes a second language, you can understand everything even from the next room, even with the door closed, with your ears blocked. You know what point they have reached, what will happen next, and you feel powerless because you cannot change the music or make it stop. I was convinced that all this anger, this resentment of hers, was justified, that he had done something terrible to her, and when I was grown-up I would punish him for it – I couldn't wait!

We had moved to New York, into a very small apartment, the walls were thin, I couldn't escape. It was hell.

It took me years to realise that excruciating score was not something she endured but what she wanted, she was the conductor of the orchestra. My mother likes arguing, it gives her a way of insulting her adversary, of letting rip and reaffirming her moral supremacy, it is a blast of vitality. Men go to war, they go hunting, they watch boxing and get into fights – but what can a woman do to give vent to her repressed aggression? My mother instigates a blazing row, that is her recourse.

She had work problems, I think. Mary was a fashion designer, she did publicity illustrations, and getting commissions became ever more difficult, she ended up being supported by her husband, a simpler solution but more frustrating. She got her own back by cheating on him, I'm sure she had affairs, but Stanley always turned a blind eye, in fact two blind eyes.

He too must have relished those scenes, I imagine – perhaps it was their way of rekindling desire, revitalising their relationship. Stanley is certainly a bit of a masochist, he should talk to Dr Klein about it.

"Do you not think there is almost always a power game underlying human relationships?" I ask her.

Dr Klein does not reply.

However, in the meantime my mother had also begun to pick on me. I was not the daughter she wanted, I was untidy, I read too much, I did too well at school, I wasn't popular with the boys, I was *strange*. When I was fourteen she asked me if I were not by any chance a lesbian.

What she actually said to me, I remember very well, how could I forget? "Look at you, you could be one of *them*. You're not a lesbian, are you?" That's what she said.

Lesbian, what a word to use with a fourteen-year-old girl. A word so fraught with abhorrence, even if technically correct.

I have never denied it, I have never said no, and this must have scared her. She has never since asked me a direct question about it, so obviously I have not been able to give any direct answers, which is just as well – or worse, I don't know.

I do not hate my stepfather any more. I have realised that he is worse off than I am. We both have to deal with this woman who subjects us to an enervating alternation between arguments and reconciliation. First of all, she systematically tears you apart, then while you are licking your wounds she comes back at you, all sweetness and light, asking whether you might happen to be mad at her.

She is afraid of losing us. If we leave her, Stanley and I, who could she torment? At a certain age, getting yourself another man is not easy, and you can't have any more children. Poor mother, without any victims her life would be meaningless. At least I can live on my own, escape her control most of the time, whereas Stanley has to serve a life sentence.

If I marry Ned I will make her happy. Not that she deserves it, but at least she will leave me in peace for a while.

Dr Klein suggests that my mother's behaviour – alternating between love and abandonment, selfishness and seduction – has affected my whole life, and obviously my amorous behaviour. According to her, I will always respond to this model, and in certain situations I will put it into practice myself.

There is a horrible bleak humour in the idea of hating my mother so much that I end up resembling her. One day it will inspire me.

NY, January 1949

I saw her, a few hours ago. The image of her has remained in my eyes, clear and precise. She was wearing a soft grey dress and she was sitting in front of the fire. There were still Christmas decorations in the garden.

The urge to see her suddenly came over me. Actually, I have been thinking about it for days but as something distant, unreal. And yet today I left home in the early afternoon knowing that I really *had* to do it, that it was the only thing that truly mattered to me at that moment.

At Grand Central Station, beneath the echoing vaults and in the midst of the crowd, a tremendous euphoria sets my heart racing. In a short while I will be seeing her, I know where she lives – Mrs Robert Senn, a tall thirty-five-year-old stranger. She is my magnificent prey.

With every step, with every sway of the train that is taking me towards her, my heart overflows with a guilty joy. My hands are sweaty, I am nervous and impatient like an assassin at her first murder.

Following the one you love is not very different from stalking your victim. Killing is like making love: you are with her, you hold her in your arms, and for a moment she alone is real to you and you to her, her eyes staring into yours, the world does not exist beyond the two of you, time stops. For a moment you have her full attention. You are everything to her: mother, God, the beginning and the end.

There is no other way of entirely, totally, possessing another human being.

Unless you manage to transform them for ever into an

image of themselves – a statue, a painting. A piece of music.
A book.

When I got off the train at *her* station I was so exhausted with
anticipation, and with a strange fear that was sweet and terrible,
I had to have a drink to give myself strength. I took a bus, then
dithered for a while before plucking up the courage to ask the
driver for the stop on her street. When he repeated the name
of the street out loud I felt faint, as if he had unmasked me in
front of everybody. As I got off, I had the feeling the eyes of
every single passenger were following me, that they all knew
where I was going, and why.

The house is at the bottom of a wide residential road – big
gardens and secluded villas in leafy surroundings. The hedges
and yards were still covered with undisturbed snow, everything
was still and white and blue in the early twilight of winter. I
stood in front of the gate for a few minutes, knowing that if
someone had seen me they might have become suspicious, but
there was no one else out on the street, not a voice or a sound
to be heard. In the end, gripped by a strange exhilarating terror,
I did the most dangerous thing: I climbed over the low wall
and walked across the vast white expanse of the garden, my
footsteps clearly visible behind me. I hid in some shrubbery
whose branches were weighed down with snow, right under
the windows.

And from there I saw her enter the warmly-lit room, of
which I could see almost every detail through the big window.

She was as I remembered her: decisive, elegant, graceful,
with a touch of pride in the way she tossed her hair back,
suddenly interrupting the gesture to look outside (making me

almost faint with the fear of being discovered in my hiding-place in the snow).

She reminds me of Carol, obviously, but less brusque, more composed and remote, and enveloped in a solitude all of her own, as if in a silk shawl.

She sat in an armchair with a book in her hand, but she was not reading it, she was thinking or perhaps dreaming, her gaze lost in space (and every so often dangerously turned in my direction, as if aware of my presence despite not being able to see me).

For how long did I remain there, my feet frozen in wet shoes, letting a sense of her life envelop me?

It was like becoming weightless, not being me any more. Cast adrift from myself, absorbed into the existence of this adorable stranger – being the fabric touching her skin, the yellow light from the lamp on her face – feeling an almost intolerable nostalgia for something that had never been.

Then a car turned into the street and stopped in front of the house. I hid among the trees, paralysed with fear. The melting snow was dripping down my neck. A man went into the house, Mr Robert Senn for sure, and shortly afterwards she looked round, spoke to him, got up and left the room. From my observation post I could not see anything else. Luckily, after a while the panel of light in the large window went out, the garden was plunged into darkness, and I was able to leave without being seen.

One thing is certain: I shan't say anything about it to Dr Klein. She wouldn't understand.

NY, February 1949

I think Dr Klein is failing to grasp one essential detail: I don't want to be *cured* – in the sense of becoming normal. (God preserve me from that!) I want to use the psychoanalysis to enable me to get married without too many problems, because I think being a married woman is going to save me a lot of trouble, and Ned is the right person to see this thing through with – though I doubt this more and more with every day that passes.

Dr Klein's faith in her profession is ingenuous and in a way irritating; she does not realise that I want to *make use of* psychoanalysis! And not as a highway through the unconscious so that it can be colonised – but rather as a network of paths through the jungle so that I can go wherever *I* want to! She is convinced there are only certain routes that may be followed in order to reach certain destinations (normality, in other words the worst form of perversion). This narrowness of vision leads me to doubt the value of the method.

I have occasionally wondered how she would respond if I were to invite her for a drink, outside of these therapy sessions. (Obviously I know this is off limits.) But not having done it before now, I discover that my desire to gain access to her private life, and possibly her bed, is ever decreasing.

She is not adventurous enough for me. Yesterday I caught myself feeling something new, for these sessions at least: for a few moments I was plain bored.

NY, February 1949

Read a couple of chapters of the novel to Ned, who made some suggestions that I intend to work on. A pleasant and positive evening, especially because at the end of it he did not insist on staying. Why can't things always be like that? Ned would be an ideal husband if we always devoted our attention to interesting things like writing, and not conflictual things like sex and the relationship between two married people.

Ned says the novel (I continue to have doubts about the title, he suggests *Strangers on a Train*, which is not bad) has enormous potential, that I must continue to explore the ambiguous and disturbing aspect of the attraction between the two men, the way in which the bad guy manages in the end to transform the good guy into a criminal, playing on the dark impulses that lurk within him, as they do within every one of us. In this materialistic world dominated by conflict and the will to power we are all potential victims of the seduction of evil, and therefore it is morally correct to expose it and demonstrate the catastrophic results of it – Ned claims.

Which is absolutely fine by me, of course.

What I cannot explain to him is that I am quite fond of the bad guy, Bruno. He is a monster, agreed, he is spoiled and twisted and mean and probably homosexual as well (this is debatable, although it would be better if we did not discuss it) but I can't help it, I like him a lot more than that dumb, boring, nice young man Guy. Pity I have to kill him off in the end.

NY, March 1949

Horrible row with Ned on the usual subject. He turns up in the late afternoon, I am in a good mood, my work has gone well, eight pages, we go out for a drink, then he wants to stay out and have dinner with friends, I prefer to go home and read over what I have written today. Ned tries to pressurise me but eventually gives in and goes off clearly disappointed and perhaps hurt, with that look that says: this is not the end of it.

And in fact a few hours later he reappears, just at the most crucial stage of my working day, while I am lying on the bed thinking about what I will write tomorrow, it is the time of day when thoughts are free to wander, creating unexpected interconnections, for days I have had Camus' stranger on my mind, a man who does not share the commonplaces and sentimentalism of the mass of the population, who speaks another language, a man whom the others deem to be immoral and cold and cruel, but who in reality is simply more honest – and I am musing on how I might be able to construct a character like that of my own, so that in the end he is not judged and condemned by society but manages to get away with it…

And just at that point Ned rings at the door making a huge racket in danger of waking the neighbours, I run to let him in and he looks at me with that tragic expression of a strong and patient man unjustly put upon by a cruel and irresponsible woman – that would be me – and it is clear, he is thoroughly plastered.

He tells me that he got into a fight with someone to defend my reputation. A guy at the bar apparently made some unpleasant remarks about me – that I am a lesbian and I have a moustache – and he felt obliged to take a swing at him, now his hand is bleeding. I take care of him as best I can, actually I would like to throw him out but it is midnight and I am afraid that Ned might create even more of a rumpus on the stairs, getting me into trouble with the landlord. I tell him I don't care what his friends think of me, I don't have a moustache and that guy had better keep an eye on his girlfriend, with whom he

85

most likely has problems. Ned tries to put his arms around me, I wriggle away, he berates me for being cold, selfish, callous, not having any respect for his feelings… the usual rigmarole. I make him a strong coffee.

Unfortunately the coffee wakes him up, at least temporarily, and he sits down in an armchair, determined "to talk".

And so, we talk. He tells me I am not "like that", it is just a phase, an attitude, stubbornness. He knows very well what *dykes* are like, he has encountered a few in his life, they are monstrous creatures, tough masculine lesbians who hate men because they are consumed with penis envy. I tell him that when we met, at Yaddo, he didn't think that, he was open-minded and accommodating and without any prejudices, but Ned carries on regardless, telling me that on Saturday nights, outside a seedy bar in his neighbourhood, there is always a little group of dykes fighting like crazy, they would gouge each other's eyes out if somebody, often the police, did not turn up to stop them. He tells me it is well known that relationships between *that type*, whether they are men or women, quickly degenerate into hate and hysteria and jealousy, to levels that *we normal* people cannot even imagine. Are they my kind of people, are they who I want to hang out with and identify with? He cannot believe that is what I really want, and he has to save me from a mistake that could be fatal to me.

And so on, for at least half an hour, in which he managed to insinuate that my work on comics, in itself ridiculous and not very serious, might have something to do with my sexual inclinations. Only an infantile and immature woman would prefer to do that kind of work rather than get married and settle down.

Unlike other occasions, tonight his words leave me rather

cold – aside from an increasing sense of annoyance.

While he is talking I am thinking: after a few months of pyschotherapy that has done nothing but dwell on the theme of "Pat and her perversions and neuroses", I am now accustomed to confronting it with a certain clinical detachment, I am more lucid and less vulnerable – and also a little bit fed up. In the end what use has the psychoanalysis been?

I tell him he need not worry about my reputation in New York as I am about to go to Europe. The much discussed trip we were supposed to make together, and which I will do alone.

Without him?

Well, yes, without him.

And we'll get married when I come back?

But since I don't even know whether I will ever come back? (I am of course bluffing but Ned seems to take this seriously.)

What about my psychotherapy?

To hell with the therapy! If I had saved that money I would already be in Europe now!

But that I did not say to him. In the meantime Ned has turned predictably romantic and started rhapsodising about what he loves about me: I am so fragile and funny and innocent and transparent, so different from all the others, I am a wild roe deer, a heron with long, white, awkward wings and so on. To what extent can I be different, I want to ask him, before I am *too* different? How long will it be before I change from a timid doe into a dangerous animal, a crocodile with long teeth, or a hyena? This idea is so amusing that I cannot help laughing but at the moment Ned is in no state to appreciate the joke.

He finally falls asleep in the armchair but by now it is

nearly dawn, tomorrow I will be shattered. Goodbye to another day's work.

If I had taken the train and spent the night in Mrs Senn's garden, with the prospect of seeing her in the morning, in her nightgown, with her hair loose and her face still soft with sleep, in the leather armchair behind the big window – that would have been a better use of my time.

NY, April 1949

I informed Dr Klein of my decision not to come any more. She remained unperturbed. There will certainly be no shortage of patients in a city full of the deranged and the disturbed. Good for her. She recommended group therapy, with a certain number of married women who have "problems of latent homosexuality".

Well, that could be interesting. I imagine all they are waiting for is to be seduced by the first woman who comes along. But why should I pay to meet women with "problems of latent homosexuality" who, on top of that, are married?

No thank you, there are too many of those in my life already.

NY, May 1949

I leave tomorrow! My first really big trip – after Mexico, but Europe is another thing altogether.

Mexico was a discovery of freedom, a breath of oxygen, and all that sunshine and those colours – so bright they become dark and dangerous – but basically it is a country that is too different and in certain respects too primitive to be anything more than an exotic refuge, a holiday from America. Europe, however, holds out the promise of new discoveries, even about myself. In Europe writers can still tell stories in which good and evil, fiction and reality, confront each other and blend into each other and endlessly play their enthralling game. Whereas in America *everything* is fiction.

The United States is a story for children, a comic strip for adults who never grow up, a collective dream.

We Americans are, all of us, waiting for a train that will never come, the train of our future happiness – every one of us in our heart of hearts knows full well this train does not exist – but still we all believe in it.

Now, however, I am waiting for a ship, or rather the ship is in port waiting for me – the *Queen Mary*! I will arrive in London aboard a queen. And from there to Paris, then Marseilles, and from the south of France I will go to Italy and at last I shall see Venice, Florence, Rome, Naples…

I shall be crossing the Atlantic in a third class cabin, alas. If I had not had to pay Dr Klein's fees I would have been able to travel in first class.

Naples, August 1949

Naples is fabulous and squalid, as embracing as a regressive dream. I stroll through the narrow streets between buildings of historic magnificence that are falling to pieces, surrounded by the smell of food and excrement, of flowers and filth, among stray dogs and ragged children, amid outbursts of voices and blasts of American songs on the radio. I hear the hiss of the espresso machines in the dark interiors of cafés and smell the fragrance of the cream pastries, and of the roses that a black-eyed girl with a dirty radiant face holds out to me insistently.

A continuous solicitation of the senses, almost to the limit of endurance, but which draws me out of myself – I feel I am floating, in dispersal, in disintegration, and therefore more alive than ever, in the decaying piazzas, in the glimpses of the sea, in the alleyways where people appear at the threshold, revealing cavernous interiors, unmade beds, stoves and madonnas in a gloom teeming with human beings.

It is curious how, as my trip goes on, I feel ever more at ease with the people I meet – as if I were able to allow myself the luxury, in the cities of Europe, of not always hiding, of not being continuously on the defensive.

Here I am a different person, not the efficient, hopeful and insecure Pat who sends her stories to the editors of NY magazines, nor the time-waster who haunts bars picking up girls (although in Paris I was that too), and I am certainly no longer the neophyte trying to meet the right people at intellectual salons and who is always afraid of not being accepted, but nor am I the solitary writer who prefers reading the existentialists to going out and meeting people, still less Ned's fiancée tormented with doubts about marriage – here I am just an American passing through, like so many others, someone without ties, who goes where she wants – and I am more sure-footed, it is easier for me to make friends and to chat – it is as if I have no identity, and strangely this makes me feel much more comfortable, more myself.

I have taken a room in a small relatively quiet *pensione*, I can hear the noise outside, the bells, the car horns and the street cries, but they do not disturb me. I have started to write my Bloomingdale story, the one I quickly sketched out the plot of, that feverish night last December.

A very young and very innocent girl, who still knows almost nothing about herself, meets a much older woman who is attractive and mysterious, and she is dazzled by her. From that moment on all she wants is to see her again... soon she will have to realise that for the rest of the world their love is a crime, that they are two offenders to be hunted down, fugitives from human justice – and she will have to decide between renouncing her feelings and pursuing a dangerous freedom.

I too, here in Naples, am expecting a beautiful woman to arrive soon, soon she will be here, in this room! I can't believe it, yet I know it is true, Elisabeth will come, she has written to me, we will see each other again after those days we had in London, days that were only too short, and here she will be all mine – no work, husband, friends, or social obligations to keep her occupied – and we will be able to wander the city arm in arm, as Italian women do, and drive over to Vesuvius in a horse-drawn trap, and listen to the sounds of the night through the half-closed window of my room – although I imagine that she will want to stay in a more decent and more comfortable place, a real hotel.

And then – after a few weeks of all that – she will go back to London and I to America. It will be a Mediterranean interlude.

Never mind. An interlude is better than nothing.

While I await her arrival in this astonishingly alien city that is yet mine, I feel close to the feelings of that night last December. It is as if I still had that fever, not the burning fever of chickenpox but a light and diffuse fever, the prolonged thrill of expectation, of anticipated kisses – and all this turns into writing with such ease and joy!

I think I will call it *The Garden of Tantalus*. Because that is the situation that my protagonist experiences: for her, love and happiness are very near at hand, on offer, within reach – but the world's condemnation and the barriers erected by respectable and normal society make them unobtainable, as the fruit and the water were to the starved and parched Tantalus.

The seed of *Tantalus*, which germinated so quickly and so vigorously in the New York winter, was put aside, forgotten and then rediscovered. Its destiny is a struggle for growth amid difficulties and contradictions, in a sometimes frenetic fluctuation between enthusiasm and despair, euphoria and panic. As the writing progresses, Pat realises that her ambitions as a writer are naive and dangerous. Writing her own truth, saying what is not yet said, and by that simple act making it visible and acceptable to the world – what a foolish and childish illusion!

The world – starting with her literary agent, her friends, her editors – not only make clear that they do not think as she does but try to make her give up this enterprise that might turn out to be disastrous. Pat is certainly no wide-eyed innocent but on this occasion she proves to be no less naive than her protagonist, Theresa, who is ten years younger than she is. Humiliated and unsure of herself, but tenacious and stubborn as ever, and almost reluctantly, she continues to pound away at the typewriter and to count the pages. She will finish the novel which she is now prepared to disown, and she will sign it with the name Claire Morgan. This puts her in the same category as females writers of this genre, for whom the use of one or more pseudonyms is an established practice, the rule, without exception. The book will be loved by a vast reading public but will not be admitted into literature's respectable circles and it will remain a bastard child, unpresentable in society and relegated to the literary undergrowth of pulp fiction.

At least for the next twenty years.

The unknown woman in Bloomingdale's will never run the risk of coming across that drugstore romance with a cover featuring a troubled young woman reclining on a divan while a seductress wreathed in cigarette smoke lays a predatory hand on her shoulder, and in the background a male figure suggestive of Frankenstein's monster looms menacingly. Nor that of recognising herself in the beautiful woman in a fur coat who one winter's afternoon bought a doll from an attractive and slightly gauche young salesgirl.

It is November 1951 when Pat, back on the Old Continent, this time in Munich, receives a letter from Rose, her loyal comforter, who continues to write to her and keeps her informed about America. Rose is the only person, apart from Dr Klein, to whom Pat has ever spoken about her Bloomingdale Muse.

In the envelope is a newspaper cutting that announces the death by suicide of a certain Mrs Senn, of Mount Vernon, aged thirty-six. She reads it in disbelief, with her hands trembling, and discovers that Mrs Robert Senn (the very same!) was found lifeless in her car, suffocated by exhaust fumes. The garage doors were hermetically sealed, locked from the inside.

For two hours Pat remains motionless in her room, incapable of doing anything but stare at the ceiling.

She keeps picturing her, seated in the dark armchair in front of the fireplace, with that air of stillness and mystery.

Watching her from outside on that winter's evening, her shoes wet with snow, she did not feel the cold. Now she does.

Would it have changed anything if she had had the courage to ring the doorbell?

What do we know of others, of their happiness or unhappiness?

Suicide is a deed she could never commit. Life has too great a hold over her. She can imagine murder – unleashing her aggression on another person – but not suicide. Maybe it is a sign of that self-centredness for which Ned has reproached her so often in recent years.

Yet at the same time she knows what it means, she feels its nearness. She knows that we are all potential suicides. What is more, if we are alive, it is because we are all survivors of suicide. And in the case of Mrs Senn, it is as if that terrible act were a confirmation of something that Pat saw in her from the very first. An impatience, a yearning that pleaded to be satisfied, a desire to fly away – elsewhere. Indeed, perhaps it was that, the woman's imperious and captive gaze, of which her character, her book was born.

But the Muse, the unknown woman from Bloomingdale's, did not manage to fly where she wanted to.

The other thing Pat learned from the newspaper cutting was her name. She was called Kathleen.

III

Sincerity is the worst policy.

What I feel is written on my face, even when I am not talking.

My life is a series of mistakes.

1951, the second trip to Europe.

In Paris she visits the tomb of Oscar Wilde in Père-Lachaise and meets Janet Flanner, correspondent of the *New Yorker*, and her friend Natalia Danesi Murray, an ambassador for Italian culture in New York, two women she admires enormously, elegant, witty, cosmopolitan. She is delighted by their scintillating and open-minded conversation. Will she manage to be like them in twenty or thirty years' time?

In London she meets up again with Elisabeth, wife of her English publisher and her lover for a short while in Naples, and it causes her no pain to realise that everything between them is over now.

But what in reality was that "everything"? Only a great dream on her part, a few moonlit nights on the shores of the Mediterranean two years earlier, and then, in New York, months of irrational and excruciating expectation of a letter telling her: "I love you, come!" A letter that never arrived. When Elisabeth did finally reply, her words were so calm, courteous, distant, that it was not even a question of a no but of a much deeper and more radical rejection.

All her yearning and her anxiety obliterated. As if they were not worthy of existence.

Yet it was not an entirely abortive affair, because it inspired a story with which she is rather pleased. It is about a man who, like her, writes to a woman far away. He writes that he has come to realise that he loves her, separation has clarified his feelings – ah, what separation can do, where love is concerned! He writes that his whole life depends on her, that she alone can bring order and meaning to his existence. That he wants to marry her.

The days go by, slow and febrile, full of false signs and omens, and every day the man looks into his empty letter-box and recalculates the agonising balance sheet of hope but the figures never add up... it is a story about waiting, about unrequited love and the delusions of hope. Delusions are the fuel of creation.

She has called the story "The Birds Poised to Fly", and it will not be published until years and years later, under another title, perhaps less suggestive but drier and more precise: "Love is a Terrible Thing".

Europe is cheap and she is frugal, she makes her savings last. Months of travelling in France, Italy, Germany.

In a charming village in the Bavarian forest she feels that she could lead a virtuous life, regular rhythms, constant writing. Self-control. The satisfaction of a day's work, and in the evening eating simple food and drinking local wine, preferably in the company of interesting people.

Interesting people, however, are a continual source of distraction. And there are always women (usually married) who become more interesting day by day. At least for a while, until, luckily, it is time for her to move on.

Suddenly, in an elegant restaurant, in Munich, among a tableful of people who have already lost the glitz of novelty, there she is: Lucy.

In her forties, slender, with clear penetrating eyes, a classic profile, well dressed.

Everything about her gives the impression of fastidiousness and of being ruled by a punctilious will. Rather attractive but of few words, with a severe gaze, she appears vexed.

Pat immediately categorises her as the only woman at their table it makes sense to look at. And so she looks at her. Out of the corner of her eye, without attracting too much attention.

After a couple of glasses she finds the courage to speak to her, a banal question about her work. She is a sociologist and works for an American agency in Europe which has something to do with military bases and aid programmes (the war ended six years ago but Europe is still grappling with the aftermath of war).

Her name is Lucy Heller and she is keen to let Pat know that she is married. Towards the end of the meal she corrects herself: divorced.

She holds her drink fairly well (three martinis, like Pat), but she is totally lacking in any sense of humour, which – Pat notes that evening in her diary – does not add to her charm. At the end of the evening Lucy proposes, wholly unexpectedly, an excursion outside the city. Pat accepts.

The following day, having dutifully visited a baroque castle with an armoury annex and a museum, they dine in an elegant restaurant in the country. Just the three of them: Pat, Lucy and Duke, a black miniature schnauzer who spends the evening begging for food under the table. (Pat will soon discover that when Lucy dines out she counts on the generosity of fellow diners to feed her dog, thereby saving on the cost of its meals.)

Unlike Carol, who seduced her even before finding out her name, not caring two hoots about details, Lucy remains serious and distant the entire evening and subjects her to the third degree.

She responds diligently, telling the truth as she usually does, leaving out only the most difficult bits. She talks about her first book, published the previous year, which has sold fairly well and attracted rather good reviews and on which a director by the name of Hitchcock has based a film that has just come out in the United States, but not in time for her to see it before leaving.

She does not say anything about her second novel, the one about lesbians, awaiting her in her hotel room like a clandestine lover who day by day becomes more and more embarrassing.

Of her stay in London she mentions only the work aspect, in which she takes a modest pride: it is a fine thing for a writer at the beginning of her career already to have found a publisher in England. A bridge to Europe.

Cautiously, she replies to questions about a friend in common, with whom she has just had a pleasant summer fling, wondering whether it is the ring of a familiar language that she thinks she detects in the words of the nevertheless very prudish Lucy.

It is, and this is confirmed when Lucy invites her up to her apartment.

Pat accepts mostly out of good manners and force of habit, following a well-established pattern of behaviour. Lucy in fact reminds her of those other women – a whole series, from Rosalind onwards – who allowed themselves to be courted by her over a long period of New York nights, almost never conceding themselves, but unleashing in her an exciting although in the long run unbearable welter of feelings. Lucy has some of the fundamental characteristics of those women: she is older than Pat, worldly, cultured and interesting – she just seems less amusing.

After a couple of hours of music (Mozart, Albinoni, Haydn), polite conversation and unvoiced doubts, accompanied by glasses of Birnenschnaps (lethal), they turn to each other simultaneously. Pat, determined to put an end to the suspense with a clear-cut question – shall I stay or shall I go? Lucy, sterner and more focused than ever, like a person who has taken a serious decision.

After one long suspended moment Lucy kisses her on the mouth.

At their feet Duke gives a whine of protest but his mistress ignores him.

The rest is a wonderful surprise.

Lucy is soft and scented like Carol. The same white skin, velvety and supple, the same enveloping embrace, the same generous daring. Infinite tenderness. Before dawn Pat is in love and she has the wonderful feeling – albeit not entirely new – that this time it is different, important, definitive.

Lucy's unconditional tenderness lasts a couple of days.

On the third day Pat, who has turned up at her house to accompany her to dinner with some friends, is given an unexpected and violent telling-off. The belt of her raincoat is back to front and what is more it is fraying. How can a young and attractive girl like her, a representative of America abroad, be so slovenly? Has she no respect for herself? Can't she even take care of her clothes?

Embarrassed, Pat points out to her that people in the street are looking at her. Lucy apologises. During dinner Lucy treats her as if they did not know each other but Pat thinks this is understandable, she has her social position to protect.

That night Lucy is ardent, passionate.

We are two exact opposites, she tells Pat after making love. That is why we are attracted to each other and why we are well suited to each other.

Pat agrees with her. They differ in their tastes, in character, even in their political thinking. Lucy is conservative, firmly anti-communist, convinced of American superiority over the Russians, indeed over the rest of the world.

Pat flirted with communism in her twenties. To her it appeared fascinating, like a half-glimpsed and unattainable woman, an ideal goal more than a reality, and yet a noble dream. Not to mention that in her pre-war youth, to be a rebel meant sympathising with the left, because the communists were like some exotic and faraway devil that alarmed American conformists. Now people are beginning to say that Russia has actually to a very large extent betrayed that ideal, which is no less pure and elevated because of that, just less realisable.

And with regard to the Americans, Pat strives in vain to explain to Lucy how much hypocrisy there is in their ostensible faith in perfection, happiness and themselves.

Lucy listens, with her perfectly plucked eyebrows arched, and tells her what she has seen in places affected by war, victims of the Nazi camps, hunger, destruction, human degradation. The Americans have come with their clean uniforms, their ration packs. The Americans are rebuilding, planning, giving a name to things, restoring order. Of course they may be limited by their own rationality, with their sights set on a future within reach, a measurable happiness – however, that is the best there is on this earth, and it is well worth the price of a few neuroses. The important thing is to preserve decorum, the capacity for control, reason. American pragmatism is a virtue and it becomes a duty to the whole world. All political and philosophical romanticism – like Pat's personal brand of existentialism – is worthless and damaging, and should be nipped in the bud.

Lucy is articulate and persuasive in argument and has been exposed to many situations and met a great many people, ordinary individuals as well as important ones, generals, diplomats, artists, intellectuals – almost none of whom she likes. The more time goes by, the more categorical Lucy is in asserting that the overwhelming majority of human beings are stupid.

Sometimes she even puts a figure on the number of stupid people: ninety-five per cent, a percentage that to the young and innocent Pat seems slightly high. (In old age she will subscribe to it herself, considering it fair or even a little optimistic.)

Pat is fascinated by these conversations. At a certain point in the discussion Lucy becomes more attractive, talking about American decorum she ends up forgetting her own, her pale cheeks turn pink, her eyes shine, she crosses her legs in a provocative way. When she gets heated in defence of her theories she makes love with more abandon and for a while their ideological debates are for Pat a source of pleasure in more ways than one.

Lucy is not only good at analysing the state of affairs on the world political stage but also Pat's personal situation.

This is not the first time that an older and more cultured woman friend has turned her inside out like a glove. Her character, her defects, her sexual tendencies have been exhaustively discussed for nights on end, with bottles of wine, cups of coffee or tumblers of whisky and soda, depending on her interlocutor. Lucy too, like those who have preceded her, comes to the conclusion that Pat is brilliant but erratic, talented but lacking in self-esteem and with deplorable masochistic tendencies.

And while sparing her, out of the goodness of her heart, a diagnosis of hormonal dysfunction, she does not fail to criticise her rejection of femininity and her insistence on making a life-style of her own homosexuality, however discreetly masked.

Yes, Lucy, too, makes Pat's difference weigh against her, placing herself a step higher because she, Lucy, is not really *queer* but merely attracted by people who could equally well be men or women.

Her bisexuality does not make her a deviant, it does not detract in any way from her being a *real* woman, just look at the way she dresses, the way she moves in society.

Pat should emulate her. Take the trouble to look like a real woman, and become one. Words that remind her a little too much of Mary.

But now and again Lucy makes observations that are surprisingly acute, for instance, she explains to Pat that when she falls in love with a woman she makes an idol of her, something whose beauty and excellence is more than human, and then when she inevitably realises that the real woman does not correspond to the idol she is bitterly disappointed, blames the woman and feels entitled to abandon her.

"You will do the same to me, I know," she tells her.

Pat swears this will never happen, and is all tenderness towards her. But Lucy is right about her need to create idols. It is true!

Lucy proves to be demanding, bossy and bad-tempered.

But the long and rewarding conversations that can be had with her would have been impossible with Carol, who would have walked out on her in the middle of an argument, bored to death. Conversation is a precious and rare delight in an amorous relationship. Lucy has the ability to present her ideas with the cold, scientific authority of a man; like a man, she is able to keep separate the personal and the general, the public and the private.

After a few months their relationship has acquired a steady rhythm of conflict and reconciliation, storms and bright spells. All punctuated with intelligent conversation.

Travelling through Europe, depending on the requirements of Lucy's work (for Pat one place is as good as another as long as she has a quiet room to work in and a welcoming bar for the evenings), they go to Italy, Germany, Switzerland, France. But mostly Italy.

There is no city in their travels that does not evoke the memory of a greater or lesser humiliation inflicted by Lucy.

There is that time at Peggy Guggenheim's palazzo in Venice. She is wearing new shoes that hurt her feet and an elegant dark-grey dress, paid for by her but chosen by Lucy.

She circulates among well-dressed people of various nationalities, who make her feel uncomfortable because, despite the years of training in Rosalind's salon, the world of the rich and famous will never be her world. She studies the paintings on the walls, some of which seem to her really bad, and others, interesting or even beautiful. She realises that she has much to learn about art, this trip will be educational. There are attractive women around her, especially the wife of an Italian writer whose name she does not remember.

Peggy, seeing her interest in what is beautiful, talks to her about the paintings and introduces her to the woman, who does not speak English but smiles like the Mona Lisa. Perhaps distracted by the charming Italian woman, as Pat follows the lady of the house who wants to show her an Ernst painting, she trips on a rug, spilling some of the contents of her glass over herself. At the other end of the room Lucy's eyes are trained on her with cold fury. As in a bad dream, Lucy comes towards her, cutting through the crowd, belligerently pointing a finger at her. She has stained her new dress. Probably no one would have noticed if Lucy had not proclaimed it in a shrill and accusatory voice.

Pat returns to the hotel with her tail between her legs,

accompanied by a triumphant and vindictive Lucy, who accuses her of having paid court to Peggy and the beautiful Italian woman and of being clumsy, gauche and unpresentable in society.

She is so good at making Pat feel guilty! Give Lucy a little stain on a dress and she will manage to convince you that the stain is deeply inherent in your life, an original sin, a defect that cannot be cured, an irredeemable genetic flaw. Naturally with Pat she has it easy, as far as a sense of guilt and inadequacy is concerned, her mother has already sown plenty of seed and Lucy has only to harvest.

In later years she will come to believe that Lucy played an important role in her life, refining and accelerating the process of self-discovery, just as a torturer sharpens the senses of the victim on whom he inflicts his torments, unwittingly inducing a state of visionary clarity.

It was during the Lucy period that what would turn out to be her most important character first appeared to her, the best known to her readers and the most loved, and perhaps the only one for whom she will be remembered when, as happens to all authors, her work is reduced for posterity to a few salient features: Tom Ripley.

Her alter ego, as journalists have said. Her stunt, as she describes him to herself. Tom Ripley is a bluff, a writer's gamble that pays off. One of the purest joys in life, like that of a child who invents an incredible story and is believed.

Tom Ripley, who is not yet called that, first comes into view early one morning in late autumn, in a village in southern Italy, while Lucy lies asleep behind her, in the room redolent of slumber and of eau de Cologne, after a tempestuous night. Pat has made the unforgiveable mistake of giving in to her demands and told her about the first time she was in this place, in September '49, with Elisabeth. She should have known better and said nothing. No use swearing that it is all in the past, that she does not love Elisabeth. That when she saw her again in London a few months ago she realised that she made a mistake, that Elisabeth is not the person she thought she was, that there could never have been anything serious between them.

But Lucy will not be placated, telling her over and over again that having fallen out of love with Elisabeth is all the more reason why Pat will stop loving her, if living together is already such a trial to her, after barely three months. She accuses Pat of having brought her to the same place in order to compare the two of them, entirely to her disadvantage, obviously.

And then from Elisabeth she moves on to Carol: she is the one you still love, you will always love her, I am only a pale substitute, you chose me because I remind you of her, but you look down on me because I am not her.

Her logic is cogent and at the same time crazy. Pat's rationality wavers.

Lucy is jealous of her past, wants to know everything, asks for exhaustively detailed accounts, yet resents her having loved anyone else, having had a life before they met. A very human trait perhaps, but very difficult to put up with.

Pat's past is held against her as something reprehensible, downright criminal.

Lucy weeping, trembling in her arms. A devastating

frailty underlying that strength. The task of reassuring her: I will always love you, I will never abandon you.

Always, never: false words, that make her feel false. But they have to be said, administered like medicine. So that Lucy recovers, and can be herself again.

That is to say, bossy and domineering.

From Pat's diary

December 1951, Positano

This morning I was at the hotel window looking out at the deserted beach. I had woken early and did not want to disturb Lucy. All at once I saw a man walking across the sand, he was young, about twenty-five, twenty-eight years old, brown hair, medium build, slim and agile, and something about his appearance and the way he walked made me certain he was American. He was wearing a white shirt, dark trousers, canvas shoes, with his jacket thrown carelessly over one shoulder. He was walking quickly in the sun, and at a certain point he stopped, looked back, then gazed out to sea, with one hand shading his eyes.

In that instant I sensed an entire life surrounding that man, a story asking to be told, which I did not yet know but I would. Perhaps what struck me above all was his decisive and at the same time furtive manner, as if someone might be following him.

For a moment I wanted to be that man – so intensely that it almost came about. To transform myself into him, to get inside his skin, into a life that was completely different from mine, unfamiliar, free of my fears, my failings, the things that I drag around with me, the burden of my own identity.

Free of Lucy, asleep in the darkened room, free of my love for her, which at this moment feels like a sentence I have to serve, a harsh punishment I cannot avoid.

Of course my man on the beach has his demons and obsessions too, but I feel that if I were him I would be able to confront them with a light touch, with a sure grip. That everything would be easier, simpler. I would be moving towards a wonderful, unimagined freedom.

I want to follow him – not the real man crossing the beach, an American like so many others – but the one who appeared to me, to me alone. I feel that he is driven by urgent and perhaps culpable desires, and it was not without some reason that he turned to look back. What he has left in his wake? A lover? Some shady business? A crime?

Where is he going, so agile and swift and alone – free as no woman could ever be – leaving behind him only his footprints in the sand?

March '52, St Moritz

This should have been a pleasant jaunt during our trip to Geneva, where Lucy has work to do. A horrible row on the way when the car stopped with a flat tyre. Tried in vain to unscrew the damned nuts, which would not budge. Lucy showered me with insults because I do not know how to change a tyre, which evidently in her eyes represents the height of human stupidity.

Well, no, I don't know how to change a tyre.

I have never been Superman and I certainly won't turn into him here, in the snow, with the temperature below zero, and my fingers frozen. In fact, I have remembered that I am not even allowed to drive in Europe, not yet having passed my test here, and seeing as an American driving licence is not good enough for the Europeans. As Lucy well knows, but for her, as a representative of the American government, all doors open with ease.

Besides, she does not know how to change a tyre either but obviously for Mrs Heller the question does not arise: this kind of problem is something the lackey is supposed to deal with, in other words yours truly.

We were rescued by a Swiss farmer on his way to market with two sturdy adolescent sons, who stopped at Lucy's peremptory request.

She did not say a word to me in the hotel, other than to give me orders in Teutonic fashion ("The case! Hurry up!"), which led me to retire to the bar with a book, a glass and a cigarette. A quiet, comfortable, masculine atmosphere, not a woman in sight.

When I got back to the room I found her in the bath with her head lolling and her eyes rolled back. A terrible fright. She had taken a dose of sleeping pills before getting into it. I carried her to bed and made her drink coffee.

I don't think this was a serious attempt at suicide but it is surely a sign of genuine distress, not just blackmail.

Fortunately Lucy recovered fairly quickly. I held her in my arms throughout the rest of the night. Hours later my hands are still shaking.

And what if, beneath that perspicuity and rationality, there really is a vein of madness?

What if Lucy is made in the same mould as my mother?

Is she too the typical American woman born to lay down the law and make a man's life hell but incapable of taking one step without him?

It makes you sympathise with the husbands.

March '52, Geneva

Have taken stock of the situation with Lucy. Seeing that our relationship is based on the attraction that comes of being so different, we must both make an effort to understand the other and meet halfway. So we have identified a number of grievances, on either side, and made resolutions which we undertake to honour, as far as is reasonably possible. The list that follows shows that this is no easy commitment:

Lucy's Grievances

I am promiscuous, unfaithful and fickle by nature, selfishly devoted only to my work and incapable of giving her security.

I have no routine or regular pattern, I am answerable only to myself, whereas she has a job with fixed hours, obligations and commitments, to which she has to devote her energies.

I am stubborn, diabolically wilful in my self-assertiveness, and incorrigible in my defects.

My sexual demands are excessive and I do not take account of her physiological need for rest.

I am a drunk; instead of confronting my problems I take refuge in drink.

I don't know how to behave in public, I have the social graces of a rhinoceros (Lucy has seen some in Africa and therefore knows what she is talking about).

I am still in love with Carol, with whom I unfavourably compare all the other women in my life. (What the hell was I thinking when I talked to her about Carol?)

Pat's Grievances

I can't stand being treated like dirt, the way she walks all over me, as if I were a doormat, especially in public. I may be masochistic, but not to that extent.

Her accusations, her constantly critical attitude towards me, make me feel incapable, good for nothing, inadequate, a failure as a writer and as a woman.

I feel inferior because she has more money, more authority, more prestige, she is more familiar with the world and its rules – and it seems to me that all this is often impressed upon me.

I would like us to choose less luxurious hotels so that I do not feel like a kept woman.

Sex is important to me but I believe that it is to her too; besides, if we make love at four in the morning, usually it is because we have spent the three hours beforehand arguing, for which she is certainly not entirely blameless.

It is not true that I am still in love with Carol. I am not jealous of Lucy's past and I ask her to accept mine.

Despite my love for animals, sometimes I resent Duke because he gets more attention than I do.

I don't like anyone reading my letters and diaries, or rummaging through my belongings; that to me is an unacceptable intrusion.

Lucy's Resolutions

To be more tolerant and respectful of my feelings.

To overcome her jealousy and never again bring up the subject of Carol, Elisabeth, or any other woman in my past. (But do I really believe she will?)

Not to insult me in front of waiters, taxi drivers, shopkeepers and especially not in front of my friends and acquaintances.

To be supportive of my ambitions and not to belittle my work.

To give me lessons in etiquette without giving me too much of a hard time and to help me in social and bureaucratic matters without getting annoyed.

Not to rummage through my belongings. To respect my privacy.

To choose hotels and restaurants that I can afford, as long as they are not total dumps.

To feed Duke before we go out to dinner and not force me to order steak to give to him.

My Resolutions

To respect Lucy's routines and to take into consideration the fact that she has to get up at eight in the morning.

Not to shut myself off but to be open to conversation (when it is a conversation and not an exchange of fire).

To accept our economic disparity without being ashamed of it.

Not to take every criticism as a total condemnation of myself (this is difficult, especially when the tone and expression of the criticism imply that is exactly what it is).

Not to betray Lucy with other women, or if I must, to be very honest with her (but I doubt she would appreciate it).

To learn the ways of the world and try, as much as I possibly can, to behave like a lady.

To be less proud and more understanding.

To drink less (not more than two martinis a day and two glasses of wine with a meal).

This is all very well, but I do not believe that it will get us very far. If we had only to put into words good resolutions in order to succeed in keeping them, we would not be where we are. However, talking to Lucy is always a pleasure, especially when we manage to examine problems dispassionately. She is able to be cold and rational, like a scientist. I admire her intellect. I love having discussions with her about economics and political theory. I like analysing current affairs and newspaper articles together.

Why can't we behave like two good friends?

Because we love each other, that is the sad truth.

Finally, we have agreed to keep a certain distance. On our return to Munich (where we will not stay long, in fact, as Lucy has to go to Paris and then probably to Italy) we will take two separate apartments and I will stay in a hotel in the meantime. This is a relief if only from the work point of view because I shall have more peace and quiet for writing.

I think it is very funny that this agreement of ours should have been drawn up in Geneva, a place particularly suited to treaties. I told Lucy but she did not find it amusing.

June '52, Paris

Lucy arrived today. She left Munich two days after receiving my letter, which is to say as soon as she had sorted out the most urgent issues at work. She did not hesitate to let me know that in order to come running to me she had to invent some story for her superiors to justify her absence and that it had cost her stress and inconvenience. She found my lodgings dirty and squalid and demanded that we move to a more decent hotel but I refused to leave my room because Lucy will only be staying in Paris for a few days and I cannot afford to pay three times what I am paying at the moment for a bed and a table, which are all that I need. This led to further recriminations.

Despite all that, I am enormously happy and relieved that she is here.

I thought I could do without her but I was wrong. I did not think that I would miss her so much, or that I would be capable of feeling the abject gratitude with which I dissolved into tears on the pillow this evening, spilling them in her hair and on her face (which annoyed her) and kissing her lovely white manicured hands. Those same hands that not more than two weeks ago smacked me violently. But I am ready to admit that was my fault.

How I have missed them in recent days – her voice, her scent, her skin. Only the happy moments remained in my memory, and all the difficulties, the anger, the rows were forgotten or seemed less significant.

Distance is a marvellous cure for love. It is simply a matter of finding the right balance between nearness and separation.

June '52, Salzburg

I have been rereading what I wrote in recent weeks and I wonder: how many lies am I telling myself?

Lucy will join me here in Salzburg in a few days' time, and then we will return to Munich together. This separation, although interrupted by our brief reunion in Paris, has allowed me the time and the solitude necessary for reflection.

I realise there are two conflicting impulses within me. As if I were two different people, an older self and a newer self, not yet completely formed, who is trying to emerge, to free herself from the deadly embrace of the other, the old me.

The old me feels guilty towards Lucy for not being everything she would like me to be: faultess, organised, successful, always measuring up, capable of earning my living by doing a proper job. That me would like to win Lucy's approval and her love, and for that reason she tries to make good use of her talents, to put herself in a good light – always with unsatisfactory results.

Because at the same time she would like to have approval for what she is, without betraying herself or renouncing herself, and she is profoundly humiliated by the fact that is exactly what is being asked of her – a mortifying demand, as well as being one that is impossible to meet.

It is the same thing that I felt with my mother: an ardent desire for the approval of not only a person who will never approve of you but a person you yourself admire less with every day that passes, until you end up despising her.

Lucy is beginning to remind me far too much of my mother.

They both impress upon me my inadequacies, my disorganisation, my lack of clear ideas about the future, the fact that at the age of thirty I still have not acquired a family or a position in the world.

But what more has my mother achieved than I have? What are her dazzling successes? She got married – twice – in order to have a man to depend on, to use as a scapegoat for her neuroses. I pay for my own keep through my work, and for better or worse I have embarked on a career to which I intend to devote myself without burdening anyone else with my financial requirements and my frustrations, which is more than can be said for Mrs Mary Highsmith.

Both of them, first my mother and now Lucy, have the upper hand with me because of my sense of guilt. Their power is based on my guilt. It is a universal process.

A woman blames a man because he is free to go about the world and decide about his own life; instead of doing the same, she prefers to accuse him, harrass him and make him pay for that freedom which she would like for herself but which she cannot or dare not experience – or the cost of which perhaps she simply and mean-spiritedly does not want to pay.

The honest man blames the lawbreaker for assuming a right that he himself would like to enjoy – how convenient it would be, every now and again, to be free of every legal restriction and moral scruple! But he does not have the courage.

The strong oppress the weak, thereby relieving their own innate sense of guilt, telling them: you are culpable, even if you do not know why, you are guilty of existing, your every gesture, your every breath is culpable, because I have decided it is so. That is the basis of every authoritarian regime. How else could a man submit to the blind and total power of another man over his life?

I believe that America, the greatest democracy in the world, is doing something similar with its citizens. Oh certainly not with the threat of arms and imprisonment – reserved only for the most dangerous, communists and spies – but with money and material goods. It hooks them with the bait of a mass-produced happiness, made of identical dreams. If you want something different, if the common dream does not make you happy, you are to blame.

The opposite of a sense of guilt is respect. Self-respect, first of all.

And within me there is another person, a new me, who is struggling to emerge, who wants to get out of playing that game and to win self-respect. But how are you to free yourself from the oppression that makes you miserable if not by killing your oppressor, literally or psychologically? If not by paying no heed to laws and throwing moral scruples to the wind?

Only by getting rid of all sense of guilt are you completely free.

That is the eternal attraction towards evil that Dostoevsky talks of. But in my case I feel that it is also something different. Because I am not interested in Evil as an end in itself, the taste for cruelty, the corruption of innocence and so on. What interests me exclusively is freedom of choice and of action. Only if you have that can you hope to build a life that suits your requirements and is not based on a one-size-that-is-supposed-to-fit-all model that does not fit you.

And then what is Evil? What are guilt and innocence? Who decides? Killing is a patriotic and even heroic act in war, a crime in peacetime. Justice, like public opinion, can punish the innocent who does not conform to the rules and reward the guilty who pretends to respect them.

Meursault in Camus' *L'Étranger* is condemned not because he has killed a man, almost accidentally, but because he did not cry at his mother's funeral. He is a monster because he does not go along with the sham of a common "sensibility".

Since her suicide attempt, Lucy's *modus operandi* – night-time siren and daytime tyrant – has rapidly altered. The siren has disappeared, to meet pressing engagements in the watery abyss, and only the tyrant remains.

Lucy is gradually ceasing to make love with me. If after only a few months she had already taken to using sex as an instrument of blackmail, denying herself in order to punish me for my faults, now it is clear that the burden of desire rests entirely on my shoulders. I am the lascivious one; Lucy is the virtuous woman who yields to my wants only to satisfy me – but ever more infrequently.

Yet if I timidly suggest a separation Lucy goes crazy, and then come the accusations, the screaming, the slapping.

Physical violence is always degrading, because it also entails a moral violence. If the person you are living with hits you, it degrades you whatever you do, whether you endure it without hitting back (thereby becoming a contemptible victim), or whether you return the blow. (And then the wave of violence rises within you and is in danger of overwhelming you – why stop at one clout? Why not go further, as far as murder?)

And if I try to turn my back on her game Lucy resorts to the ultimate weapon: the threat of suicide.

We cannot go on for much longer like this.

Something has to change, and soon.

Perhaps it is I who have to change.

The sense of duality and multiplicity is a phenomenon with which I am very familiar but now I sometimes feel like Dr Jekyll and Mr Hyde, two distinct personalities, the quiet American who is correcting for the umpteenth time the draft of her forbidden novel, and a potential criminal who fantasises about drowning Lucy in the bath.

The dark side, Mr Hyde, is bent on coming out into the open, and what is new is that I no longer wish to restrain him and control him, on the contrary. I am cheering him on.

One day sooner or later I will write a story that I have been wanting to write for some time. My hero will be the young man on the beach at Positano – agile and determined, well versed in the process of constructing his own life and his own moral universe unaided, of literally constructing *himself* – and he will be capable of committing a crime if necessary, without feeling guilty, in order to attain his goal. And since it is the sense of guilt that draws condemnation, my hero, who is devoid of any, will get away with it.

I want readers to see things through his eyes, to feel his emotions – and for them to be happy to see him escape justice.

November '52, Trieste

What do you feel when you discover that someone is reading your diaries?

The first emotion is anger, mixed with a sense of indignation and impotence. You feel the victim of a violation. More serious than theft and perhaps scarcely less so than rape. Because what has been violated is your private life at its most secret and most fragile.

And your initial response immediately gives way to shame.

You have been seen; your most private moments, your uncertainties, your doubts and your outpourings, your least noble thoughts, have been spied on, they are the object of constant observation on the part of someone else. Someone who intends to use them to get the upper hand over you, to criticise you and blackmail you; because such a low deed is not done out of a disinterested love of knowledge but in order to gain an advantage.

You are the victim of an abuse and, as often happens to victims, you are blamed for the situation you are in: why would you ever be spied on if not to catch you out, to have proof of your guilt?

The person reading my diaries in secret is like a prison guard who silently opens the peephole into the cell in order to observe the prisoner when he thinks he is alone. That person ought to know that the more serious and the more flagrant the deprivation of freedom becomes, the more the prisoner's thoughts concentrate on one thing only: escape.

From today I will strictly limit myself to jotting down what might be useful to me in my work so that, not being able to get her teeth into anything juicy, the spy will be induced to abandon her futile and shameful behaviour.

I have rallied my mental resources to react with the utmost possible coldness in this situation. And it is with coldness that I add an observation that the person who reads these lines would probably never arrive at by herself: a diary is not only a collection of ugly thoughts, compromising deeds, betrayals and infamies; it is above all a work on oneself, on one's own unconscious, in search of the truth. I am not a scientist – I would like to have been one, if I had not had a greater aptitude for literature and artistic expression – but that is no reason for me not to feel a need for knowledge. The only true science accessible to me is that of the mind, of the human psyche; and it is that which I am constantly striving to pursue, through observation of myself and others. Drawing on the inner self, digging deep to discover hidden layers, roots, stones, fossils, subterranean rivers – that is part of my job.

I do it humbly, modestly, in the most prosaic way possible: trying to tell myself the truth about my experiences and feelings. And if I discover that I am made of common dirt and hard stones, and if I find worms in the dirt, well, that too is the truth. Perhaps all my discoveries are no more than insignificant details and mean nothing to anyone else but me; however, I have chosen to believe, and I do believe, that if I am ever to make anything of my life it will be founded on this.

So, whoever is spying on me, don't think that you make me feel as guilty as you would like. It is true, I am ashamed of being seen in the nakedness of my core self – who would not be disturbed by that? But on a deeper level I remain perfectly indifferent.

December '52, Trieste

Frightfully cold. At night the thermometer drops below zero. That hateful wind they call the *bora* has been blowing for days. What am I doing here in this city?

Once again I have followed Lucy. She is here for work, with me in tow. It is true, a writer can write anywhere, all she needs is a table and a room, and a bit of silence – and hopefully someone to spend the evening with – but even I, a rootless creature who likes change, have reached my limit.

The place where we are staying ought at least to be welcoming – but it is cold here, and I do not understand a word of what people in the street are saying, and when I go into certain bars I feel I am being watched because women in Italy do not go out alone, they stay at home, making soup and giving birth.

Not to mention the fact that I am fed up with not having an address, and having to queue in the American Express in order to get my post.

I must take some decisions, be more independent. In a few months' time Lucy's contract will end and we will be going back to America, it will be an opportunity to rethink all of this.

The young American on the beach in Positano. His indeterminateness, the fact that I never saw his face but have retained only a general impression of him – build, gait – stimulates me, suggests to me a great adaptability in him. He does not have a well–defined personality; he is in search of a life, a place in the world. He knows what he would like – and it is very difficult to obtain – but he does not know *who he is*. He could become a thousand different people, and perhaps he will. He is dissatisfied with himself but he is also proud and ready to seize every new opportunity that fate offers him. Nothing ties him to America and it is in fact Europe with its promise of freedom that attracts him.

How familiar I am with that situation.

And how well I know him too, I feel. It is only a fleeting glimpse, and then he is gone, leaving me empty-handed. But for that brief flash I am truly inside his life, I scan it from top to bottom.

April '53, Gibraltar

Gibraltar, the pillars of Hercules; once symbolising the end of the known world, now for me the gates of Europe. Today they mark the last stage of our journey before our return to the USA, but I will soon be travelling through them again, heading towards the Mediterranean.

Tantalus, which has become *The Price of Salt* along the way, and has cost me so much trouble, doubt and anxiety, in the end has turned out all right and the publisher is asking for another book straightaway. But I am not even considering it: to write a second lesbian novel, now, would mean losing friends and a respectable career in favour of another, perhaps a more remunerative one, but much more ambiguous and obscure, in which I would always have to use pseudonyms and remain behind the scenes of "real" literature.

May '53, Atlantic Ocean

Fortunately, Lucy is suffering from seasickness so I am nearly always free to retire into a corner of the deck and write. The idea for my next book is rapidly taking shape, cradled in its development by the rolling of the ship.

I am thinking of a man trapped in a marriage, a man who once loved his wife very much and now hates her. He hates her while continuing to love her, or rather hatred becomes ever more mingled in his love, it thoroughly pervades it. The man cannot forgive his wife for not being the woman he used to love, a woman who actually existed, she was not the fruit of his imagination. The smiling and fascinating young girl has given way to a despotic woman impossible to please. The passionate lover has become a cold tyrant who accuses him of being a sexual maniac every time he dares to show his desire and consequently he has turned into a supplicant who is perpetually rejected and made to feel ashamed of his natural instincts.

It is not her fault, she does not do it deliberately, that is simply *the way she is*. After the courtship phase is over, the metamorphosis takes place, irreversibly, revealing the truth: for her, as for so many other women, sex and seduction are only tools for binding a man to them, tools that once the goal has been achieved are no longer needed and are therefore abandoned.

So why not let him go? But no, of course not. She needs him to stay. The strong and bossy wife who dominates her husband is in reality the more dependent out of the couple. As with most women, her weakness is also her strength, and it is a noose that draws ever tighter. In the end one of the two will be strangled.

How well I know that type of woman. A year and a half of my life has been devoted to a battlefield study. I feel the book growing inside me, taking possession of my body and my mind, perhaps it is something like what a mother feels when the child is kicking in the womb. I am imbued with a sense of physical well-being, I sleep well, I enjoy my food. At night I wake up, dwell fondly on my not yet fully formed idea, and go back to sleep cherishing it. During the day I spend hours by myself on the deck allowing my imagination to work on my story, and when I return to the cabin where Lucy lies on the bed looking miserable I try without great success to hide my euphoria.

Every now and again doubt assails me: will it be too close to reality?

But no, my plot will be totally different from the facts of my life. My man is a respected professional, mild-mannered, well-read, polite – a man incapable of committing a crime. However, despite this – or perhaps because of it – he is attracted to dangerous individuals, by the ambiguous and powerful rapport between opposites. And one day he reads a news story that disturbs him and at the same time fascinates him: a woman has been brutally murdered and the police suspect the husband but do not have enough proof to charge him.

My gentle hero at once feels sure that yes, it was definitely the husband, and he is overcome with the irresistible desire to confront the probable killer, to spy on him, to discover his secret: how has he managed to carry out the great deed of liberation?

July '53, Cherry Grove

Lucy is in hospital. Two days ago she swallowed a bottle of sleeping-pills after a terrible scene by which I remained unmoved. After a certain number of terrible scenes and suicide threats, their power inevitably decreases.

I knew that she might do it, but I went out all the same. I left her lying on the bed in tears, with her bottle of pills on the bedside table and Duke whining pathetically at her feet. Poor dog, if his mistress were to die, I do not think I could keep him; but I would find him a good home and perhaps that would be better for him.

If I am a monster, it is she who has made me become one.

The point is that I have had more than enough. I cannot take any more criticisms, insults, slaps and violent arguments – after a while the reconciliations, the wet kisses and the tremulous promises begin to lose their charm, and tenderness and sex seem to me no more than a bait to hook me before giving another tug on the line.

Her jealousy has become pathological, to say the least. Not just Carol and the past but every woman I know, in fact every person, every occasion of amusement and entertainment becomes a pretext for a scene. What has kept me with her till now has been the recollection of the Lucy I first knew in Munich, with her magnolia skin and her scented kisses, a Lucy who could smile and every now and again even laugh. But in reality that woman ceased to exist some time ago, she is confined to my memories.

I thought: if Lucy wants to die, well let us allow her desire to be satisfied. Has she not always done exactly what she wanted to?

I left and I went to that old bar in the Village, where there is always someone to have a drink and a chat with.

I spent a couple of enjoyable hours with Liz, then – more out of a sense of tidiness than anything else, and so as not to leave things half done – I decided it was time to get an update on how Lucy's suicide was going. At about ten o'clock I went back up to her apartment and I found her inert, her eyes staring, her breathing raspy.

I called for an ambulance. I noticed that as I dialled the number my hands were steady, they were not shaking.

Together with Liz, who was waiting for me downstairs in the car, we followed her to the hospital, where after hours of waiting they told me that she would probably pull through.

It was just typical of her to commit suicide on July the fourth, ruining everyone's holiday. By then it was almost five in the morning and Liz had fallen asleep with her head on the steering wheel of her little red sports car. Dear sweet Liz, always so kind. Liz is the easy-going type, friendly and amusing, the type of girl who doesn't ask you for promises or proofs of love, and who is here today and gone tomorrow. You have to take her as she comes – so after a coffee, we decided to go to the seaside.

Even if I had stayed at Lucy's bedside, what difference would it have made to her? Indeed, my presence might actually have been harmful, in view of the rather unkind thoughts I have with regard to her at the moment.

A few hours later we were here in Cherry Grove, eating croissants in a little café with French pretensions, overlooking the harbour, where the sails on the boats were a brilliant white in the sunshine of a perfect summer's day. It was Rosalind who introduced me to Cherry Grove – and to so many other things – this place is a little too classy and fashionable but perfect for the couple of days I intend to spend here. You need only look around to realise that all the *les girls* with a little money and a few social connections come here, it is a kind of lesbian colony, Liz is keen on it.

After a lazy afternoon on the beach and a light supper we came back early to the cabin by the sea that we have rented. In a few minutes Liz will come out of the bath, wet and fragrant, wrapped only in a towel, and the sound of her bare feet on the wooden floor will send a delicious shiver down my spine. In a moment she will be here, lying beside me, a beautiful girl trembling with desire. Can there be anything more wonderful in the world?

And what if Lucy dies? The thought fills me with horror and dismay but – I have to confess – it also gives me a delightful little quiver of revenge and liberation.

If I am sober the horror prevails; but if I drink, the sense of liberation triumphs. So I drink.

IV

*The only thing that makes me happy
is trying to attain the unattainable.*

There was a time in her life when waiting was everything, expanding until space and time were entirely filled with it. It was sweet and bitter, fulfilling and unbearable. It created a parallel world for her, of greater reality than the real world, and compared with which the real world pales.

She has known the taste of madness – she has felt it melt on her tongue during those hours when she lay stretched out in her room immersed in the world created by waiting and imagination – and it was as exquisite as a poisoned sugared sweet.

She might genuinely have gone mad. But a writer has better things to do than go mad, there are stories to be written. And then she is too sane a person actually to fall into the trap of madness. She is like an explorer suspended over the red-hot cone of the volcano: she looks directly into the fiery abyss but she knows that she will go back to tell of it.

It is the end of the 1950s, those years that were so troubled for her and for America; the McCarthy era is over and already you can sense in the air the stirrings of that wind of novelty and rebellion that will blow in the 1960s, but a woman in trousers is still not allowed into an elegant restaurant and the American dream is still a well-paid job, a pretty little wife, children and a suburban home.

In every house there is a television, a refrigerator and a washing machine, a car or two in the garages. Commuters coming home from the office are greeted with appetising smells from the kitchen and a martini on the rocks with an olive, often followed by another, and when suburban happiness becomes particularly unbearable, by a third and a fourth.

The remedy for creeping unhappiness and for neuroses is still being sought in psychoanalysis but there is also ever greater recourse to psychiatry and its miraculous pills. There continue to be sightings of flying saucers and Americans still dream of Europe, but it is now easier and more convenient to get there by aeroplane than by ship.

Rubbing shoulders on the streets of Manhattan and the Village are celebrities and obscure poets and artists, emancipated women, crazy women writers, tramps and the homeless; whites and blacks live in close proximity but they rarely mix and at night certain bars become meeting-places and temples where an intimidated community celebrates its rites. To be different in any way is still dangerous, as it ever shall be, even though Pat is quite well known now and when she goes into one of those bars there is always one of its habituées who turns to whisper her name in another's ear.

She is quite well known in those places for that sole forbidden novel that came out a few years earlier, that *Price of Salt*, formerly *Tantalus*, which was her great reckless defiance, her disgrace and her gamble. The book whose existence she would have kept from her mother (but failed to), and which she will never give her married women friends to read.

The paperback edition sold nearly a million copies and for months Pat received letters from grateful readers, women and men. They thanked her for having written a book with a happy ending, a story whose protagonists are two strong and courageous women who do not lose their self-respect. She has not read all of those letters.

Often victory contains the bitter taste of defeat.

She does not want to think about that success of hers. At least not for the time being.

In the official world of letters her renown is still far from well established. She is spoken of as a promising newcomer who may become a brilliant crime writer. (She does not want to be a crime writer, she wants to be a writer, full stop. But the world needs labels, so better to be a crime writer than a lesbian writer.)

For years fame, with its corollaries of a reliable income, public admiration and self-confidence, has seemed to be playing hide-and-seek. There are books that write themselves, like the first Ripley, and they are the best – but there are others which require doggedness, effort, a blind perseverance deaf to doubts. There is no formula for books, every one is different, a unique case. What it takes is for an idea, a seed, patiently nurtured, to germinate and blossom into a story sufficiently interesting to keep her engaged for months, the time needed to reach the last word.

And her love affairs too are all different from each other, although with worrying similarities, and they retain their grip on her for a limited period, in the happiest or most inveterate cases for the duration of one novel, maximum two.

Pat is poised on a threshold, several thresholds. Between obscurity and fame, America and Europe. Between solitude and being in love, between the freedom of travel and the security of a quiet port to return to. She leads a double life in every sense, she is a serious and promising author and an habituée of louche bars, and she no sooner has a stable relationship with a partner than already in her thoughts another clandestine love affair is beckoning.

Things cannot go on like this, particularly as she is not so young any more, she is approaching forty, and on every birthday the notion of taking stock of her life (who am I, what have I accomplished, what is my goal?) leads to reconsiderations, self-criticisms and good resolutions that will soon be broken.

In this frame of mind, torn between hedonism and penitence, anxiety and determination, she might happen to come across another girl she has already run into a number of times, in that casual way that is almost the norm in their clandestine community, someone who like her sits alone at the bar in a smoky nightclub.

The flame reignites and Pat is once again seduced by the idea of someone she can spend her days with, doing things together, sharing literature.

Rose, too, writes for a living, she is the literary equivalent of the *commercial artist*, a category created by industrious money-making America, people who, to sell their talent, are prepared to settle for doing art with a small a – fashion design, advertising graphics, manuals or genre writing, from gardening columns to pulp fiction, which are simply a kind of craft.

Actually, Pat is not at all sure of the difference between art and craft, between pulp fiction and "real" literature. Perhaps her own books are not so very different from those yellowish paperbacks that sell millions of copies, like her *Price*.

Pat is sceptical about Art with a capital A, perhaps it does not exist, perhaps it exists only in relation to the past and includes people like Poe and Dostoevsky, people who perhaps when they were alive did not know that they would be admitted to the Olympus of Art and had they been told they might have considered it a joke in bad taste. And so better not to think about it, better to remain in familiar surroundings, those of daily work, half creativity, half patient craft.

Yes, they will live together, she and the girl who earns a good living writing drugstore novels. Since Pat has had enough of New York, and would really like to go away on another long trip to Europe and the Mediterranean, whereas the girl – who is sweet and very much in love – cannot go far because her job entails frequent contact with editors, they seek a compromise solution: they will take a house in the country not too far from New York, where they can write in peace.

It is a deal that is flawed from the start because in fact it dissatisfies both of them: no Europe for Pat, no New York for Rose.

But they will have a garden and develop routines, it will be lovely, comforting and productive, thinks Pat who is struggling with a novel set in the Greek islands, where she has frolicked to her heart's content in recent years. A story that is not going well and is giving her a lot of headaches.

When, laboriously, she has finished it, she will call it *The*

Two Faces of January; actually she would like to have called it *The Two Faces of Janus*, the two-faced god, but she feared that would be too trite.

There are so many two-faced things in her life! In love her greatest passions have been for women very different from herself, like Carol, who rather than read a novel preferred to pilot an aeroplane, or like Lucy, who never read more than ten pages of one of her books because she was bored by them. But she now once again feels a strong desire for sharing, for a more rational and self-controlled love, without the thrilling but destructive highs and lows. This time she wants a companion, one who accepts her and understands her for what she is deep down: a writer. She had deluded herself that she would be able to find a companion in Ned but she had been forced to acknowledge their sexual incompatibility, which then became an emotional incompatibility as well; with Rose, on the other hand, everything works wonderfully from that point of view.

And so what on earth can prevent them from being happy together?

A question it is more than legitimate to ask.

Rose is real, tangible. Rose is American. Rose is the everyday, the assurance of the present.

Rose very soon becomes her prison.

And shimmering between the bars, more seductive, more beautiful and cruel than ever, is her dream. It is cloaked in waiting, it feeds on distance, it fuels her writing.

> *Men put passion into action.*
> *Woman put it into waiting.*

From Pat's diary

March '58, New York

Looking for a house with Rose. Have sifted through various possibilities, all about an hour from NY. Very undecided, especially because the really lovely house where I could live very happily, with a bright studio that looks out onto a garden, and a big bedroom, very quiet, is too small. It is in New Freedom, Pennsylvania, and it is actually only part of a house, with a separate entrance; the owner seems very discreet to me, and not too grasping. But it is truly impossible for two to live there.

Rose is very determined. Our relationship, according to her, is now sufficiently solid, and living together can only consolidate it further.

I wish I had her certainty. I admit that the idea of waking up in the morning beside the person you love is pleasing and comforting, as is the prospect of long quiet evenings in front of the fireplace with a good book and good conversation. But will all that be enough for me?

I feel that I love Rose. I appreciate more than ever her steadiness, her good sense, her constant calming affection. Heaven knows, I need calm after so much tempestuousness.

Yet doubts remain. I dare not speak of them but the prospect of sharing a house provokes in me a sense of apprehension, at certain moments even anguish.

Foolishness. I need tranquillity for my book. The

important thing now is to carry out rationally drawn-up plans. The rest will follow.

Tomorrow we will go and see another house in Old Faith.

March '58, Old Faith, Pennsylvania

First day in the new house. Rose is enthusiastic and has already organised the kitchen and our bedroom. She says that it is good to have two bedrooms in case we have family or friends to visit. I am all for having a guest room but why pretend it is *my* room?

But if that makes her feel better, fine. What does it cost me, after all?

Yet I feel I ought to draw lines and I tell her that we will never do the same as Isabel and Leah, who since they have been living together have had a timer installed in the guest room. So every evening at a certain time the light in the empty room comes on and the neighbours think that two bedrooms are occupied and not just one, as is the case in reality.

Fortunately Rose, too, thinks this is taking circumspection too far.

Old Faith is a quiet town where everybody knows each other and most families have been living here for generations. The men meet at the bar of the country club, the women exchange visits and homemade jams. The buildings are well maintained, the fences recently painted. People take pride in their gardens, their family, their new car. Or they pretend to. Inside, the houses are polished and full of new electrical appliances. The children speed around on brand new bicycles.

The neighbours came to introduce themselves today,

bringing a walnut cake. We offered them tea. They went away duly impressed by our status as freelancers from the city; independent women, courageous enough to live here without a man. They made great efforts to show that they were so modern as to approve of us. Intolerable.

In retrospect, the charming little independent studio in New Freedom seems like an ideal refuge, a remote island.

April '58, Old Faith

A letter from my editor: the book is weak, unconvincing, it lacks rhythm and suspense.

The implication is that for her there is nothing to be salvaged. But I do not believe that. I am determined to work on it for as long as it takes. Rose encourages me.

Spent the afternoon browsing in a couple of junk shops where Rose found a small old table which she got very excited about. She is delighted with the idea that we will paint it together (blue, I fear).

Cocktails and dinner with her friends Etta and John who have a house nearby. Nice, but deadly boring. In the kitchen, while we were drying the dishes, Etta told me all about her two pregnancies, sore nipples included. (Ugh!)

April '58, Old Faith

Wonderful day, spring at last. Did some hoeing in the garden, made a shelf to put up in my studio, prepared lunch.

At midday I cook, Rose clears the table and does the dishes, in the evening she cooks the main dish and I prepare the salad, set the table and take care of the drinks, and afterwards we tidy up together.

In bed together after lunch for a pleasant siesta. Living with someone else can be truly satisfying.

In the afternoon I worked well. Rewrote almost ten pages.

April '58, Old Faith

Alone the whole day. Rose is in NY, where she goes about once a week to pick up and deliver her work to the agency. I cannot help fantasising how it would be to live here without her. If Rose lived a little distance away, in town, we could see each other frequently.

It is curious how reassuring it is for her to establish regular habits and routines, whereas for me it is not at all reassuring. I can easily imagine the moment when doing something for the hundredth time (for example, having coffee together every morning, or putting out the napkins folded in a particular way) becomes intolerable to me, makes me want to overturn the table and run away.

It is like when you get stuck with someone at a party who talks and talks and talks, about themselves and about stupid things that are of no interest to you, and you sit there, trapped, and feel your lips have hardened into a smile and that they could crack at any moment, and you have pins and needles and cramp in your thighs, and a silent scream rises from deep in your throat.

If you were not a cowardly creature in a civilised world, at that moment you'd kill to get away.

I do not know if I will ever feel this house is truly mine. After a month it is now full of furniture and all sorts of things: a chintz-covered sofa, two armchairs, an old rocking chair, a multitude of vases, picture frames, mirrors, tablecloths, plates and glasses, not to mention an enormous wicker cage, which has no canaries inside it but takes up half the verandah. All these objects are really too much for me. Rose keeps insisting that I put something more than just the table and chair in my study but I am not giving way: I need a refuge where my eyes can rest on uncluttered walls and bare floors.

It is true, however, that I need a wardrobe, I cannot keep my clothes in a suitcase for ever.

May '58, Old Faith

Living in some isolated place in the country, with no noise or distractions or social obligations, is certainly ideal for work because it allows you to reach the level of concentration required to keep reality at bay and to live in your imaginary world. But then why is my book not progressing, not getting beyond this impasse?

The answer is: because activity, disturbance, passion, turbulence are just as necessary as peace and quiet, if not more so. Stagnation is bad for creativity, it is only out of movement that ideas are born.

I think of the pages I have written in a squalid room in a Marseilles pension, where the noises of the port woke me early in the morning, or in a rented house in Positano, among screaming children and mothers calling out to them from the windows and starving cats that would come into the house begging for food. I think of the sea crossings, of scribbling notes on the deck or in my confined cabin, with my notebook on my lap. Of the sounds of Mexico: dogs howling all night, cocks crowing, drunkards creating a rumpus in the street. Yet after a while I did not hear them any more and everything seemed to me idyllically peaceful because I was free to write when I wanted to and to go where I pleased.

Calm without the storm is deadly. Stillness requires movement: without dialogue between opposites, life is intolerable.

What is a prison if not a place that you cannot leave, where everything repeats itself in exactly the same way for ever?

May '58, Old Faith

Mentioned to Rose my idea of a trip to Europe. She cannot do it at the moment, her deadlines are too pressing. Suggested that I might go alone, I would be away for a few months, three or four at most.

I cannot bear female tears. Not even when they are totally sincere, in good faith, as Rose's are. There is in a woman's weakness an element of aggression that puts me on the defensive, makes me withdraw into myself.

I cannot make Rose suffer like this after all she has done for me. I promised her that tomorrow we would both go and look for a chest of drawers for my studio.

May '58, Old Faith

Installed in my room now is an old chest of drawers with four drawers and brass handles, which has put the smile back on Rose's lips (less so on mine: I have the distinct impression it is infested with woodworm). Also, in the corner, there now stands a grandfather clock that does not work even if you kick it but it is a genuine nineteenth-century piece.

All this activity is preventing me from thinking about my novel, which, like a ship run aground, is not going anywhere.

Beneath my calm and almost cheerful exterior a creeping desperation is building up, a lack of self-confidence that takes me back to my darkest moments.

May '58, Old Faith

Guests for dinner yesterday evening: Isabel and Leah, with a friend of theirs, Ellie Kraft, who lives in New Freedom. Ellie is about thirty-five, light blonde, with a perfect face, and above all perfectly serene. She has a soft, musing, very melodious voice. She is married, with two children, aged six and nine, and a relationship with her husband that from what she implies is more affectionate than erotic.

Ellie is dazzling. A bolt of lightning in a cloudless sky. With Carol's cheeks and eyes that are clear like hers but a golden hazel rather than light grey. A beauty less untamed but just as proud. Two divine dimples when she smiles. And that way of slightly tilting her head when she listens to you!

I told her that we had come very close to being neighbours in New Freedom, where there was that little house I liked so much. She agreed it was a shame but the distance was not so great that it should become an obstacle to seeing each other again. She invited us to pick cherries in her orchard when they were ripe.

Before she left, while Rose was in the kitchen, I asked her for her address in order to send her the sketch I had drawn of her and which I intend to do more work on to improve it. I shall make a copy so as to be able to keep the original for myself.

May '58, Old Faith

A good day's work. I have faith in myself, I know I am going to make this work. Sent the sketch off to Ellie, with a long letter (three pages). I hope I don't appear to her to be out of order or, worse, offensive. She showed some curiosity about me so I told her something of my life, my travels – and my dreams.

I hope she does the same soon.

May '58, Old Faith

Wonderful letter from Ellie. She writes about her love of music and poetry, her ambitions as a young girl and her family life. Her husband is a decent man, retired from the military, much older than she is, with heart problems. Her children are blond and beautiful like her (she sent me a photo of the three of them in the garden, with the children on a pony).

She likes Bach and Chopin and sacred music, and she paints watercolours (but she does not want to show me anything because, she maintains, she is only an amateur, unsure of her tastes and with no technical skill).

I sent her a poem (an old one, which talks of distant seas and as yet undreamed of beauty) and a musical score. She plays the piano a lot better than yours truly, it would seem, so it will be of more use to her than to me.

I went to post it in town. No need to get Rose upset.

June '58, New Freedom
One in the Morning

I am in the guest room of Ellie and her husband Frank. They have a lovely big two-storey house painted white with a colonnade at the front, a real country mansion, not a cottage like ours. The children played in the garden all afternoon with the nanny while Ellie kept an eye on them from afar, a benevolent queen ruling her subjects with a light but sure hand.

I felt an instinctive sympathy for Frank, a kind and humorous man in his sixties, who with Ellie behaves more like a father than a husband. Before dinner he and Rose went to inspect a local antique dealer's stock; I declined and Ellie rescued me by saying that she needed me in the kitchen.

But we stayed in the sitting room, alone, enjoying a moment of total intimacy. With a spontaneity and a sweetness I have never come across before, she invited me to sit on the large sofa, and after having exchanged a few insignificant words we simply sat looking at each other in the golden light of late afternoon.

I could have stayed like that for the rest of my life, my eyes gazing into hers, caressed by her smile.

Then she did something incredible: she took my hand which was lying on my lap and brushed my fingers, one by one, examining them as if she had never seen a human hand before. Then – to my amazement – she raised them to her mouth and slowly kissed them all.

I was motionless, transfixed. If I had died at that moment it would have been a happy death.

How much time passed before Ellie let go of my hand and got to her feet with a tired and far-away look, like someone who has spent all their energy in some beautiful dream? Come on, she said, or the cherry tart will burn.

I do not know what happened during the rest of that evening, except that there were glow-worms and from the fields came an intense fragrance of grass and earth. Frank insisted we stayed the night, and Rose was clearly happy that I raised no objection and that I liked her friends! Now she is asleep and I am at the little table next to the half-shut window writing by the light of the moon – and of the torch that since I have been living in the country I always carry around with me.

I do not feel guilty towards either Rose or Frank. What happened today between Ellie and me is so pure and perfect and inevitable that it has nothing to do with anything or anyone other than the two of us.

June '58, Old Faith

Argued with Rose. This afternoon I moved my typewriter on to the verandah to work outside (there is a heatwave and my study is south-facing, which is not entirely an advantage as it had seemed to be a few months ago), and there I am, hammering away at the keys when our neighbour, Mr Rodgers, appears, trimming his hedge, and he starts chatting away as usual. At first I responded in monosyllables, then seeing that he did not take the hint I got up and said to him: "Excuse me, but one of us is busy", picked up my typewriter and went back inside.

Rose accuses me of being tactless and of trying to antagonise the Rodgers. But if that man is so stupid he cannot see that I am working and cannot take it in even when I *tell* him, what I am supposed to do, according to her, waste half the afternoon listening to him chatter on about the weather and golf?

Rose says that it is important to build good relationships with the neighbours, we cannot alienate ourselves from the community in which we live, heaven knows, we are in a vulnerable position, they could make life impossible for us.

Well then, we will leave, who is going to stop us? I point out to her that we can move somewhere else, there are hundreds of other places in Pennsylvania with houses for rent or for sale (I am thinking of New Freedom).

But we have not even finished furnishing this house yet, she complains. And she reminds me that arriving in three days' time is the made-to-measure wardrobe she ordered from the local carpenter. (A huge waste of money, in my view, but who has the courage to tell her?)

Made up with each other this evening. Fortunately Rose is one of the most accommodating and amenable women I have ever known. She is ready to forgive and accept almost anything if you reassure her about the things that really matter to her, like undying love.

Besides I do not want to waste time and energy arguing either. I am in a decidedly better mood since Ellie has taken up residence in my thoughts.

June '58, Old Faith

A ridiculous and unpleasant scene this morning. In the kitchen, just after getting up, both scantily clad – very hot again today – we are exchanging a kiss – more affectionate than passionate but unmistakeably conjugal – when we hear the sound of shattering crockery and an exclamation, we turn and discover with horror the Rodgers brat standing in the doorway, wide-eyed, her hands over her mouth, at her feet a plate with a large piece of cream cake on it, now broken. Shattered crockery and cream everywhere. Having dropped it, the wretched girl ran off into the garden, back the way she came, slipping through the hedge, damn her, instead of walking up the path and ringing the doorbell.

I am furious. How dare the Rodgers take such a liberty?

Rose has an anxiety attack: what will happen now? Well, I don't think they will shoot us or set fire to the house, I tell her, at most they won't speak to us any more, which could be an advantage. I pretend to be blasé but I too am bothered. From now on we will close the doors leading into the garden – even though, on reflection, I don't think the Rodgers will be taking it into their heads to send us any more cakes.

June '58, Old Faith

Wonderful long letter from Ellie, to whom I replied with one just as long and, I hope, wonderful.

She tells me about herself, about her childhood, her college years, how she dreamed of becoming a poet. I tell her about my adolescence (which becomes less horrible and unhappy when I recall it for her) and about my love for E.A. Poe. She says she realised from the very first moment that I was someone special to her, that our meeting was predestined.

I asked her when we will see each other again.

June '58, Old Faith

No chance of going to see E for the month of June, her mother is visiting and we would never be alone.

She knows, obviously, all there is to know. She knows Isabel and Leah, and has a fairly clear idea of the relationship between them, so she immediately understood that Rose and I were a couple. In her last letter she assures me that she does not disapprove at all, even though she could never live like that herself. She is too attached to her children, who will still be needing her for many years to come. And she genuinely loves her husband, even if there is nothing romantic between them

146

any more; they are united by a pact of loyalty and devotion. This by no means prevents her from feeling deeply attracted to me and experiencing an "almost painful" happiness in thinking about me, remembering our meeting and reading my letters.

She asks me if I feel the same, with the same intensity.

Oh Ellie!

June '58, Old Faith

I look at her photo, her divinely serene face. She is so calm and patient – self-contained, like a statue. She wants for nothing, she is not troubled with countless yearnings and contradictions, she is not tortured by doubts. She sits there, calm and smiling, immersed in secret thoughts – a work of art, perfect, the highest perfection it is given to human beings to reach.

Sent off the new version of the novel. Now all I have to do is wait and hope. But anticipation of the publisher's response is almost eclipsed by the even more eager anticipation of another event: seeing Ellie again. The agreed date is approaching.

July '58, Old Faith

Back from New Freedom.

A long afternoon, and a very short one, harrowing and wonderful. The two of us alone in the house. Her husband took the children over to their grandparents, who are back from Connecticut.

The pure and simple joy of seeing each other again is followed by a chat on the sofa, and then she comes close, takes my face in her hands and caresses it for a while. She dreamed about me, she says. Several times. Almost every night. I can't speak.

She explores my face with her fingertips, with her lips.

I'm afraid of fainting.

We kiss so long we are left breathless and lose all sense of time. But when I clasp her more tightly she gently frees herself. I can't go any further, she says. I'm sorry but I can't.

It doesn't matter, I say, going back to kissing her.

The whole afternoon a long and exquisite torture. To think of the women with whom I have made love before now and of the incredible and sometimes even brutal initiatives I or they have taken. To think of myself and Rose – no, that's just it, I cannot think of Rose, because what I do with her now seems to me to be merely sex, conjugal sex, a more or less pleasant act but now irredeemably reduced from passion to mere habit, something entirely physical. Whereas with Ellie the physical aspect is only the tip of the iceberg. What happens between us, as we kiss, as I breathe in her scent (she smells of lilac and new-mown hay), as her caresses release pent-up shivers in me, is only partly physical, but in essence transcends sex and the body and attains a higher dimension, where we meet without reservations or boundaries.

Ellie tells me she cannot and will never be able to be my lover, not only out of loyalty towards her husband or consideration for her children but because she does not feel capable of braving such a lonely and difficult path, of taking decisions that would make her different from most of the people she knows. Loving me, she says (yes, she loves me, she has no difficulty in confessing it), loving me is as exciting as flying. But she is an earthbound creature, she does not have wings, she does not have the courage of Icarus, and she does not want to come crashing to the ground – she cannot, if only for the sake of her children.

No, she tells me, closing my mouth when I tell her that is not true, no, she repeats, she does not know how to fly, and worse still: she does not even believe it is possible, for any human being.

Which does not leave any hope for me: am I, then, not a human being?

Oh yes, she assures me with that very sweet smile of hers – the slight gap between her two front teeth investing her with something childlike and touching – oh yes, but special: you are an artist, you have the talent and the strength to live outside the norm. I am an ordinary run-of-the-mill person. (How can she say such a thing? She! Perfection! The absolute ideal!) I have to follow the rules and walk on the ground, like everyone else, she says. I can only watch you fly and be happy for you. I know my limitations and my place, and I know where that is: here. Don't try to convince me, it will only cause both of us needless suffering. I know I am asking a lot of you, perhaps the impossible, but can we not be happy with what we have?

Oh indeed we can, Ellie. If those are the conditions, who am I to question them? How could I declare war against your clear eyes and the humility of your voice?

The pact between us fills me with pride and joy and at the same time with desperation. I am proud and happy because what E is offering is so far above the petty world of *les girls* with their jealousies, resentments, arguments, deceptions. Ours is an accord of ideal purity, a passion that will never be eroded and diminished by everyday life…

But obviously the thought of never being able to make love with her except in my dreams, of never clasping her in my arms at night, never feeling her naked body against mine,

never waking up in the morning enveloped in her lilac scent
– is terrible.

No one can live without hope, Ellie. Out of every state of
despair hope rises again, stronger, wilier and fiercer.

July '58, Old Faith

I was right: that damned chest of drawers not only has woodworm but also moths. My favourite woollen jacket and a new
jumper ruined beyond repair. I do nothing to hide my irritation.
Rose, upset and confused. One point to me in the domestic
querelle. Which in some way increases the wretchedness of it.

There is in the friction between two people living
together something terribly oppressive, a kind of compulsive
doggedness. Why is it not possible simply to disagree, have a
good row and then move on, acknowledging our differences?
But no, we have to clarify, explain ourselves, reassert our
arguments, chew over the reasons for the disagreement ad
nauseam, like dogs fighting over a bone already stripped bare.

We are seeking an impossible harmony, a fusion that
would turn us into one sole being with two identical heads. A
monster. Why not simply admit that our tastes and desires do
not coincide, that we are not cut out for living together?

Yet I myself am unable to, perhaps because this game that
it takes two to play has also taken hold of me, infected me and
I do not know how to extricate myself from it. And now added
to my mean-spiritedness, for which I despise myself, I also
feel a sense of guilt towards Rose because I ought to tell her
about Ellie, and yet I say nothing.

(Do I say nothing so as not to hurt Rose? Because I am
afraid of her reaction? Or because I am afraid that the thing I

have going with Ellie will burst like a soap bubble the minute I try to describe it?)

So I feel as if I am two different people: one is the person who lives here with Rose, a hard-up writer afraid that her career is permanently grounded, and who right now would like to be on the Côte d'Azur or in Naples or London but who hasn't the money or the nerve to leave.

My other self is a much calmer, stronger, more assured woman who knows that things will turn out all right, who carries within her a trust and confidence in tomorrow, together with a dream whose name is Ellie.

July '58, Old Faith

The book has been accepted. Hallelujah.

I cannot help thinking that it is thanks to Ellie. It was my love for her that gave me the strength to keep going with the revisions and rewriting, through those weeks in May and June when I was about to hit rock bottom and perhaps be grounded for ever.

I shall not be seeing her until October because in a few days' time she is leaving for France with Frank and the children. Rose and I will probably spend a couple of weeks in Cherry Grove and then come back here to work before our trip to Mexico, planned for September – and which now does not seem to me so desirable any more.

August '58, Old Faith

The most terrible thing is knowing that, as in a prison, tomorrow will be just like today, that every day is an identical slip of paper in the calendar and nothing unexpected will ever happen, can ever happen. Knowing that I will be here because I am not allowed to be anywhere else, that I will be what I am thought to be and therefore I will be a sham, I will be wearing a mask because my face too becomes a mask if I am not free.

Rose thinks she knows me, she is convinced of it, and so she implicitly asks me not to change, not to be to her that stranger of a thousand faces that I am to myself.

August '58, Old Faith

Marriage is the great leveller, the Procrustean bed from which no one escapes.

No matter whether you are a genius or an idiot, your fate is sealed: you will have to toe the line, submit to the social order. Be measured by the yardstick that applies to all.

Convicts, too, are chained together in pairs to prevent them from escaping.

August '58, Old Faith

What disgusts me is my capacity for pretending to play the game. Every day, every moment, I want to put an end to all this, yet I don't. It is as if I had decided to see how far I can take this pretence.

My real life is when I write. And when I reread Ellie's letters and the time I spend with her in imagination.

I am returning to an old idea for a novel: a man creates a double identity for himself in order to collect an insurance payout. His old self will die (a staged death) and his new self, the beneficiary of the policy, will live the life of a rich man. It is worth working on.

Death as a fiction and a way of escape. A dark corridor between the rooms of life, so brightly lit and false.

To have two existences, to create a second identity, to breach the suffocating and at the same time artificial walls of reality – I know that I can go away from here, that I will go, that I do not belong to this life, that I am not like this, that I am a different person – I know it but I continue to play this game, without anyone realising…

Like me, my protagonist is poor and rich at the same time. He is a poor man who expects to become someone else and to collect a great sum of money. I am imprisoned and free, I am here and elsewhere – and which is the truth?

August '58, Old Faith

She writes that she has painted my portrait from the photograph I sent her – that every brushstroke was like a kiss.

At the moment she is in Juan-les-Pins, in a few days they will be going to Paris, where they will stay for three weeks. Then they return to the States. Perhaps, before Rose and I leave for Mexico (what I would give not to be going any more!) I will be able to have a whole afternoon with Ellie.

But is it possible to live on that?

It is possible to live on much less.

Fantasy expands to fill the space entirely. In the sultry afternoons I lie motionless for hours on my bed, dreaming with open eyes. Her presence gains substance at my side, I smell her scent, her breathing cradles me, her hands touch me lightly.

Her voice – how alive, how real! – whispers words of love to me that she may never say.

At this rate, I could go crazy.

September '58, Old Faith

But it's obvious! How did I not think of it before! The whole plot will centre on a woman. It is she, not the money that will be the prize. She will be his secret strength, the nucleus of his double identity.

A woman you cannot have, yet who is more yours than anything else in the world, even more than yourself: my novel is already all there. My hero lives in imagination what he cannot live in reality. He wants a quiet spot, an isolated house, where he can be left in peace with his dream.

Perhaps then he could attain a measure of equilibrium, live a quiet madness. And seemingly, at the beginning, that is exactly what happens. But the equilibrium is only illusory because imagination and reality are like two neighbouring states at war with each other, perpetually trying to invade each other's territory. So he can never help trying to make the dream come true, forcing reality – which in turn will burst into the fortress of his fantasies, endangering it.

I think I am on the right path.

The atmosphere at home is tense. Rose is practically not speaking to me. Yet I have done my best to be kind and obliging (including an evening with the Prestons, during which I nearly died of boredom).

We have not heard a peep out of the Rodgers, which is a blessing – but according to Rose they have certainly not kept their mouths shut, insinuations have been made, so much so that she does not go to the post office or even the bank in Old Faith any more, but drives over to some nearby town because she feels people here are looking at her "in a strange way".

She may be exaggerating or she may be right – the other

day the guy in the drugstore started chatting and at a certain point, with a smile I did not like at all, he said, "So you two girls live here all alone?" And I replied, "Not exactly, we two girls live all alone *together*." That shut him up but I think that I too will go to a different drugstore from now on.

September '58, Old Faith

Row with Rose. The reason: my countless shortcomings. I am cold and selfish, I think only of my work, I drink too much, I am rude to the neighbours, I take no interest in her friends. No use telling her that she does not find friends of mine very likeable, friends I have practically stopped seeing since I have been living here.

As for drinking, which of us gets drunk more often? But Rose says that I have much greater tolerance of alcohol and she just tries to keep up with me. So, it is supposed to be *my* fault that *she* drinks. Hell!

(The argument about alcohol arose from my own stupid mistake. Yesterday morning at breakfast I mistakenly passed her my glass of orange juice, slightly laced with vodka, instead of hers. I should pay more attention to certain details.)

I try to explain to her that this may not be the right place, the right life for me. That I loathe barbecues in the yard, I find the country club stressful and I don't care whether our hedges are perfectly trimmed and our furniture is polished to a mirror shine.

That I am fed up with America, with its pretentious houses and bad taste, fed up with the stupid arrogance of provincials who have been to college and are no less ignorant for that, but who think they are perfect, that everything connected with them is perfect and superior, their children, their houses, their damned washing machines are perfect. I hate this mass-produced happiness, it is fake and hypocritical, it is a nightmare, it could be the death of me, it will be the death of me if I do not cut the cord as soon as I can.

I want to go to Europe, where the countryside still exists and there are country folk and villages and people do not pretend that life is some wonderful thing that can be bought at Walmart.

I did not manage to tell Rose all this.

Why do I feel like a criminal set on breaking her heart if I try to say a word against her country? She believes blindly in America or at least that is how it seems, she loves this place and this house and all that it contains, right down to the confounded bedpan with little flowers on it, bought at a jumble sale.

Miserable evening. Drank three martinis, a whole bottle of wine and an indeterminate quantity of bourbon. Rose collapsed and I had to help her to bed. Once she was in bed, her eyes clearly expressed a plea for an affectionate reconciliation but this time I would have found it impossible, and not only because I had been drinking. Fortunately she almost immediately fell into a drunken and merciful sleep.

For the first time I appreciated the fact that I had a room that was "mine" (that is to say, the guest room). What a treat to sleep alone.

Alone with Ellie in my arms.

September '58, Old Faith

Fortunately the problem of Mexico has more or less resolved itself. Rose does not insist on going any more and implicitly accepts the idea of an indefinite postponement. Just as she has accepted almost without discussion that I should sleep in "my room".

Ellie is with me always. She is at my side while I write, she moves silently about the room, she entirely fills it with her calm and smiling presence. Every now and again she brushes past me, deliberately – it is a game between us – and that gives me goosebumps, waves of little shivers run down my spine and down the back of my neck.

It is indescribably pleasurable, like a light fever that keeps your thoughts ebullient, makes your body languid, loosens your anchorage in reality just enough so that you no longer notice the oppressive weight of it.

I imagine her so vividly – her smile, the whiteness of her teeth in the shadows, her golden irises, the warmth of her freckled arms – that I know – I am certain that I know – things about her I could not possibly know: her gestures in the evening when she undresses, the way in which she abandons herself to sleep, the sound of her bare feet on the wooden flooring…

To think that I have never seen her asleep, never been to a restaurant with her, never walked along a river or down a street with her! In reality I know nothing about her, the time we have spent together alone comes to four or five hours in total – during which a great deal and not enough has happened.

Yet nothing and no one is as close to me as she is. She is part of me, she breathes to the rhythm of my breathing, the heat of my blood warms her.

Perhaps I am going mad but I don't care. I will let this sweet sickness run its course.

September '58, Old Faith

Ellie has written to say that we cannot see each other until October. She is visiting her in-laws in Maine.

Why am I so bitterly disappointed? Even though I had been expecting it. It is like a test – crazy, absurd, yet in a way it makes sense.

I shall be patient, as I have been until now.

Sometimes her presence beside me is so tangible I think I am having hallucinations. I hear the swish of her skirt, the sound of her footsteps. I catch her reflection in the mirror, just a glimpse, but clearly visible. And immediately afterwards I despair because my desire, albeit so strong, is not strong enough to make her appear at my side in substance.

At night she comes to me, she lies down next to me in bed, her blonde head leaves an impression in the pillow. Her breathing caresses my face in my sleep.

Waking up from a dream in which she is at my side, stretching out my hand and finding nothing but empty space – is a torture.

But only for a moment: my desire is so strong I immediately conjure her up again.

Fever of the imagination has a tidal rhythm: rising and falling, it fills me and drains me, incessantly.

All this is extremely useful for the new novel I am thinking about.

September '58, Old Faith

A bad-tempered outburst with Rose, who in her mania for tidiness has moved my papers. For a moment I was afraid she had laid hands on Ellie's letters.

Poor Rose, it is not entirely her fault if there are moments when I cannot stand her. But the fact that she is "innocent" – that she does not see, does not know, does not want to know, anything about my disquiet, about the sense of anguish and suffocation that overcomes me when I am forced to admit this is my present reality – infuriates me even more.

October '58, Old Faith

Visiting Lucy, who is back at last from her long honeymoon in South America. Her husband, Charles, is younger than her (about forty, I would say), pensive and slight, kind and taciturn. I think she married him because he generally keeps to himself (he is a naturalist and spent almost the entire honeymoon on expeditions to study butterflies and beetles and the like) and allows himself to be easily ruled. And above all, he offers her the security and social respectability to which she has always aspired.

I explained my plight to her. Lucy says that I am mad, as usual, and that Ellie Kraft is stringing me along. With my complicity, of course. Lucy does not at all underestimate my capacity for getting into impossible situations.

In any case, according to her Rose is the least suitable person for me: too steady and conventional. She loves me too much and therefore indulges all my quirks. Lucy is convinced that I need someone to stand up to me to get the best out of me. I reminded her that *her* way of standing up to me had not turned out to be particularly successful for either of us. She shrugged her shoulders with a grimace of disdain.

However her analysis of my present situation is not entirely wrong. In particular, she thinks it was a grave mistake to have rented out my apartment in New York, which leaves me with no place of my own in which to take refuge and spend time by myself recovering now and again. She is one hundred per cent right about that.

I tried to explain to her the strange viscidity of the couple – which suffocates you, makes you want to run away as fast as you can, and yet you stay, almost as if it were a challenge, or a mad game for two. A game whose only possible outcome seems at times to consist in eliminating one of the players or both. (But why should I have to explain this to her? Is she not a past master at this game?)

No comment on her part, other than the fact that I look "pale and run down" and have got myself involved in yet another relationship that does not make any sense. Within three months, however – she says – it will be over. I ask her what makes her think that. And which relationship is she referring to, the one with Rose or with Ellie?

Both, she says, looking at me pityingly. Don't you realise that they are both keeping each other going?

It is an irritating remark, even offensive, but I don't think I can dismiss it without giving it some consideration.

October '58, Old Faith

Rose has found the letters. Not by accident, it is obvious. She took advantage of my absence to rummage through my belongings.

When I got back, she was drunk, shattered, she had got over the stage of anger a while ago and was now in the stage of despair and self-disparagement. She asked my forgiveness, she accused herself of not being able to make me happy, and so on.

Apparently she has understood nothing about my relationship with Ellie. She thinks we are lovers, that I will soon leave her and this house and go and set up home with the woman I love in another little house like this one, in another town in Pennsylvania or in the state of New York, and that the only thing about our arrangement that is not working is her, Rose. That only one little piece needs changing, Ellie put in place of Rose, and everything will be perfect.

I remained calm. I was trembling but I controlled myself.

Poor Rose, she will never know that I wanted with all my heart to kill her that night. What's more: I did.

While I watched her, wringing my hands until they hurt, waiting for her to stop snivelling as she sat slumped on my bed, there was within me what felt like the emergence of a double. And my alter ego grabbed the nearest object to hand (an enormous, heavy, fake-antique pewter jug, bought at a jumble sale because "it would go really well in your study"), lifted it up with both hands, then brought it down heavily on her bowed, sobbing head.

She fell to the ground without a moan. There was almost no blood, only a little drop on the floorboards that would certainly come out with a good scrubbing, leaving at most a faint trace that could be anything, or even just a darker vein in the wood.

And then I wrapped her in one of her handmade quilts (her favourite, the one with the grapevines and birds of paradise) and put her in the cupboard among the pillows and sheets and lavender bags. She will be happy there, with her beloved bedlinen. Later, between three and four, at the darkest hour of night, I shall carry her out into the garden and bury her in the flowerbed under the dahlias on which she has lavished so much loving attention these past few months.

And perhaps, as I carefully replant the flowers on top of her so that no one notices that the earth has been disturbed, I will explain to her what I have never had the heart to tell her while she was still alive: that I did not kill her in order to be free to run away with Ellie but because she violated something that did not belong to her, never belonged to her. Because she sat on the bed in the guest room, which is now mine, in which I have slept with Ellie. Because she fumbled among the bedding that held the memory of Ellie. Because she sullied Ellie's letters by reading them without understanding them.

Because by her hand, through her being, the destructive violence of what we call reality invaded my dream, spoiling it for ever.

Obviously she did not kill Rose, but she parted from her after a number of other more or less painful scenes, and Rose, hurt and broken-hearted, turned in on herself for a while, and then remained friends with her – as women tend to after the end of an affair – and was still even a little in love with her for some years, *she* now waiting, vainly, for an improbable return of her lover, as if Pat had transmitted to her in blander form the power to dream and the magic tension of that long summer of suspended reality.

But the most immediate consequence of those feverish months was the novel *This Sweet Sickness*. The protagonist, David Kelsey, is a silent and lonely thirty-year-old, apparently devoted to his work alone but with one secret thought ever in his mind: Annabelle, the woman he loves and who is not at his side only because of an absurd combination of circumstances, misunderstandings and wrong moves. They are kept apart by what he calls *the Situation*, that is, an horrendous and temporary state of affairs that is denying both of them true happiness – but not for much longer…

The Situation is the following: Annabelle has married another man, lives in another city with her husband, and is expecting a child by him.

The Situation is reality. Which cannot be true.

Annabelle does not know, has never known, that she is David's one great love – or if she knew, she has forgotten.

But David will remind her. He will be persistent, he will be patient, he will be able to wait until she realises her mistake, understands her true feelings and returns to him.

Like all lovers, and like Pat several times in her life – but especially during the summer of '58 – David is convinced that love cannot be mistaken or defeated: if I love her, then she loves me. It is only a question of time and she will come to realise this.

This reality that is mine, this faith that keeps me alive – they cannot be wrong.

In the grip of the most wonderful and fatal delusion and determined never to be cured of it, David bides his time, equipped with what his author knows to be necessary in such situations: intense imaginative concentration, an almost scientific application to the creation of a double identity, and a private place, a sanctuary in which to fulfil the secret rites and invoke the metamorphosis of the imaginary romance.

From Monday to Friday Pat's character is a shy, secretive, small-town engineer who shows no interest in women and prefers to shut himself away in his room in a boarding house, reading and listening to music. But at the end of the week David turns into the confident and determined William Neumeister, who has bought a fine house and furnished it tastefully in order to spend his weekends there with Annabelle.

There she awaits him, to live with him their personal version of the American dream: a lovely country house, a man who is not himself, a woman who does not exist…

What will the neighbours say? But there are no neighbours, the house is isolated, protected from prying eyes. Which does not prevent someone from knowing, from noticing…

What will the real Annabelle's husband say, seeing that David in the meantime continues to write to his wife and tries to meet her and get her back, as if he, the husband, were just some stupid inconvenience to be got rid of?

David will die – not before he in turn has killed the defilers of his temple – by throwing himself off the window ledge of an apartment building in New York in order to escape the police. At the last moment there is "nothing in his mind but a memory of the curve of her shoulder, naked, as he had never seen it".

Pat is satisfied with her book and David will always remain one of her favourite creations. A loser, a bungler, perhaps even an idiot – but a poet and in his way a pure soul.

She smiles when she realises that almost without thinking she has chosen for David's ideal woman the name of Annabelle, with its echoes of the poem 'Annabel Lee' by Edgar Allan Poe.

I was a child and she was a child,
In this kingdom by the sea,
But we loved with a love that was more than love
I and my Annabel Lee
With a love that the wingèd seraphs of Heaven
Coveted her and me.

Annabel dies, the child lovers are parted by celestial envy. But the lover does not accept reality:

And neither the angels in Heaven above
Nor the demons down under the sea
Can ever dissever my soul from the soul
Of the beautiful Annabel Lee.

Annabelle is a homage to the venerable alcoholic madman Edgar Allan. Who was someone who knew about child love, having married a fourteen-year-old. Indeed, Pat, too, when she fell in love for the first time, with an older girl at her school, was nine years old. Since then, she has done nothing but pursue those feelings, so intense and so exhilarating, again and again, without ever rediscovering them in the pristine purity of that very first experience.

Impossible to escape the imprinting of desire: the eros of childhood continues to function within us for ever, branding our entire existence.

This is well known to another writer, Vladimir Nabokov, who round about this time introduces to the world his tormented and grotesque hero, Humbert Humbert, whose destiny is marked for ever by his pre-adolescent love for a twelve-year-old, also called Annabel. But Pat does not read *Lolita*, either when it first appears or later, because the novel is steeped in a sulphurous atmosphere of sex, and Pat, that puritan sinner, does not like sex in books or films, it annoys her, disturbs something in her that, for want of a more exact term, might be called modesty.

V

Discipline, solitude, an ascetic life cost me no effort.
It is the accompanying sense of virtue that grates on me.
Virtue is stupid.

Women, women everywhere around her, and never enough of them. As long as there are beautiful women in the world, who could ever be depressed? She is nearly forty and simultaneously in love with two women – not counting wonderful easy-going Liz, but perhaps Liz is the one she is actually in love with, sweet Liz, the girl who never says no, who comes and goes, Liz with whom everything is simple, laughter and lovemaking, with no strings attached.

But her affairs are no longer enough to light up city skies.

Melancholy, depression, loneliness.

Do not let yourself go to pot, nurture the will to live – that forced sentiment – like a delicate plant that has to be watered with extreme care, drop by drop, so as not to damage it. Always remember, it is only after touching rock bottom that you can resurface, just as, often, it is in suffering and desolation that the seed of beauty is to be found. Writing is this also, it is this above all.

Highs and lows. As ever, but the oscillation is becoming frenetic, the rhythm takes her breath away.

Having woken from the unbearable wonderful dream of Ellie and finished the book, she throws herself back into life, into bars, into affairs. Into another attempt at cohabitation that soon fails. Into more travelling.

She discovers the grey boring face of Europe, the traveller's solitude. She likes it.

Another novel. It is about a man who has been demoralised by his ex-wife, a manipulative and deceitful bitch; a wounded man, whose sole panacea consists in spying on a stranger, a young woman in her house, watching her unseen as she performs everyday tasks, immersed in a peace and serenity he feels lost to him for ever. Like his author who, with her heart in her mouth, stole into the garden of the woman from Bloomingdale's, so Robert hides behind a clump of trees outside the young woman's house, with the sole purpose of capturing the image of her moving behind the lighted window.

Who will ever understand what extraordinary power the vision of that graceful and distant figure has over him? She is the incarnation of the ideal woman, poised and unattainable, and Robert wants nothing of her except to watch her, with the racing heart of a guilty man who might be discovered from one moment to the next, because he knows very well that no one would believe in the innocence of his intentions.

And in fact once he has been exposed, public condemnation is immediate, local people consider him a pervert, a madman or a criminal. Robert suddenly finds himself the focus of an entire community's suspicions and persecution, and his dream turns into a nightmare...

This was not how she wanted her protagonist to be. This is not how she wants herself to be.

Robert is too weak, too good, a victim, and she cannot bear victims, all they need to do is rebel, to strike back in turn. They are accomplices of the persecutors, inviting them, luring them into victimisation.

However, the public and critics like the book, they see in it a commentary on society and the individual, on marginalisation and racism. Critics need to give labels to what they read. Let them. Reality does not interest her.

Pat is far from having any intention of documenting an era, confronting this or that social problem, fastening on to fashionable issues. For her, there has only ever been one theme: what goes on within ourselves, in our innermost depths, regardless of period, logic or ideology.

At the end of the story Robert finds himself alone in the ever more narrow margin of an improbable unprovable innocence, and it is not without some relief that Pat leaves him to his fate. Sooner or later guys like him pay for all the sins they have not committed. She on the other hand once again gets away with the satisfaction of having killed off another harpy, Robert's ex-wife: one of those invasive and oppressive women who want nothing other than to tear you to pieces with their long sharp claws. It is good to be able to do it publicly and with impunity, exercising the writer's power of life and death over her characters.

Killing by writing leaves her with a clear conscience, unlike what happens in the dreams that she notes in her diary: I killed a woman, she was old, I slowly raised the hatchet and brought it down violently on her head, which split in two. And then I continued to strike, again and again, until there was nothing left of her but a shapeless, bleeding heap. Why did I do it? Who was that old woman? I did not know her, I knew nothing about her, but it is obvious that I did it, they all know, the police are arriving, I can hear the sound of the siren approaching, in my street. In a moment they will be here, they will come and arrest me. What will my friends say when they read the news in tomorrow's paper? What will they say about me?

One day I might do it, if I were very drunk, if I lost control, one day I might.

Damn her Dostoevskian conscience.

But readers do not judge her, they are not shocked, on the contrary: they like her murders and they like her. At least English, French and German readers do.

However, American readers are baffled and appalled, not by the violence and the number of victims, men and women, in her novels – tame stuff compared with some hardboiled American fiction – but because her characters are too weird, misfits, from whom the ordinary American wants to keep his distance: I'm not like that, this woman is a bit cracked, she only likes psychopaths, perverts. Give me a detective who is likeable, a bit of a rogue, who treats women badly and takes deliquents apart, all the rest is intellectual rubbish.

Yet she continues to publish, the money comes in, not huge sums, but enough to keep her going, for a few months, a few years, the time it takes to write another novel. Her fame as a thriller writer is becoming more consolidated, whether she likes it or not; how to explain to the public, to editors, to anyone who reads her, that her books are not mysteries or suspense novels, but stories of life? Because suspense, violence and crime are part of everyday life. People do not want to know. And so she might just as well accept the label: all right, she is a thriller writer.

The woman who remains the constant in her life, her mother, is becoming ever more insufferable. During a trip to Europe together – at Pat's expense – Mary prevents her from working, criticises her appearance and her lifestyle, gives interviews to journalists in place of her. She loses everything, her bag, passport, gloves, traveller's cheques.

"You're neurotic, you're abnormal, you're mad," Mommie Dearest tells her.

"Me? Have you looked at yourself in the mirror? If I am, it is only because I take after you," screams Pat, on the edge of a nervous breakdown.

There is not a woman she likes that Mary does not attack ferociously. Only to take her side as soon as Pat breaks off the relationship and loses interest in her.

Every visit from Mary is a battle, at the end of which she feels like a wounded soldier who needs care and rest to recover and forget. And who wins? Who can say.

There is always that phrase ringing in her ears: when are you going to sort yourself out? Nothing has changed since she was fourteen. No, that is not true: her mother is worse, she gets worse every year. What a pity that in reality you cannot pick up that hatchet and bring it down on Mommie Dearest's head.

(When will she be strong enough to do it without dying herself?)

And then suddenly, at the age of forty, in the midst of this chaos that is her life, without any mainstay or anchor, without having reached any real objective, she is ready to repeat the mistake she swore she would never make again: share a house with another woman.

In 1962 she writes in her diary: I will never live with anyone again, I have realised once and for all that cohabitation is not for me.

In 1963 she settles in England to live with Catherine.

No, that is not quite true. She only wants to be near Catherine. It will be a part-time cohabitation.

It seems to her the perfect solution. A sensible compromise, too sensible even, considering the intensity of her desire. Catherine will come and stay with her at the weekend and during the holidays, and the rest of the time she will be in London with her husband and daughter. That way, separation will strengthen love, at the same time allowing her to write without any distractions.

The house is one of those picture-postcard cottages, almost unbelievably pretty, and very different from the house in Old Faith, which was more of an old converted barn. Her new residence is in Sussex and has a thatched roof, windows framed by branches of wisteria, a garden with fuchsia and foxgloves growing in it. It is impractical and freezing cold in winter. But Pat is reasonably happy living there for a couple of years until things deteriorate.

Catherine is a sudden, rampant blaze. A brief encounter during a trip to the Mediterranean, a headlong passion without even time to get to know each other, and then both immediately having to return to their respective homes. During their separation desire grows hugely, expectancy of their next meeting becomes a religious frisson. It is the second time she has fallen in love with an Englishwoman, and again the ocean that keeps them apart can only strengthen her feelings.

But while with Elisabeth, fourteen years earlier, the feelings were one-sided, Catherine has responded to her in the most delightful way since the very first moment.

Back in America, Pat can only dream of the gentle touch of those little puffy hands, of her soft chestnut curls, of the warmth and languor in her eyes.

Catherine had been waiting for no one else but her, just as she had been waiting for Catherine. They were a godsend to each other, a miracle – or a misapprehension, depending on which way you want to look at it.

The Englishwoman is bored to death with her husband, her family, her life in the home. She has reached the end of the line: she has nothing more to do, no experience to try out, no illusion to live for. Pat is exhausted, sick with anxiety, drained and depressed by her attempts to build a professional and private life. She lives in financial uncertainty, and knows only two things for sure: that women and America have left her shattered, and that being a writer is not so much a profession as a punishment.

And suddenly it seems that Catherine is the solution to everything, the universal remedy.

A woman, a real woman at last, who knows how to hem a curtain and serve tea gracefully, and whose sole desire is to do so for Pat – albeit only on Saturdays and Sundays. Pat asks for nothing more, tea every day would be too much – anyway she prefers coffee – and what use are curtains when between you and your neighbours there is a honeysuckle hedge?

Their first meetings.

Pat falls into her arms as if into a soft bottomless cavern. Catherine is full of allure, with honeyed looks and intoxicating words.

I have never been loved before, you are the best lover in the world, sighs Catherine.

A declaration to be put in perspective, assuming her experience is limited, as it probably is, to her husband Oscar and a couple of harmless suitors before him. Which detracts nothing from the engulfing and satisfying quality of having sex with her.

It is curious how sex is an entirely independent variable in a loving relationship. The person you love most, or the one most suited to you, is not necessarily the person with whom you have the best sexual rapport. And vice versa, obviously.

With Carol, it was always a more mystical experience than a truly physical one. With her, Pat was not so much interested in pleasure – in fact her body was often silenced, dazzled by the excess of sensations – as in absorbing her presence. Carol was a magic potion that transformed her into herself at last.

Carol was her elixir of life, her holy communion. Her demon. She would have followed her to hell. At least that is what she thought, but then she didn't. In Carol's hell, there was no room for Pat.

Poor Carol, she died years ago now, in a clinic for rich alcoholics where her family quietly confined her and threw away the key. Pat found out belatedly and almost by chance.

A numbness, a sadness, no surprise – not real grief but a rekindling of the nostalgic flame that burns before the picture of her. The ideal Carol cannot die, and in fact continues to live in her dreams and will be reincarnated in her novels. If anything of the real Carol survives somewhere, Pat wishes her well.

With Rose the sex was enjoyable and affectionate, a little humdrum from the start, a little too tame and domesticated with no surprises, until it became a habit and as such a duty, which made her feel obligated and vaguely despicable. Yet it was precisely the controllable aspect of their relationship, the certainty of being compatible – with some compromises, of course – that had seemed to both of them the attractive premise of their partnership, the basis for living together. They were on the same level, peers: the same age, the same professional choices, the same problems and ambitions – and therefore similar in the things that mattered.

Wrong, they were very different, because they had very different ways of confronting life. In actual fact, they were incompatible.

Making love with Lucy on the other hand was wonderful, like being crowned winners after a long, tiring and bloody tussle. Or like a hot shower after an interminable cold bath. And for the same reason, it became intolerable over time. A certain dose of suffering intensifies passion, that is undeniable; but if the dose is excessive, the passion is killed off. And with Lucy the dose of suffering was decidedly out of all proportion.

But in the case of Catherine, you could call it "chemistry". From the physical point of view, they were made for each other. Every gesture of Pat's elicits moans of ecstasy from

Catherine; every desire of the one is mirrored exactly in the other. No need of words.

This leads them to believe in absolute total love. Even though in truth there is never any real conversation between them about anything more elevated and abstract than the weather, when would be the right time to repair the roof, the best make of biscuits, or why Catherine's son is not doing well at school (a subject that soon becomes taboo; Pat cannot bear indolence and self-pity, and Catherine cannot bear her off-spring to be accused of laziness, her maternal instinct is roused).

Pat's attempts to talk about the British government or the war in Vietnam or the existence of God meet with banal and vapid replies, not very different from what you might hear in casual conversation at the grocer's or the post office. And this is not because her beloved is too stupid to think but because she is serious, reserved and respectable. Everything that Pat is not. And apparently a respectable woman – especially a respectable Englishwoman – has no personal opinions, she adopts those of her class, or the social group with whom she associates.

Or perhaps yes, Catherine is indeed too stupid to think. As time goes by, Pat begins to lean towards this second hypothesis.

After a while she begins to wonder what she is doing there, on her own five days of the week if not six, in a rainy village in Sussex where there is no one to talk to, and where, if Catherine does not manage to see her off first, the draughts in that doll's house will be the death of her. Gradually the idyll becomes a state of friction, and Catherine, conscious of not being the uncontested sovereign and goddess any more, feels the need to reassert herself with a little high-handedness, whingeing and aggression.

Pat will tell herself that attributing so much importance to sex was a mistake. Love does not live by sex alone, in fact it can very well do without it, just as sex can do without love.

And Catherine has used sex, has fallen into the habit of deploying her feminine allure to get what she wants. How can you say no to a woman who gives you that languid yielding smile, who entrusts herself to you, who looks at you as if you were her saviour?

Traps and ruses. Tricks and turnabouts.

At first Catherine accused her husband of being the cause of her unhappiness: dear Oscar with his no-nonsense coldness, showing no feeling, made her miserable. Now it is the other way round and Oscar has become a treasure and Pat a nasty selfish monster.

Maybe Pat is actually a monster? But is she the only one?

Why must the majority of idylls come to such an absurd and painful end?

From Pat's diary

May '67, Frameborough

Catherine arrived at four today, and without even taking off her hat complained that the house was freezing cold and damp and that she had caught a chill. Not a brilliant start, it seemed to me. (It has been raining for days, something that does not have a positive influence on anyone's mood, certainly not mine.) I reminded her that, since she had asked me to meet the expenses for the cottage on my own – when according to our original agreement they were supposed to be shared and paid for by both of us – it was up to me to decide whether to light the fires or not, as I am the one who is paying.

Catherine looked displeased, like Queen Elizabeth herself before an act of *lèse-majesté*: according to her, I should have got the house warm anyway, in anticipation of her arrival. *I* can live with the cold, but *she* can't. I lit the stove in the sitting room but since it has not been cleaned recently the room filled up with smoke and we had to take refuge in the kitchen so as not to die of asphyxiation.

This set the tone for the rest of the afternoon. We had tea (she still in her hat, coat and gloves – I laced mine with a drop of whisky, knowing what was to come). I was scolded for never asking about her family; but what is the point of asking, seeing as she always gives me the family bulletin anyway, whether I want it or not? Answer: to show that I am interested.

I took a deep breath and I told her what it seemed to me I had already made clear since the very beginning of our relationship: I am not interested in her as the mother of a family – if anything, it is *despite* her being one. Her family is definitely not among my chief concerns.

As usual, my honesty was interpreted as deliberate bitchiness and a desire to hurt her; I don't love her any more and so on, leading up to the accusation that I was a common drunkard (she could smell the whisky in the tea – obviously she has not got as much of a cold as she claimed).

Supper was a wretched affair: she wanted to do the cooking but was "too upset", so she burnt the (very expensive) roast I had bought especially from the best butcher in Frameborough.

When it was time for bed, without a word she headed for the guest room. A relief.

May '67, Frameborough

Dreamt of Liz. Beautiful and vivacious, as she was in 1953, that time we went to Cherry Grove together in her red sports car. (Fourteen years ago!) Very enjoyable, half dream and half fantasy. So intense that this morning I had a clear impression of her presence. Liz was there, just behind the door leading into the hallway, I could smell her fresh scent, hear the amusement in her deep carefree voice.

Ah Liz, if only I could have you here for a few days, just a few hours! I am certain that you would restore my energy and faith in myself, and give me the necessary strength to escape this mire.

Her majesty appeared on the landing at nine thirty, wearing a dressing gown (mine), and informed me that the toilet in the bathroom was not flushing properly. Which is odd, because it was working until a moment before. Perhaps, like me, objects when confronted with her become confused and reveal their worst side.

As she delivered this complaint she grandly started descending the stairs – but she missed her footing and fell, and ended up in a heap at the bottom of the staircase.

I could not help laughing – at last a little amusement in this miserable story! – which convicted me once and for all, even though I helped her up at once. Apart from a few bruises there was nothing wrong with her.

She has gone back to London without even staying for lunch.

It is evening now and my thoughts continue to dwell on that

fall. She could have broken her neck. A providential accident in the plot of a novel. She falls down the stairs and dies, and it is not a crime because no one pushed her (this would have to be proved, preferably by a witness). What actually pushed her were her own passions (anger, a sense of having suffered an affront), and even if someone did undoubtedly provoke those passions, no one is to blame.

Would that not be a just end for a harpy? To fall from a height, to feel herself stepping into the void and then slam into the ground – just the way it happens when deception is exposed, ruses are revealed – a perfect death for a bitch, a witch, who for a while was, or seemed to be, or could have been, the Ideal Woman.

Ah, my Liz, if only I had you here!

May '67, Frameborough

Have written to Catherine a long and reasoned letter in which I suggest breaking off this relationship which clearly cannot go on. I will pay her back the expenses she has incurred on the cottage, and then I will put it up for sale and I will go away. I do not yet know where, but certainly not anywhere in England.

Another failure, both emotional and financial. In recent years I have earned more (because I have worked more, I have worked nonstop) and my finances are almost on an even keel at last. Ironically, this now allows me to bear the cost of this separation – and leaves me more or less where I was three years ago, in other words, broke. At least until I have sold the cottage.

When will I be capable of making solid investments?

May '67, Frameborough

Still no reply from Catherine, which does not reassure me. Yesterday I contacted an estate agent about selling the cottage.

Dreamt of Liz again. I have got everything wrong in life, *she* was the woman I should have stayed with. I am thinking of writing her a letter asking for her news and possibly inviting her to come and visit me in England. Why not?

She will be surprised to hear from me after such a long time. But perhaps it is worth a try.

June '67, Frameborough

Received a visit from Oscar, who turned up on my doorstep with a funereal look on his face to announce that his wife is deeply depressed and very unwell and has a cracked rib (a result of her fall from the landing a week ago) and that all this is the fault of yours truly. He then formally asked me to show some responsibility and to reconsider my attitude towards his wife.

"In what way?" I asked him. (I could not believe my ears.)

His wife, Oscar informed me, is a delicate and sensitive woman, and those individuals who have a place in her affections should show how gratified they are and not contemptibly betray her. Thereupon he stopped and coughed. He seemed nervous and so more human than usual. Maybe that is why I felt a vague sympathy towards him.

"Oscar," I said, "this is all ridiculous."

He looked at me resentfully.

What was I supposed to say to him, that I did not intend to continue my affair with his wife, not even to please him?

I could not help thinking that if that fall down the stairs

had had more serious consequences, today Oscar might have been a free man.

But freedom is something you have to earn.

I have decided not to write to Liz after all. Too much time has gone by, and she is surely not as I remember her.

VI

Why do my books not sell in America? Because they are "too psychologically subtle", says my American agent – and there is not a single "likeable" character in them. Perhaps that is because I don't like anyone. Next time I'll write about animals.

And so the affair with Catherine is over, with the by now familiar unpleasant sentimental and bureaucratic aftermath. What on earth prompted her, more than once, to want to share her bed and her purse with a woman, only to find herself on her own, saddled with a house where she no longer lives?

The curse of houses! This urge to possess, to settle down, combined with that other urge to go away, to spread her wings, to break free of every bond. It would be so much easier to be a snail that carries its shell around with it, and is masculine or feminine at will – not to mention the fact that snails make love with delicate concentration, with slow and ecstatic movements, for hours, as if nothing else existed in the world.

Snails are Pat's next favourite animal after cats. She breeds them, she even takes them with her when she travels, having to smuggle them because the customs authorities do not allow it. All her predilections, it goes without saying, are forbidden by law.

She likes cats more and more: they are soft, elegant, mysterious and sensual. Like women. But unlike women they make no demands, and with cats there is no recrimination and no blackmailing.

As soon as she settles in France, she gets herself a splendid Siamese cat she calls Sam.

Together with a friend, Evelyn, nicknamed Madame because of her grand manner, she buys a house in the Île de France. It is a little house tucked away in the middle of an old neighbourhood and squeezed in between other buildings, almost invisible to anyone who does not know of its existence. It is like her life: she tries to blend in with others, not to be noticed.

Without ever succeeding.

Evelyn, another huge mistake. Cohabitation turns the charming and witty woman who in recent years has been a delightful travelling companion into a possessive harridan, always upbraiding her and creating violent scenes inspired by jealousy.

Within a few months she finds herself with another wife. As if there were no escape.

And they are not even lovers, only friends!

She is definitely bedevilled by bad luck, even though she is prepared to admit it is partly her own fault.

It is true: Sam, who is still a kitten and uncontrollable, has pulled the threads in Evelyn's carpet – in fact, Evelyn has actually asked to be compensated for the damage.

And yes, when Pat types she makes a noise, but how was she to know that Madame was so sensitive that she would not be able to sleep because of it? Furthermore, Madame cannot stand her English girlfriend Violet, and the antipathy is reciprocated.

Violet is the first woman in her life who approaches Pat with the reverential awe of a true fan: heavens above, what a thrill to be near Miss Highsmith, the writer!

It is not bad to be treated like a diva just for a change, although it is disconcerting.

It was Violet who sought her out, to interview her. After barely a few minutes' acquaintance and a few questions, Pat knows exactly who she is dealing with: an ambitious English girl, twenty years younger than her, only too willing to fall into her arms.

But who does Violet talk of when she talks of Pat? Who does she see with that wide-eyed look of hers?

"Oh gosh, can I really call you Pat?" Big Eyes says to her. "But can you imagine? It would be like calling Shakespeare 'Bill' or Dickens 'Charles'."

Which is delightfully stupid, Pat thinks, kissing her.

Violet turns out to be a fault-finding little know-it-all. And a conservative one, what's more.

Fortunately she is in England and they only see each other for a few days once in a while.

At last she scrapes together the money for another house, all of her own.

And it is like a paradise to her, until she realises that in order to buy meat for Sam or a new typewriter ribbon she has to go miles, which means she needs a car. And in winter it is cold and humid, just like Sussex. And the neighbours, an Italian family with an incredible number of children, are rude and noisy.

But she holds out.

She wants to put down roots.

And she wants to put them down here, in Fromoncourt, a few dozen miles from Paris, on the edge of the forest of Fontainebleau.

She chose the place, as ever, with a mixture of haste, fatalism, impulsiveness and casualness.

It will do fine.

It will do. One place is as good as another.

She is not alone. Sam keeps her company and shows her affection without expecting her to give up her freedom, the way human beings do. She is not without friends, or even lovers: partially overlapping with Violet and after her there is Josy, an attractive madcap Parisian, and a few others besides.

Pat certainly does not stay put: she travels back and forth between the village and Paris, the village and London, New York, Berlin...

The inhabitants of Fromoncourt do not like her, they barely greet her, do not read her books, and will wait until she is dead before taking pride in their local celebrity – if the ambiguous sentiment that will prompt them to name, with unintentional humour, a dead-end alley 'Impasse Highsmith' can be called pride.

Her life too, on bad days, is a dead-end.

You must be proud of what you have become, writes Constant, the loyal friend from her college years, now her American correspondent.

Constant is her girl Friday, who keeps her supplied with black ruled notebooks and news of home, her woman in New York. There has never been anything between them, thank heavens, so Pat can now speak to her freely.

Or almost freely. Constant is puritanical, some things she would not understand.

You are a famous writer, Constant tells her, you must be proud of yourself. How many languages have you been translated into? Twenty?

But Pat is tormented by her unfulfilment, and consumed with fear of failure.

Being is decidedly not her strong point. She prefers doing.

Writing is pervasive, invading all space and time. Sleeping, moving about the house, taking care of the garden, travelling – everything is a preparation for writing, all being good and positive when it is useful for her work, a cause of bad temper and a waste of time when it is of no use to the novel she is writing or the next one taking shape in her mind.

Writing increasingly rewards her dedication, giving her moments of pure enjoyment. That vein of cynical and cruel humour that she has been carrying around with her since adolescence finds expression especially in her short stories, which provide her with the warrior's recreation after the exertion of a novel. She finds herself more and more often laughing out loud as she writes, ha ha, and despite her darker moments would not swap her life for anyone else's because this is the only life that suits her.

She has become a real writer. For some, like Violet, even a great writer. Someone has described her as the poet of apprehension.

Is she a *real* writer? What is a *real* writer? Does such a thing exist? Or is it only the product of others' imagination, of chance, of distance?

Again, she ruminates, as she did years ago, on this insoluble problem, again she tells herself that no one, least of all her, could ever call into question Dostoevsky, Poe and James – but the fact is: they are dead. How to distinguish between what each of them really was as a writer, from what each of us, as readers, sees in them? From the layers that accumulate on top of them, like dust, every time another pair of hands opens one of their books, and another pair of eyes reads it?

Their books are still read and that is all that counts.

Chance, luck – she is old enough to know that these play an important part in the success of a writer, perhaps even more important than talent. And perseverance. Perseverance, the only virtue she acknowledges in herself and which she exercises at some cost with triumphant doggedness.

As for her contemporaries, living writers, she prefers not to know much about them. She does not want to measure herself against anyone, even though she would like to be paid and recognised like some of them, such as Graham Greene – incidentally, it has recently come to her knowledge that Greene has sold all his documents and manuscripts to some American university for a tidy sum. It would not be such a bad thing if she managed to do the same.

Why leave things to your heirs, for free, after you are dead, when you can sell them while you are still alive and get the money for them yourself?

And what does she care what becomes of her work after

her death? She won't be here any more to be pleased or hurt by it so it is pointless to waste time thinking about it.

Nevertheless the idea of leaving something, of not altogether dying, continues to work on her. There are books that she cherishes, her favourite children, and what parent would not want to provide for their children before dying? She would like to know that at least they would survive for a reasonable length of time. Her Ripley, David Kelsey and his mad love for Annabelle, and of course *The Tremor of Forgery*, the work of her maturity. The one the critics – out of the kindness of their hearts – finally deigned to regard as a *novel* rather than a mere crime story.

It was a great experience writing about Howard Ingham, who goes to Tunisia, to places with which she is familiar, having stayed there with Madame Evelyn a few years ago.

Ingham is an American writer, summoned to Africa to work on the screenplay of a film, which will never be made. When he is left with no reason for being there, his trip becomes a period of waiting that makes less and less sense with every day that passes. Ingham waits, without knowing what for, and in the meantime he writes a novel. Writing feeds on periods when nothing is happening, it is rooted in unplanned situations and casual encounters. Writing is nomadic, like nomads it carries its home around with it. Ingham is an outsider, in an alien environment, his sole belongings are his typewriter and his love for a woman who is distant and impossible, a little like Carol...

It is good to choose as a protagonist someone who does something that is familiar to you, in which you are well versed, so there is no need for any flights of fancy to know how he operates, what he does, what his everyday routines are. Just as it is good to have some familiarity with the deep core of the events recounted, to know from long experience their texture and flavour. Ingham finds himself alone in a foreign and dangerous country, every footstep heard outside his door could be a threat... when she lived on her own in New York in an apartment with access onto a fire escape, which thieves or prowlers could have climbed without any difficulty, she used to imagine defending herself against possible intruders by hurling her heavy Olympia at them, the typewriter being always within reach on her bedside table. And this is exactly what Ingham will do: he will throw his typewriter at the judgemental old beggar who is stalking him and about to break into his room, hitting him on the head with it. Did he kill him or just injure him? He will never know. The hotel staff will take care of removing all trace of the incident, perhaps even of burying the body, they being much more interested in not disturbing the tourists' tranquillity than in getting the law involved...

Like all her characters, Ingham derives from her, and in a game of mirrors and transformations she herself becomes Ingham. In writing, the writer creates her own double, a psychic experience without equal. Feelings past and present; emotions hoarded in notebooks and rescued from the archive of memory; images glimpsed when the door of reality stands ambiguously ajar, not quite shutting out the possible and the improbable; strange coincidences dreamed up when the mind wanders freely and without restraint – everything turns out to be useful, everything contributes to form that other self that interpenetrates with Pat, delineates her, echoes around her.

The only solitude she really fears is to be deserted by her creations, to be left as just herself.

In Tunisia, with its hotels for wealthy tourists and alleys where violence and wretchedness hold sway, Ingham at last feels at home, in other words an outsider, different from everything and everyone, far from America. Beneath the sun and in the desert wind, which carries with it the intimation of a more primitive and cruel life, or perhaps only less hypocritical, the American dream and *the American way of life* can be seen for what they are, conventions and illusions. Cages, invisible prisons, glass cells. And what does it matter whether Ingham has actually killed the old beggar or merely injured him or scared him off? What counts is that he does not feel guilty, on the contrary: he is happy to be rid of him.

Why should we ever feel guilty for destroying the ghosts that prey on us, for striking first against the enemies who are intending to waylay us?

Morality, legality, justice – do not exist in nature. And that includes human nature.

How many crimes are punished? A very small percentage. And has the world stopped turning as a result?

Justice is a phantom that haunts only the conscience of sensitive individuals (such as she, Pat, used to be, when she was young, and heaven knows it is not a very comfortable state to be in). To most people it is of no real interest. They pretend, perhaps unconsciously, owing to that mass hypocrisy that controls all of us.

Book by book her vision has become clearer and she more audacious. The critics are starting to take her seriously, it seems. The time is now ripe to return to her favourite creation, Tom Ripley, whom she brought into the world some fifteen years ago and who is there just waiting for her to revive him.

In the fifteen years he has been left in suspension, in the dense hypnotic fluid of fantasy, Tom has not aged, or only just enough to settle down and marry the beautiful and wealthy Héloïse, a European cousin of Carol, poised and enigmatic like some French actresses, the ideal woman among whose virtues is that of almost always being somewhere else, mostly on trips with friends. The couple live in Belle Ombre, a château set in the countryside near Fontainebleau, a stone's throw from Fromoncourt.

Now Pat and Tom are neighbours, travelling the same tree-lined roads, doing their shopping in the same local stores, they might meet in the café, in fact she would not be surprised if one day, going into the village bar-tabac-épicerie, she were to see him leaning against the counter, intent on reading the newspaper, or exchanging a few jocular words with the tobacconist Madame Jolie.

Tom has the qualities that Pat attributes to herself or that she admires unconditionally: he is witty, inventive, loyal to friends, tender and respectful towards his wife. He is an art lover and connoisseur, he likes gardening and plays the harpsichord. He is also detached and cold, an outsider, like Ingham, but much more adventurous than Ingham. Brisk and without scruple, he is impervious to any sense of guilt, which means that he has nothing to defend other than appearances, something that makes him so much more honest and sincere than the majority of his fellow men. (Who like to regard him as an amoral degenerate.)

Behind the appearance of a respectable American citizen abroad, Tom lives the shady life of an habitual forger and occasional murderer.

Like her.

Tom gives her a sense of power and of lightness. When she is among people she finds boring or oppressive, or she is faced with journalists harassing her with stupid or invasive questions, when she finds it terribly burdensome to impersonate herself, the writer, and she knows she is doing it badly and gracelessly, when she is afraid of being exposed for her faults and shortcomings past and present – it is at that moment that Tom sidles up to her, like a cat, and whispers in her ear some irreverent comment or points out to her some ridiculous detail about one of her tormentors, and suddenly everything changes, becomes more bearable, almost amusing.

"Oh my god," Catherine says to her one day, "how could you have invented that totally preposterous character, that what's-his-name, that Ripley? He's repulsive, you must admit, and totally unprincipled, he has no moral sense."

She and Catherine have started to see each other again. After some ten years' rift, a mutual friend told her of poor Oscar's death, and Pat had the decency to send the widow a note of condolence. Since then, they see each other every now and again, whenever she goes to London, short somewhat formal visits, in the course of which they almost never mention the past. Strange that Catherine should have bothered to read one of her books. For the first time, as far as she knows.

"You're getting more and more neurotic," Lucy has declared, on receiving a photo of her, with a cigarette clamped between her teeth, looking shifty and cocky, signed Pat, alias Tom R.

Lucy is a remarkable woman but completely devoid of any sense of humour.

Toinette, her new French girlfriend, roars with laughter reading about Tom. *"C'est merveilleux,"* she says. "And you are a reprobate, like him."

Writing is not a neutral act.

You write with the brain but also with your blood, your past, your sex life.

What it cost her, that *Tantalus*, all those years ago! While she was still writing it – before it had a publisher, a cover, before it was called *The Price of Salt* and became an object that you pick up in your hand, when it was still inside her, attached to her body and mind by thousands of invisible filaments – shivers of joy alternated with anguish. Fear, shame, sudden anxieties that overwhelmed her, and made her feel dizzy.

She would suddenly look up from the page and find herself confronted with that look of triumphant disgust in her mother, in Rosalind, in Ned, in Lucy, in how many others? No one was with her in that endeavour, she was alone.

You are always alone when you write. But in the case of *Tantalus*, solitude was not a privilege, it was a sentence of doom.

The judges – Ned, her mother, Rosalind, again her mother, especially her mother – were a tribunal, unanimous in their sentence.

Why write *this*? Is this how you want to be known, and remembered? What do you need this for, where is the sense in it?

(Yes, *this* is exactly what I want to write, about Carol's courage, the way she would brush her hair off her face, the way she smoked, her bravado. Carol and Therese's love, magnificent and fragile, always in danger. The joy that pulses in Therese's veins at the sight of Carol...)

Even before she brought it into the world, she sometimes hated that *Tantalus*, to which she did not put her name.

Years later they would ask her to recognise it, as one might recognise a bastard child who has done well for himself in some shady way.

She will hesitate for a long time. But why? What do you want of me?

They will tell her that times have changed, that certain subjects are no longer taboo. She will reply with one of her grunts of scepticism. They will tell her that readers are eager to read her, that if it has her name on it critics will at last give it the attention it deserves, that it is a fine, courageous, important book.

What will prove decisive is the argument that the book continues to be published in pirated editions and the pirate publishers get away with it because there is no name, no definite attribution. No one can lay claim to it, if she doesn't.

She will take the last drag on her unfiltered Gauloise - she always smokes them right down until she almost burns her fingers on them – and stub it out with an angry headstrong gesture.

And in the end she will say yes.

As long as they stop bothering her.

It will be republished for the nth time, with her name on it. They will also change the title, it will be called *Carol*.

No female protagonists. She has never written that down in her black notebooks, and in any case it is not a rule or a conclusion but a point of departure. The recognition of an impossibility.

Women are not free to move about, to act and to change. They are tied down to one place – the home, the family – and to their human bodies. To their crystallised immutable identity. A prison.

Carol and Therese have been the only exceptions. Because they are not women. Not in the usual sense of the word. And they are not *les girls* either. They are that rare and perhaps only dreamed-of thing, complete human beings.

But now, in her fifties, in the seventh decade of the century, she begins to think of writing a story that does in fact tell of a woman, one apparently like so many others. A housewife.

What happens, she wonders, if the housewife is a woman who thinks? Who reads the papers, gets interested, becomes outraged, has opinions?

A woman who cooks, washes, irons, cleans, is a servant to the men of the house – who are not even aware of her working – yet who thinks. A woman who could be her, Pat, if she had married Ned all those years ago.

If she had taken a dead-end road.

She will call her Edith. She will still be young, educated, full of energy and plans, as women in those years seem to be, ready to criticise and change the world but incapable of taking a look at themselves, of seeing the wall that confines their existence on all sides, that every day becomes ever more restrictive…

It will be fun, she thinks, putting another sheet of paper into her typewriter.

For Pat Highsmith, normality is the dead end. Which her fellow citizens might have sensed, when they – perhaps reluctantly and against the opposition of conservative local councillors – named that wretched alley after her.

My mother, she writes at the age of fifty to her stepfather Stanley, expected me to be a girl like any other and to marry Ned.

I wasted my breath telling her that we would both have been desperately unhappy. Years later she was still coming out with: "That poor man, you destroyed him!" No use repeating that *if I had married him* I would have destroyed him.

She has always disapproved of everything I did, the company I kept, my travelling, my successes. "I wouldn't live the way you live for a million dollars," she said to me one day. Absurd, as well as offensive. I told her I was happier than a great many others, that I loved my work, that I had a lot of friends, that there were probably some people who would consider me enviable. Deluded fool that I am! What did I expect of her, a rational response?

As with many American women of her generation, what she cared about was not my happiness, or even hers, but a neurotic, shrill pretence of happiness. And in the name of that pretence I was supposed to relinquish everything of any truth in me.

She is not talking to her mother Mary any more, she does not answer her letters of recrimination. Stanley is the only tenuous link with her dreadful dysfunctional family.

She does not tell Stanley that she has killed her. It has taken her fifty years to go through with this long-drawn out murder. Now that she has finally found the courage to do it, she is not at all ashamed of it. It was high time.

She is free of her, she has stopped loving her and therefore stopped hating her as well.

Murdering women has by now become one of her favourite sports.

A brief and incomplete list of the women Miss Highsmith has killed in the course of her career would include:

– The unfaithful Miriam in *Strangers on a Train*, who does not want to grant a divorce to that hopeless gentleman Guy. Miriam is a harpy who deserves to die and whose execution gives Pat moments of enjoyment. Miriam is strangled to death by Bruno, the likeable and perverse villain, because that is how she would do it, and that is how probably anyone would do it, in those moments when love turns to hatred, the hands become hooks.

– Clara, the wife of Walter *the Blunderer*. Neurotic, frigid and a blackmailer, Clara is exactly like Lucy, and like Lucy she attempts suicide. But while the flesh and blood Pat saved Lucy, albeit with reluctance, Pat the writer looks on with sadistic satisfaction while events take their course.

– The nymphomaniac Melinda in *Deep Water*, a serial adulterer and protagonist in a ruthless war between a couple. Her husband is a gentle sadist, who carries within him a few Ripley chromosomes.

– Leila in *A Game for the Living*. Leila is actually an exception, an intellectually and sexually liberated woman, and so there is no room for her in this world. There is no pleasure in her death, which takes place offstage, even before the story begins. Anyway, *A Game* is a boring and unsuccessful book which its author prefers to forget.

– That bore Effie in *This Sweet Sickness*. Effie is a clingy and tiresome girly woman who is in love with David Kelsey and does not realise that he loves only the unattainable Annabelle. She has to be got rid of, like all those who do not understand dreams and want to force you back to reality.

– The umpteenth harridan, Nickie, in *The Cry of the Owl*, closely related to Miriam and Clara. And, a collateral casualty in the same novel, Jenny, a feeble-minded, idealistic girl, incapable of facing up to life and sick with the will to die. Pat is intimately familiar with the Jenny type, there is a little Jenny living and languishing inside her.

– Colette, Chester's indecisive little woman who is attracted to the young Rydal in *The Two Faces of January*. Actually, Colette was not that bad, but at a certain point she interfered with the struggle between the two men, and so it was better to have her killed accidentally in the Minoan palace in Crete (as always, Pat does not collect souvenirs on her travels but crime scenes).

– Alicia in *A Suspension of Mercy* dies twice over, first fictitiously in the literary imagination of her husband Sydney (just like when Pat hit Rose with the pewter vase at Old Faith and wrapped her up in a carpet), and then for real, committing suicide.

– The fragile Peggy in *Those Who Walk Away*, another suicide. A precursory death, offstage, like that of Leila, that triggers the action: the conflict between the two adversaries, Peggy's father and her husband, set against the backdrop of Venice in winter…

And so many, many others.

"Do you realise," that little Miss Smarty-pants, Violet, says to her one day, "that in almost all your novels there are two men pitted against each other, who love and hate each other and try to kill each other, who are locked in a struggle that resembles a dance or a coupling…"

"I've been told that before," she says in irritation. The alter ego, the *Doppelgänger*, the angel and the devil. Trite observations.

"…but all this takes place over the body of a dead woman. And it is they, the two men, in a way, who kill her."

She does not say anything.

"It's as if they have to rid themselves of her before they can kill each other."

Pat listens in silence.

"The women as you describe them, monsters, harpies…" Violet continues.

"Bitches," she obligingly suggests.

"…bitches, if you like," (Violet cannot bring herself to say certain words, and only with her lips puckered if she has to). "They're grotesque, exaggerated, they don't exist."

"That's your opinion," she retorts, thinking how much of Violet there is in some of her women.

"Do you *really* believe that women are so stupid?"

Pat emits a grunt that could be interpreted as: "Well? Aren't they?"

"And those feeble girls who commit suicide… you have to admit, that's disturbing, it's sadistic on your part."

"So what?"

"Take Peggy: she kills herself for no reason. Why on earth

would a beautiful, healthy, wealthy girl, married to the man she loves, who loves her in return, kill herself?"

Pat remains silent. She is vexed.

She could give various answers. Because Peggy wants more, she wants the impossible. Like her author. Because she cannot bear reality not measuring up to her dreams. Peggy lives in a world of her own and thinks making love is an act of mystical union with the beloved. Like Pat, years ago. When she realises that reality is not so perfect, she despairs. And she has no other resources because, like ninety-five per cent of humanity, male and female, without distinction (according to Lucy's realistic estimate), she is stupid.

"I needed her to die. The story begins with that. I write thrillers," she says, puffing smoke in the girl's face.

"You've constructed a story around her but without her. You made her commit suicide. Why?"

"Because that will teach her not to be so unreasonable."

And with that she gets up and goes out into the garden. Her espaliered pear tree needs a good pruning. That Violet gets on her nerves. Who does she think she is? Miss Literary Critic?

Peggy is not the only one to have ideals. Pat also has them, yet she has learned to deal with the harshness of reality and to tie her own shoelaces. There is no room in this world for the weak, for idealists, for those who cannot bear pain, guilt, who don't get their hands dirty. Better for them to die young. Otherwise they risk becoming a great nuisance, capable of ruining a life, as Peggy was beginning to ruin her husband's. And Violet, hers. Not that Violet is idealistic, she is just tiresome. Fortunately their relationship won't last.

She turns to the girl, who has followed her into the garden.

"I don't want to talk about my books!" she hisses. "And don't stand there, you're trampling on my plants."

"It's you I'm talking about," says Violet. "You're a misogynist, you're worse than a man."

Then, looking at her muddy shoes, she says, "What plants? There's nothing growing here. You know, there's too much shade in your garden."

These days everybody talks about women, and above all women are talking. They are having their say. They are creating a disturbance. The so-called feminists are protesting loudly about male oppression.

But not a word about their own dependency, about the despicable contrivances of complicity and the squalid little ploys of seduction.

Poor defenceless victims, thinks Pat angrily, sawing the piece of wood more furiously. In the cold and damp cellar the only glimmer of warmth is the glow of her cigarette. Clouds of smoke and vexation escape from her mouth, the ends of her scarf sway violently in sync with her abrupt movements.

That Violet!

Little Miss Perfect! You want freedom, you want a life of your own? And how do you think you'll get it? By being a little know-it-all with those pursed lips of yours?

Challenge the world! Assume your responsibilities! Stop blaming others and seeking approval!

The wood splits.

"Aargh!" roars Pat.

Then slowly, with resolute determination, she starts on another piece.

Two hours later, the stool has taken shape, it is ready to be sanded and then varnished. Pat holds it up by one leg, observing it with satisfaction.

When she closes the door to the cellar behind her, she goes straight to her desk and sits down at it.

Misogynist, Violet called her.

A good idea. For some years she has been writing short stories that make her split her sides laughing, the only moments of good humour on some bad days. So far she has read them only to her most trusted friends – with varying responses, it has to be said.

She will call them *Little Tales of Misogyny*. Take that, Miss Violet.

When you feel sad, depressed, your work is not going well, your teeth hurt, nothing makes sense and you feel you have achieved nothing in life, when even Sammy looks at you through slit eyes as if she does not know you – murder a woman.

It will boost your spirits enormously.

A young man asked a father for his daughter's hand, and received it in a box – her left hand.

...So the young man was locked up, and once a month the girl whose hand he had received came to look at him through the wire barrier, like a dutiful wife. And like most wives, she had nothing to say.

He realised what a horrible mistake, crime even, he had been guilty of in demanding such a barbaric thing as a girl's hand.

Lying on the living room carpet, Pat wipes away a tear with the back of her hand. Her stomach hurts from laughing. She feels good, at peace, happy.

Laughter is an explosion that breaks your chains. The prison that is the world bursts open, its falsehoods are blown to bits, the fragments come down in a dance of joy.

You are free, for a sublime moment you are in the face of the elusive truth.

At the other end of the carpet Sammy is crouched with an air of expectancy.

Pat raises herself on one elbow, grabs a frayed cloth ball with the stitching coming apart. "Come on," she says, "it's time for our evening game."

The cat pricks up an ear, the vague look in her eyes becomes focused. The muscles tense beneath her silky fur coat.

For a moment they stare at each other like two adversaries ready to attack. Then Pat throws the ball into the air and with an absolutely vertical jump, making no visible effort, the cat uncurls like a leather belt and grabs it between her front paws.

A hoarse cackle of love and pleasure rasps Pat's throat.

Her relationship with Toinette starts in Paris, during a press reception.

Their first meeting is not at all romantic. Toinette gets a friend to introduce her, on the grounds that she is too shy to make any approach by herself. Pat does not know what to say to this girl with dishevelled curls round a chubby face. Toinette for her part stammers something incomprehensible and does not stop staring at her, then she spills a glass of Burgundy over herself and laughs inanely with an air of desperation, which raises a little tenderness in Pat and a great deal of alarm.

After the reception she is taken to dinner in some pretentious place where there is nothing else to drink but French wine, no beer or whisky. Toinette is not there, she is not one of the important people invited by the publisher. Pat finds this, like all social occasions, a trial. She asks for a pizza instead of the elaborate meat dish that she is served, and which she would like to take home for Sam (but she does not have the courage to ask). After endless delay and misunderstanding the pizza finally arrives, but Pat no longer has any appetite and does no more than scrape off some of the topping, olives and other stuff that she does not much care for.

She has forgotten about the girl with curly hair but when she finds herself face to face with her again, on the train to Moret-sur-Loing, she realises this is no coincidence.

Toinette has followed her.

Sat in the uncomfortable seat in front of her, clutching a huge shapeless bag, she asks her for an interview. She says that she works for various papers, that being allowed to interview her is her dream, and so on, and so on. Pat revises her opinion of her: she is not shy.

What is to be done? She certainly cannot make her get off the train, or indeed let her go off on her own in search of a hotel in the forest of Fontainebleau (Toinette has cooked up a story – obviously invented – about having friends who live in the area who she is on her way to visit, at this hour of the night).

She invites her to stay the night with her. They both get into the beaten-up Saab that Pat has parked, as always, at

Moret station, and together they drive through the undulating countryside of the Île de France to Fromoncourt, five miles between fields of corn and walls of greenery.

Pat is vaguely irritated, what worries her most are the neighbours, it is after midnight and she hopes that the girl tones down her chatter, she does not want to wake the numerous brood (even if the Italians deserve to be woken every evening with cannonfire). In fact it has been quite a while since she last had a visit of this kind. She is embarrassed, she does not really know what to do, how to react.

But incapable of discretion, Toinette trips and falls over the threshold, making a huge racket and spilling on the ground the contents of her bag, as big as a suitcase. Pat is furious, but the girl's laughter is disarming, contagious.

Together they pick up the pitiful remains of her tape-recorder (smashed to pieces in her fall), and go and sit in the sitting room, where a semblance of a conversation very soon dies away. Hell, it is all terribly obvious! But Pat does not want any complications. So she knocks back the remains of her whisky and announces that she is very tired and is going to bed and Toinette can do the same, she will make up a bed for her in the guest room.

Then, to make it even clearer, she adds that in any case she is too old for her, she could be her mother.

Then Toinette gives her a big hopeful smile as if the absolute banality of those words were confirmation that everything is going just as she would wish.

And actually she is right. Half an hour later they are in bed and Pat is wondering how she has managed to do without a woman, a feminine body to hold close, for… oh, it's not worth trying to work out for how long. Too long, in any case. More or less since her fiftieth birthday.

Toinette is not exactly her type. Not at all.

She is a plump thirty-five-year-old with a bright and ready smile but with an underlying sadness in her hazel eyes. She is young, it is true, but perhaps not young enough for Pat, who as a girl used to fall in love with mature women and now that she is almost old fancies only radiant youngsters.

And one thing is certain. Toinette is not radiant.

She is messy, disorganised, a little overweight, unreliable and unsure of herself. But she has a sense of humour that makes her shortcomings tolerable. They often laugh together, and exchange opinions and advice about their work.

In reality, the advice, almost never followed, is mostly given by Pat. Toinette likes to regard her as a model to be looked up to with admiration, in a when-I-grow-up-I-want-to-be-like-you kind of way.

Despite her initial incredulity, Pat realises that Toinette is truly attracted to her, that – in her way, a kind, flattering and sometimes exasperating way – she loves her.

A strange and novel situation. Pat has always found herself in the position of the lover, more in keeping with her character than that of the beloved. Obviously reciprocity would be better but since you cannot have everything in life Pat's choice would still remain the same: to love is so much more interesting than to be loved.

But at her age you cannot expect too much. You have to be satisfied with what you have got.

However, being satisfied does not form part of Miss

Highsmith's talents and she knows this only too well. For decades she has striven with all her might to make a virtue of necessity: to enjoy, to content herself with what she has, to give prominence to the positive aspects of reality.

For decades she has been pushing herself: to eat regularly, to breathe, to rest, to think positively.

Mantras repeated in pursuit of an impossible and in any case despised well-being.

In life Miss Highsmith has been Tantalus, condemned to see her desires perpetually unsatisfied. She has been Sisyphus, groaning with the effort of beginning her ascent anew every day. And Prometheus, her liver constantly gnawed by the eagle of worry and anxiety.

Toinette comes and goes without creating too much disruption, both in regard to the house and to Pat's life. She too is in the grip of the joys and pains of writing but she has not got the same attitude and perseverance as her American friend.

Her first and laboriously written novel is now in its fourth (or perhaps fifth) draft. The publisher – Pochette, for whom she also has a temporary job as a proof reader – continues to keep her in a state of uncertainty. The problem, it seems, is that the novel is about two lesbians, who never have sex, but go on a journey through a kind of hell, and are involved in a series of amusing and macabre incidents. Her editor has told her that if they really have to be two lesbians they ought at least to have sex together. Toinette is trying to introduce a few sex scenes but, according to Pat, the one she read out to her was too grotesque and farcical to satisfy Pochette.

Maybe she should advise Toinette not to write this novel

or at least not to publish it? To find another subject for her first work so as not to start off her career on the wrong foot? She talks to her about her *Price*, which caused her such worry and humiliation. But the homosexual theme is not what bothers Toinette. The world is changing and apparently is becoming less bigoted and oppressive. Even if Toinette is ahead of the times, better to be ahead than behind.

"Carry on then! Don't give up!"

Toinette shakes her head. "The difference between you and me," she tells her with that little smile of both sadness and amusement, "is that you believe in what you do, I don't."

How to make her understand that "believing in what you do" is by no means a gift of nature? To write, you have to build up the will to do so. To make a declaration of faith every day that is based on nothing. No supporting evidence. I believe. I believe in this work of mine that is of such little substance, I believe in the incredible, I believe in the story I am telling, in its capacity to become more real than reality.

But Toinette sighs and says that she has had enough of her novel, she hates it, she would like to burn it. Pat suggests that she throws it on the fire then, that would save her a bit of firewood on this cold afternoon, and for a moment her friend seems to take her seriously. Then she collapses on the sofa, clutching the typescript, in a fit of laughter.

Pat is concerned: Toinette is not so young any more, by the age of thirty-five a writer ought to have some idea of where she is going and how she intends to get there. She tries to encourage her, she clears the desk in the guest room for her, she listens attentively to the pages that Toinette reads out to her, and she does her best to make suitable suggestions but Toinette loses heart so easily! She is lazy, capable of abandoning a sentence halfway through to go out into the garden and lie in the sunshine, leafing through a magazine and treating herself to sweets. (Which explains her very feminine curves!)

Not that a writer necessarily has to have an orderly life and a stable job. On the contrary. Pat does not look back with any nostalgia on her years under the yoke of comic strips and she is proud of having deliberately avoided learning useful things like typing, so as not to be seduced by a steady job: better to go a little hungry in freedom rather than earn your crust in slavery.

But Toinette goes too far: she is always short of money and on the brink of losing her job and the apartment where she lives (temporarily). She does not choose the right friends and seems to attract misfortune with her scattiness and victim mentality.

One evening she telephones at a quarter past eleven from Moret station and asks Pat to come and pick her up. They were agreed that Toinette would arrive the following morning but she decided to come earlier. However, the voice on the phone sounds terrified: "There's a man following me, I can't get rid of him," she says. Pat rushes to her aid in a panic, seeing menacing shadows in every bush, beyond every bend in the dark country lanes. She finds Toinette talking to a skinny sinister-looking fellow who apparently started chatting her up in Paris and has not left her alone since.

"All you had to do was not engage in conversation with him," says Pat, incredulous and irritated.

"But he was so nice to begin with," she says.

Then it emerges that the guy lent her the money for her ticket because she had her wallet stolen at the station – the wallet she keeps in an open shoulder-bag!

And this is only one of many instances of her courting misfortune and putting to the test those who love her. Sometimes Pat thinks that with her masochistic tendencies she would be better off finding herself a man and settling down in a quiet marriage. At least she would know what tribulations she was going to encounter every day, and besides she would have someone to keep her.

Toinette – bisexual, promiscuous, vulnerable – has something in common with the women she has satirised in her *Little Tales of Misogyny*. Despite her intelligence and the energy of which she is incapable of making any disciplined use, she could be one of those creatures tossed about here and there by fate (and by men), like parcels, and finally dumped, not just metaphorically, in those deep black waters in which her characters are prone to disappear.

In fact, Toinette is about to disappear into the dark waters of oblivion and she knows it.

When Pat falls in love with her *golden girl* – the last love of her life, if not the last girl in her life – without needing to be asked, Toinette will silently step aside. She is not the type to fight to the bitter end, with her talons sunk into the flesh of her prey, and for that Pat can only be grateful to her.

There will be a certain graciousness in her departure, an underlying generosity, once again a form of love – the love of a loser, perhaps the only true love.

VII

The days of my youth, which seemed turbulent and dangerous, were happy days. It is now, now that I live a quiet life, in the absence of risk, that the real danger begins. It is in safety that I have my back against the wall, and fate holds a knife to my throat.

From Pat's diary

October '77, Fromoncourt

Reading and book signing in a bookshop in Paris. Journalists. Awful.

The dentist has decreed that my lower right molar must come out. That's final. It is too painful to keep it any more so I have made an appointment for the extraction; but I will have the implant done in New York by a reliable dentist.

I feel I am coming to another standstill. I am so exhausted that everyday tasks weigh on me unbearably. My nerves are exposed – and not just my tooth nerves.

On top of which, with this damp weather and the central heating not working properly, I have caught a cold and I have a nagging cough.

Yesterday the builders finally resumed work on the extension of the garage. Today there is a big hole where the wall used to be and white dust everywhere, getting into the kitchen and even the bathroom. The Italians have momentarily interrupted their yelling, arguing and listening to the radio at very high volume to protest about the noise of the demolition work.

Toinette is no help to me, with her passive and fatalistic attitude. She should get on with it, instead of crying over the job she has lost and the book on which she is still, eternally, waiting to receive a verdict. Instead of just sitting there, moaning, she could offer the novel to a different publisher.

The thought that in two weeks' time I have to leave for an extended tour in Germany fills me with panic.

From: "The Face of Crime" by Rüdi Lothar
(*Süddeutsche Zeitung*, 8 November 1977 – press cutting pasted into notebook number 37, 1977-78)

...the consecrated mistress of suspense meets her readers who flock to hear her at the Krimi & Co bookshop in Munich. Reserved, as usual, she seems unaffected by the wave of success that has overtaken her work: her latest novel in the bestseller lists, two big films in production, based on her books. "That is the writer's profession," is all she says. "In my career I have had at least as many rejections as successes."

She looks tired, her face strained and slightly swollen (a result of minor dental surgery).

Nevertheless, the work of this indefatigable weaver of plots continues. What other dark sides of the human spirit is her fervid imagination exploring now? "My next book will be set partly in Germany," she reveals. "This country stimulates my imagination. Munich was one of the first German cities I visited..."

From: "What's eating this woman?" by Konrad Gift
(*Bild*, 14 November 1977 – press cutting pasted into notebook number 37, 1977-78)

They call her the queen of suspense and indeed it is as if she wants to confirm this title by her appearance and to frighten us by the mere sight of her. She has come to Berlin from her house in a small village in France, where she lives as a recluse (to escape the American tax authorities, impertinent rumours suggest), surrounding herself with cats. She is here to promote her latest book in which a provincial housewife goes mad because her husband has left her, the son is a good-for-nothing drunkard and she is the one who has to change the invalid old uncle's bedpan. Being obsessive, tormented and incapable of living a normal life is what distinguishes her characters.

What impels this dissatisfied woman to present such a negative portrait of the couple and the family? Perhaps it is the all too familiar sour grapes syndrome? Or is it market forces that inspire her writing?

How long before you write a story for happy healthy readers, Miss Highsmith?

(The words: "to frighten us by the mere sight of her" have been underlined in ink and written alongside the cutting is the comment: "Ha ha!")

November '77, Berlin

Back in Berlin, this strange city – cold and wealthy and damaged, blighted by the ruins of war and by the long scar that divides it in two. West Berlin is an island, an artificial world apart, where everything is allowed and possible.

Yesterday evening towards the end of a reading I was giving in a bookshop in Charlottenburg the director Dora von Geissen and her actress Andrea Stern turned up. I met them last year. Dora von G, loftily distant manner, resembles Louis XIV with his long tresses – the girl Andrea, about a dozen years younger – beautiful, blonde, delicate features, too perfect even – dressed bizarrely but in an attractive way.

They invited me to a showing of one of their films in some underground festival. (Ugh!) Dined with them and some friends of theirs in a Kneipe instead of the formal restaurant suggested by the bookshop (I hope they don't take offence; too bad if they do – the Kneipe was much more fun).

November '77, Berlin

I did go in the end. The film began (behind schedule) at half past eleven. I was sitting next to A. Film a bit too surreal for my taste but von G certainly has a great visual talent. Bizarre, sumptuous images, extravagant, improbable costumes. Incomprehensible plot, which takes place on a beach, with dwarves, black slaves and a prince in blue evening dress (the prince is a woman, some famous model named Veruska). A plays the Princess Andamana, who appears dressed only in coloured feathers and anklets. She is the queen of the island, as far as I could understand, and she likes to seduce and kill any sailors who land on her shores.

Andrea, beside me, smells of Chanel and chewing gum. Restless, she keeps kicking the seat in front of her.

After the film, another beer, a little tour of West Berlin in the car, from the ruins of Kreuzberg to within sight of the Brandenburg Gate, which you cannot get near because it is in the East, and then returning to Ku'damm. Back at the hotel at three thirty. Not at all tired.

November '77, Berlin
five thirty in the morning (!)

Out again with von G and A, and their friend Werner. Went to a place on Oranienstrasse, a dark passageway, walls decorated with graffiti, a big room full of light and shadow, people, noise, and smoke suspended above our heads. The Wall runs close by.

Men in women's clothes, girls with shaved heads, young people of both sexes with multicoloured crests. I saw a guy come in wearing a dark suit with a bag under his arm, looking like a bank clerk, who headed for the toilets. After a while a flashy creature in a platinum wig and sequins came out of the same door – it was him. The same guy. The same bag under his arm, which of course now contained the clothes he wore to work.

The ease, the informality of the transformation. The innocence of it.

I feel that anything could happen here, no restriction is placed on the imagination. Everyone plays out their personal desires, dreams or fantasies in public. Here, everyone is self-invented and any switch of identity is possible.

A, in a man's suit, with a pencilled-on moustache, dances

with Werner (who is wearing a tulle skirt over tight trousers and high heels). Her movements are coldly precise and smooth, like those of a complete robot.

It is wonderfully theatrical.

Dora von G does not dance, she leans against the wall and takes photos of the girl and of other people. I myself would like to make notes, it is all so stimulating.

The time flies. Blurred snapshots. Andrea clasps Werner, leading him (she takes the man's part) to the rhythm of music that is soft and enervating, like a feather brushing against your skin, a chorus that suggests taking a walk on the wild side. Then the girl removes her beret and her long hair comes tumbling down over her shoulders, a golden cascade.

Around two we went to get something to eat because Andrea was hungry. Back at my hotel at three, where we talked and talked, and drank a bottle of whisky, and (Andrea and Werner) ate the box of marzipan I had bought for Toinette. *Tant pis*. Toinette won't miss it, every day she vows to go on a diet.

They left at five. A *very* special evening.

(Underneath is pasted the label of a bottle of Bell's special reserve whisky.)

November '77, Fromoncourt

That almost forgotten sensation. A little flame that burns in the depths of your mind, a point of light that gives off heat, always visible in the corner of your eye, wherever you are, whatever you are doing.

A light that illuminates and warms the blood. And your dreams.

That instils in you renewed desire to be doing something, renewed confidence in yourself. New life.

A warmth that runs through your veins, and ignites diamond-like sparkles in the first frost that settles on the trees in the garden. Thinking is a bridge over the coming weeks, the coming months, to the next time…

Remember it is only a dream.

December '77, Fromoncourt

Toinette was supposed to get here on the evening of the 24th to spend Christmas together, as planned. But she telephoned at the last moment to say that her mother was very ill so she had to go rushing to her bedside. It later turned out her mother simply had a stomach ache due to indigestion (like her daughter, she enjoys her food) and they spent Christmas Day watching television and playing cards until her mother, feeling bored, decided suddenly to get better and to go and visit a friend near Paris – after borrowing Toinette's last hundred francs. Result: Toinette, depressed and penniless, was left on her own to look after her mother's little dog.

I sometimes think I made a mistake: it is the mother not the daughter I should be having an affair with. The only time I saw her I found her very amusing. And not bad physically. A lively woman, enterprising and unscruplous. The kind I prefer. At least you don't get bored with them.

I'll be in Zurich for the New Year. My publisher has invited me to a New Year's Eve party, and I have decided to go. If Toinette wants to come with me, she is welcome; otherwise, she can do as she pleases. I won't worry myself any more over her continual indecision and changes of mind.

There is a tiny star – but of such brilliance! – that shines just for me up in the sky above Berlin…

February '78, Fromoncourt

Back from New York, where the dentist fitted me with a temporary bridge, which will be replaced in a few months' time. NY very cold, crowded, extremely expensive.

For weeks I have not been able to devote myself to my novel. I have a series of articles to write (on the relationship between literature and cinema, on the French countryside in winter, on a typical day in my life, and other bullshit) and some reviews and – I don't remember what else. I don't know how to say no to work.

I *cannot* say no. The tax authorities are fleecing me, the dentist in New York cost me an arm and a leg, I have to earn my living.

In a few days' time I will be leaving for Berlin (one pleasant thought, at least).

Invited to chair the jury of the Berlinale. I'm not the right person, I told them – I don't know anything about cinema. Most films annoy me. I don't like cinema.

They say they don't mind. That cinema likes me, and that is enough.

I hope they know what they are doing.

They are paying me.

February '78, Berlin

A whirlwind three days. Everyone very kind. Rushing frantically from one thing to the next, with no time to stop other than for sleeping (a little). Meetings, interviews, discussions, and obviously the films: two or three a day. Exhausting.

At night, after the film showings, A and the Kneipen of Berlin, which have amusing names, such as the Pregnant Ostrich or the Ass' Tail.

February '78, Berlin

Tonight, at Ax Bax, a little chorus of transvestites wearing pink tutus sing a song – I grasp only a few words but to judge by the reaction of the public it must be very funny. Next to me a young man with sequins on his eyelids enjoys the performance; is he an artist, a prostitute, a respectable professional in nocturnal guise – or a criminal with multiple identities?

Who really is this man? Does it matter? No.

Just as it does not matter who A really is.

The only thing that counts is being able to spend the evening with her, to drink beer and talk. I don't care about anything else.

February '78, Berlin

Over to East Berlin with AS and her friend Werner. Checkpoint manned by sullen blond soldiers, then we are on the other side. Everything seems poorer, the shops bare, people's clothes grey and shapeless. Imposing in its desolate squalor, the great parade route, Karl-Marx-Allee.

Coming back into the western world gives you a strange feeling, a kind of instantaneous jet lag. Passing through the checkpoint again, in the opposite direction, is like returning from the other side of the globe.

With A until dawn.

THE PRICE OF DREAMS

February '78, Berlin

Andrea came back to the hotel with me and stayed until nine o'clock in the morning.

March '78, Berlin

I haven't the time or the desire for analysis. Live for the moment, nothing else exists.

March '78, Berlin

Again in my room from one till two thirty in the afternoon. Her perfume, mingled with the smell of orange peel in the wastepaper basket. A smear of lipstick on the sheet.

A dream from which you would never want to waken.

March '78, Berlin

I leave the room with A and take the lift with her. Her nearness in the confined metal cabin. As in the latest film she is making with Dora, she is the *Jungfrau*, the girl-mountain, ever rising above our petty desires, never to be possessed by anyone. Radiant with white snow. I am dazzled by the reflection of the light on those rocky slopes, I am caught in a blizzard. The bitter cold makes me numb and euphoric.

Is it the euphoria that comes before freezing to death?

A lump in my throat. My fingers become transparent, like ice. I am standing beside the Eternal Girl, I am going down to the lobby with her, isn't that incredible? It is good reason for laughing with delight, for trembling with fear.

I watch her walk away down the street, the world plunges into silence.

When you are in love, at every parting words once again become what they were when very first uttered, poetry.

Your kisses fill me with terror.

Die berliner Krokodile
(Typescript on hotel notepaper, pasted into the notebook, undated)

A glorious winter's day at the Berlin zoo.

I walk beside my blonde guide.

Behind a glass wall two crocodiles drag their heavy bodies through the winter-hardened mud around a pool. The water, I learn, is heated so that they can swim, however I imagine that the biting cold of the north cuts through the thick carapace of these creatures from the south. They are a couple, male and female; and if you look carefully you can see lacerations and wounds in their armour, with rivulets of blood running from them, glistening brightly on those dark scales.

Obviously the two animals, which now lie motionless and apparently sleeping – sole sign of life is a darting black eye and a pulsing vein in the neck – habitually bite and harass each other, as lovers and couples all over the world often do. A grotesque and at the same time very realistic image of love: animals that crawl, in captivity, united by fate and deprived of freedom, keeping each other company and wounding each other, each one the lover and potential killer of the other.

Zoos ought not to exist, I think, feeling a sudden and unbearable sadness for the animals from all over the world that spend the rest of their unhappy lives here, with no prospect of ever returning to their native land and regaining their freedom. I wish them hope and the gift of dreaming – which may be all that keeps them alive, remembering the savannah and the taiga, the prairie and the desert – and I would like to be able to tell them their fate is no worse than that of many human beings.

Do they know they are in Berlin, a city where walls and barbed wire demonstrate that man is able to create for himself the same kind of prisons and cages to which he subjects other, non-human creatures?

March '78, Fromoncourt

Impossible to work. I am listening to the Lou Reed disc Toinette gave me, which takes me back to Berlin. "Take a walk on the wild side" – that is exactly what I am doing.

Wrote two poems. One about A when she leaves my hotel room and we go down in the lift together, and I am beside the Eternal Young Woman, *das Ewig Weibliche, die Jungfrau.* Fear and trembling. Panic and euphoria.

The other about the desire to disappear into the void.

Love strips you naked, it leaves you on the ropes. It reduces you to your essence. It does away with all the padding, the habits, everything inessential. It severs all superfluous connections. And what is the essence of a human being without all the clutter in their life? A beating heart on the edge of the abyss.

Love frees you from every deception. The greatest of illusions has the paradoxical effect of exposing all the others, and suddenly you are aware of your solitude, your separateness from the most familiar things – this garden, these trees that I have nurtured will survive when I no longer exist, they will retain no memory of me, and besides they have no need to, nor the power to do so. It is a sad thought but at the same time terribly calming.

The partition between life and death is a very thin one. Much thinner than that which separates man from his fellow human beings.

Incomparably thinner than the stone wall at the far end of the lawn that separates my garden from the Loing canal, with its deep dark waters.

I, who have always feared drowning as the most horrible of deaths, am attracted by that apparently calm surface beneath which the currents flow swiftly. I sense that I could disappear in those waters without any sadness – as if death, nothingness, were the only possible fulfilment, the only response worthy of such an immense question.

Unfortunately – or luckily perhaps – nothingness and death are not the same thing, even though we tend to think of them as synonymous. In practice, to attain nothingness it is necessary to pass through death, a painful and messy process, and dreadful in so far as it involves the unknown.

March '78, Fromoncourt
Recovering from a weekend with Toinette, who arrived Saturday and left this morning. What seems most remarkable to her is that I should have fallen for a person I actually already knew. According to her, infatuations of such a kind only occur

at first sight. (I do not know on what grounds and with what authority she maintains this.) Well, in my case, that is not how it happened.

Perhaps it was a mistake to talk to her about it but, on the other hand, why shouldn't I? Our relationship has always been based on honesty and she certainly has not spared me the details of her affairs with men and women. If for once I have something to relate she may as well try to accept it with good grace.

But I have to admit the thought of A is so omnipresent, it is with me all the time, and the confident and jaunty image of her makes Toinette's perpetual shilly-shallying even more insufferable, though I try not to show it.

It may be cynical to say so but when you are in love everything else – longterm girlfriends included – seems to be a distraction, and distractions are the last thing you need.

March '78, Fromoncourt

My friend Julian, who works for the BBC, has offered to lend me his apartment in London. I am awaiting definite confirmation from A, which should come soon. My commitment with the BBC is for Tuesday, May 2, so we could arrive a few days earlier and stay until the end of that week – or as long as she can.

April '78, Fromoncourt

Love is the only way of attaining the absolute, of escaping for a while the grip of incompleteness, inadequacy, the prison of oneself.

(It is not true that it's the only way. There is another way, the main one and the most reliable: work.)

When you love someone and you are loved in return, then you look into your lover's eyes and you see the world through their eyes: and it is only then the beauty of that which exists appears to you perfect and complete, and you yourself feel worthy of living and capable of great things. Without that reflection, if you cannot see yourself in the gaze of your beloved, everything is imperfect, spurious, corroded with doubt. And life is nothing but anxiety, incompleteness and guilt.

But how to keep intact your faith in the object of your love, if not at a distance?

Closeness erodes and destroys the ideal.

Yet it was to be near Catherine that I left America. (Not just for that reason: also because I had had enough of America.)

A thoroughly ordinary woman, a middle-class British housewife, she seemed to be my salvation, the universal remedy to all my ills. And she was, for a while.

Countries are like women: distance makes them seem more desirable. I was attracted to England until I lived there for a few years and discovered that it is cold and rainy and inhospitable. So then I came here, to France, a more cordial and down-to-earth nation, or so I thought – before experiencing its cynicism and appalling bureaucracy. Latin countries are corrupt, inefficient and exasperating, and France is like Italy in this respect, although not to the same extent; for its beauty, Italy would have been my first choice, if I had not realised in time that I absolutely could not live there.

I am jotting down these lines and wandering round the house and garden looking for more or less useful little chores to do because at the moment it is impossible for me to work.

In my mind there shines a star, *ein Stern*, so brightly that I cannot focus on it. So I concentrate on the stars and constellations of the past, whose light has dimmed with time and familiarity, so that I can look at them and think about them rationally.

April '78, Fromoncourt

What has always upset me most about women is their pusillanimity.

There is in the spirit of women a lack of breathing space, a narrowness of perspective; it is inevitable that anyone who lives in privacy, in the confined space of a house, should relate everything to themselves and to their own daily life, diminishing anything of greater proportions.

A woman may appear to be the very picture of perfection and harmony, as something excellent and ideal: but this is only a vision in the eye of the beholder. In all probability that same woman will at the first opportunity take a great idea and turn it into something small, just as she will harshly criticise any one of her kind who departs from conventional behaviour and will tyrannise whoever loves her. It is the only means she has at her disposal to exercise power.

But A is not like that. And not only because of what she is, a splendid isolated example, but because she belongs to a different generation of women. The young women of today are not like those of my day, thank heavens.

Andrea is not afraid of confronting the amplitude of the world and of ideas. A seeks perfection in her art, not marriage to a man who will keep her. She has experience of inspiration, the exultation of the creative moment and the daily sacrifice required of anyone who wants to make serious use of their own talents. The women of my day existed only in relation to a man – and this was so even if they loved women – because all too often, almost always, it was a man or men they depended on for approval, support, a career, permission to be in the world.

But she, Andrea, is at the centre of her world, and her human and artistic journey will be built on her own personal experience, *her* mistakes, *her* ambitions and discoveries. She does not want anyone else to vouch for her or to protect her from the vicissitudes of life. She knows that the most important thing, without which a human being cannot really claim to be such, is freedom.

Freedom and truthfulness to oneself – in other words, to something fluid and changeable, manifold and hidden, and often unacceptable to society and its so-called morality…

A and her friend Werner belong to a different race of young men and women, who are more courageous and will refuse to be victims or oppressors. Who will not acquiesce in hiding their own feelings, even when these are not approved of, and they will not be afraid to fight.

At one time my strong and victorious Nike had the features of Carol, beautiful and unhappy Carol. Who was never pusillanimous – in spirit she was anything but small – but she was self-destructive.

I realise now that Nike cannot but resemble Andrea.

Andrea is different. From Carol, and from me – luckily for her.

And her future too will be different.

April '78, Fromoncourt

Everything is fixed and so I will go in a week's time – because in any case I have that commitment with the BBC on May 2 – but I still don't know whether A will make it or not.

And I probably won't know until the very last minute, and I shall set off, holding my breath, waiting on events.

That is the way things are, I have no choice but to accept them. I certainly can't ask her to upset her work schedule for my sake. The situation – her relationship with Dora von G is not only a romantic attachment but also a professional relationship – is complicated and I don't want to create any problems for her.

Her life, her work, come before anything else. Myself included.

It is I who am attracted to her. She is the centre around which all my thoughts gravitate. I do not delude myself that my feelings are reciprocated in the same way, on the same level. How could I expect to have such a beautiful woman, so young and desirable, all to myself?

I am fifty-seven, she is twenty-five.

She has her life ahead of her – when I look ahead I don't see life any more but an enclosed, limited space – like that of my garden.

One day all I will see is a window and – if I am lucky – the top of a tree outside that window. And the fading light of a day that is drawing to a close.

I want what I can have of her, everything I can have, nothing more and nothing less.

It is so much more interesting to love than to be loved.

April '78, London

Julian's apartment is a real disaster, it is small and none too clean, the windows let in draughts and it took me half an hour to get the damned boiler to work so that I could have a bit of hot water. Spent the morning cleaning and scrubbing, certainly not my favourite activity but one that calms the nerves if need be, and gives you the sense of occupying your time doing something useful. Then I went down to buy coffee, whisky and beer, and also some fruit and chocolate, because there was nothing here except a can of tea and some dry bread.

After a clean-up the apartment looks a lot better but it is still a bit of a rabbit-hutch. However, it's better than staying with friends or in a hotel. At least we will be on our own here.

Or I will be on my own if A does not come.

Whether she is coming or not, I shall not know until three o'clock this afternoon, the time her plane is due to arrive. This uncertainty until the very last moment is enervating, last night it prevented me from sleeping. Every time I dozed off I would wake up with a lurch of my heart, thinking that A would not be coming and picturing myself waiting for her, for hours and hours, in vain, at the airport, and being lost in increasingly empty and echoing corridors while time dragged on, afternoon turning to evening and then to night.

I think back to when I used to wait for Carol, who was always late, always unpredictable, her life strewn with obstacles to overcome. To when I would prowl back and forth in front of the letterbox, looking out for an envelope with Elisabeth's fine elongated handwriting on it. I think back to the endless days with Ellie on my mind, to her phantom behind me, which would disappear when I turned round. To the afternoons before Catherine's visits, such organised visits and yet at the same time full of complication.

I think back to all the other periods of waiting in my life and it seems to me they were nothing, nothing compared with this.

April '78, London

She arrived at ten to four, the last of the passengers on her flight. She was stopped at customs, they went through her luggage with a toothcomb.

I was on the brink of despair.

When I saw her the earth started rotating again.

The moment we got in we both collapsed, side by side, on the sofa. We slept for an hour without even taking our shoes off.

That sleep was a communion, a sacrament that unites us. To fall asleep together, at the very same time, after so many sleepless nights, after the long-lasting tension.

I see her and I fall asleep. She sees me and she falls asleep.

It is an enchantment. A simultaneous departure, drifting off together, away from the riverbank, in the boat of dreams.

This is our first day.

May '78, London

Day two.

London is dreary and wonderful. The greatness of England resides in its pubs.

Dinner with Arthur Koestler and his wife, who found A "charming". I am proud of her English, of her casual elegance. A is my trophy to be kept hidden, to be shown off only to those able to appreciate her, to those who love me.

Before we set out, A asked me: But what can I say to the famous writer? I've not read any of his books!

I reassured her: the last thing a writer wants to talk about at dinner are his books.

I had thought of introducing her to Catherine but I am afraid she would be bored. And Catherine, regardless of the minor detail that we have not been together for more than a decade, would certainly be jealous.

May '78, London

Third day.

My interview took up almost the whole morning. When I got back she was different.

In the afternoon nothing seemed to please her.

Is it me she finds tiresome? Does she regret being here?

In the evening I ask her if for her I am just one of many conquests. A name to add to her list.

Miss Highsmith, the writer. You are like Gertrude Stein, she said to me in Berlin.

What was Gertrude Stein like?

A legend.

It's horrible to be a legend, I tell her.

She gets mad. She gives me a terrible look, then suddenly, unexpectedly… a precious teardrop. If only I could mount it in gold and wear it round my neck for the rest of my life.

May '78, London

Day four.

How green the trees are in Chelsea Physic Garden, shaken by a stormy wind, against a grey cloudy sky.

I have given her a green and purple scarf and a bracelet

that she liked. Now her wrist is encircled with a silver band. Something more than an object that lay gleaming in a shop window: a talisman.

May '78, London

Fifth day.

We go looking for a bar *for girls* and find a miserable dump where some twenty women of various ages seem to be profoundly bored. Andrea can't take even as much as half an hour of it. We're off, we're not going to waste time here. We have nothing in common with any of these women.

At home, snacking at two in the morning. Beer and chocolate. Playing (quietly so as not to disturb the neighbours) the song I imagine having been written for her, which says: your face when sleeping is sublime, and then you open up your eyes, and then comes pancake factor number one... rouge and colouring... although those references to coming out of the closet suggest it is not actually about a girl but what difference does that make? For Andrea and her friends, male and female, make-up is a game, a mask, a way of going beyond identity and sexual gender, and I watch the transformation with a trembling heart...

May '78, London

Sixth day. Why are there only six days in our week? Who has robbed us of one day?

Before she woke, I got up and drew a sketch of her in my notebook.

She is wrapped in the sheet, with just one bared shoulder and a bent arm emerging from it.

Her face, in profile, is barely suggested, a few curved

strokes for the forehead, the nose, the eyebrow, the hair falling on her neck and caressing her other shoulder.

This may be the last time I see her like this.

I want to steal an image of her in her sleep with sufficient accuracy to facilitate the work of memory in the future.

May 1978, Fromoncourt

I read in the *International Herald Tribune* that a woman by the name of Anita Bryant, a former beauty queen and some sort of public figure (she is an ambassador for orange juice products for that great state, Florida), has been protesting against a law that prohibits anti-gay discrimination. For what personal reason this woman should find the meaning of her life in a crusade against homosexuals, I don't know and I don't care, but I feel this is no longer the time to remain silent, even at the cost of paying a price on a personal level.

Gore Vidal has done it, he has made a stand publicly – why not I?

(Typed letter – carbon copy pasted into the notebook)

Fromoncourt (France), May 1978

To Mrs Anita Bryant, USA

Dear Mrs Bryant,
(although the 'dear' in this case is only a rhetorical convention) News of your valiant endeavours have reached even this side of the Atlantic Ocean and prompt me to write to you,

as an American citizen and as someone who feels personally offended and injured by your actions and declarations.

Having successfully promoted a political campaign to repeal an anti-discrimination law protecting homosexuals in a Florida county, with the support of a Republican politician who issues delusional statements, you have launched a crusade of hatred on the national level. You say that homosexuals should be banished from society with the aim of "saving our children" who are in danger of falling prey to their grooming and proselytising. Moreover, you have declared that "if gays are granted rights, next we'll have to give rights to prostitutes and to people who sleep with St Bernards and to nail biters."

This only demonstrates how narrow your vision of the society in which you live is. I can guarantee that in this society full rights are granted not only to nail biters but also to those who groom little girls and adolescents, frequent prostitutes and those who do a whole lot of other things that are not entirely creditable, although they almost always do so surreptiously. I am talking about respectable fathers of families and citizens beyond all suspicion in case you have not realised. And how many times, dear Mrs Bryant, does prostitution take place within the family, by women who prefer to sell their bodies legally – or are forced to do so – rather than earn their living honourably out in the world? As for the St Bernards, I refrain from expressing any opinion because I do not know what you are talking about. However, I would rather you left animals out of your hate-filled rantings – they have a dignity and a purity unknown to mankind.

With the laudable intention of "saving our children" you thunder from the pulpit of your cheap notoriety, railing not only against homosexuals but also against science and against the only truly sacred and respectable thing that exists: human thought, its capacity to dispel ignorance and darkness and to lay the foundations of reciprocal understanding and cooperation between all human beings.

It is only from a position of profound ignorance, in fact, that you can assert that gays recruit young people, and "convert" them. Modern science, especially regarding the study of the psyche, assures us that this is totally false: no one becomes homosexual by "conversion" or by recruitment but because of very deep-rooted factors relating to the individual's personal history from the earliest years of life, about which you can do absolutely nothing, Mrs Bryant.

You want to save the children of others from us but I wonder who is going to save yours from the hatred and lies you are consumed with. Who will save young Americans from agitators like you, full of fury and venom?

Fortunately, it seems they can take care of themselves, if reports of the boycotts against you and your sponsors are true. (A toast to you, Mrs Bryant, but not with orange juice!)

If my name does not mean anything to you, go into a bookshop and ask. It is possible that not even booksellers know much about me in America but in Europe I assure you that is not the case. We can pursue this argument in public if you like, I am ready to accept the challenge.

Patricia Highsmith

May '78, Fromoncourt
A has promised to come and stay with me in June, as soon as

she can get away from Berlin. Production of the film she is making with Dora von G is taking longer than envisaged.

It is difficult to contact her. I am reluctant to phone, seeing that she does not live alone and there is no telling who might answer; Dora has until now been very sporting but I feel I am in an awkward position. Obviously I am expecting a letter from A but it has not yet arrived.

I am planning where to take her. She would be bored here, alone with me.

We will go and stay with Martin and Geoff in their lovely house in Provence – they are entertaining and she will like them. We will make day trips in the car, visiting the Côte d'Azur, which she doesn't know.

What a terrible seesaw being in love is. Hope sends you flying up into the air and then immediately doubt returns, the certainty that your desires will not be realised, and you are plunged back down again.

She will come. She won't come.

She cares about me. She doesn't care about me.

And so it continues at an ever faster pace. It's enough to drive a person crazy.

At what point does it become unbearable?

Have hope, but not too much. Despair, but in moderation. And how to manage that, when I am flung high and low a thousand times a day and I have no sense of measure any more?

I will survive.

June '78, Fromoncourt

Andrea will come of course, she tells me in her last letter (the fourth since I met her), but she is not yet able to say exactly when. She assures me that she will make every effort and I believe her, I want to believe her…

She sends me a film still of herself dressed as a gangster, striped suit, dark glasses, two-tone shoes. She looks great in men's clothes.

It is not a girl I have fallen in love with, but photos of her, seductive images, a sailor's cap, a crazy black moustache, a parrot on her bare shoulder.

July '78, Fromoncourt

Still nothing.

Last night I phoned Werner, Andrea's friend. It was one o'clock in the morning. He was at home. He was understanding.

He was the only person I could ask for news of A. I told him everything – that for weeks I have been housebound, I hardly dare go into the garden for fear of missing a telephone call. There is no question of getting any work done, of course.

She has actually written recently – a note, rather than a proper letter – saying that she would be in touch as soon as possible. I don't know what she means by "as soon as possible", as it has already been ten days now, and I have not heard anything more.

I tried her number in Berlin but no one answered.

I don't want to put Werner in a difficult position or make him think that I am asking him to play the intermediary between me and A – I only wanted to know whether my assumption about the phone being out of order was correct – or whether something had happened that meant she had to be away from Berlin.

Werner does not know anything – but he was sweet, amusing, funny – he almost succeeded in making me forget what a fool I am making of myself. An old woman hopelessly in love – is there anything more pathetic?

These last weeks have been among the worst of my life.

There is no help for it but to live, to carry on, to work. She spends the day making good resolutions, drawing up lists so as not to slip into the void:

1) Keep moving, avoid sitting still and falling into the usual pattern of thought; do something, clean the kitchen.

2) Remember to eat – at least twice a day, better still three times – every time you feed Sam, have something to eat yourself.

3) You are a writer, you have published lots of books, people admire you, you are not a failure: remember that!

4) Don't always expect the impossible of yourself, be content with taking small steps.

5) When you can't take any more, listen to music, Mozart especially.

6) Think of those who are in the same boat as you, idiots and poets.

7) Take deep breaths.

8) Remember: it is not important what others think of you but what you think of yourself (this slightly contradicts point 3, but life is full of contradictions).

9) One day all this will be in the past and you will start writing again – have faith.

The longest and hottest summer for years in these parts is almost over when a letter from Andrea arrives, in which the girl tells her what she should have known from the start: that she will not be coming. She also tells her this is the way she is, her affairs never last more than a few weeks, four weeks to be precise, statistically speaking. She actually says that, "statistically speaking", and Pat studies at length those words written in a hurried imperious hand.

A sample of which handwriting she sent a few months ago to a friend who is an amateur graphologist, in the same spirit that a superstitious peasant from the south of Italy might have sent a lock of her beloved's hair to a fortune-teller, in the hope of being told: your beloved will soon come running after you.

The friend's response was that the girl was very talented, had a strong character, was ambitious, independent, and that she needed lots of *Lebensraum*, living space. In other words, she does not want to be tied down. Nothing that Pat did not already know. Anyway, in such cases, friends only tell you what you want or are prepared to hear – what you don't want to know they hide in a short silence, which you pretend not to notice.

So, statistically, how long did their affair last? What are the criteria for making the calculation? Do only the hours actually spent together count? No, the days and weeks of separation also count. Separation is the most important part of a love story.

Since she has not thrown herself into the canal, and will not do so, she just has to get on with her life: but how? Who will mend the broken thread of her dreams? How to avoid falling into a state of despair blacker than the waters of the Loing?

The thread that one girl has broken only another girl can mend. From her brief experience of psychoanalysis she has retained a few concepts, such as that of transference. The transfer of feelings and emotions from one object to another. There is something good to be said for psychoanalysis, if only that it is not set on normalising people. Transference is a concept borne out by reality, it is part of the cunning of the unconscious, a technique for survival. Pat very soon has her own proof of it.

It is the end of that hellish August when she gets a telephone call from someone she met on one of her London trips, one of those mannish women with very short hair and checked shirts, the girl-guide type, in other words a deadly boring old dyke, and even though she has no intention doing so Pat finds herself inviting her to come and visit. And the old dyke turns up with an unexpected gift, a young French acquaintance, a fresh-faced beauty with a gentle mysterious look in her eyes.

The gift's name is Valérie, and she is as calm and silent as Andrea was volatile and joyful, but her skin is just as soft and smooth to the touch. Valérie is a welcoming refuge, cool shade after too much sun. Meek and patient Valérie keeps her company over the following months until the point in her life when the wounds begin to heal.

Pat realises that if she had not met her at that moment, in those circumstances, she would never have fallen in love with Valérie (no matter how sweet and intelligent, Valérie is not her type). But at the end of that dreadful summer what is she to do with the burden of love on her exhausted shoulders that she has not been able to lay down. Valérie is her salvation and for that Pat will always be grateful to her. At the end of the affair, having unburdened herself and just about caught her breath, they will remain friends. Thank god for friendship, friends are the only thing you can count on in life – apart from work.

In the meantime she has started to write again, finishing one novel and embarking on another. She is enjoying great success, her books have never sold so well, and two films based on her novels have won important prizes in Germany. The young director Wim Wenders has adapted *Ripley's Game* and made a strange Hamburg drama out of it, in which her Tom Ripley, so suave and elusive and European, has become a graceless Texan in a horrible cowboy hat, ugh! (Later on she will become reconciled to the film but not now, it is too soon.)

She is herself again, the old Pat – perhaps not so very different from the awful English dyke who came to visit her in August but at least she is not so garrulous and is more amusing and a little better dressed. (Obviously the old dyke had her eye on Valérie and was making a play for her but who did Valérie choose in the end? Ha ha!)

Thinking of Andrea is like stroking a fresh scar. But she does not feel resentful towards her. Andrea is what she is, it is not her fault.

As ever, the important thing is to love.

She will settle for that, and it will keep her going in the future. Was she not able to make do for a couple of years with the imaginary company of an English actress she never met?

One day in London, while talking of relationships and affairs, she produces a photograph of the actress to show how beautiful she is, and the friend she is staying with exclaims, "But she lives on the floor above! Let's go and ring her doorbell, she'll be pleased to meet you."

"No!" exclaims Pat, leaping up in horror. "I don't want to meet her!"

The friend insists. Pat becomes agitated, losing her temper with this silly fool who does not understand: she wants an *imaginary* love!

That woman looks perfect in the pages of an illustrated magazine: she gazes at you provocatively and rather sultrily, as if to seduce you, to make fun of you, she lets you glimpse a world of insatiable desire. She is a bit like Liz, her former lover, only moodier. (Liz, her Liz, was a good-natured girl.)

Go upstairs, ring on the doorbell, see her appear perhaps in slippers with the sound of the television in the background, and make small talk… unthinkable. Sacrilege.

Pat hurriedly pulls on her coat, stammers out an excuse, and flees.

The last thing in the world she wants is to contaminate dream with reality.

It would be like starting to court Madame Jolie, the tobacconist in Fromoncourt, a plump forty-year-old with a bright impish smile, as pretty as her name suggests. Who knows how Madame Jolie would react, Pat wonders, giggling to herself, if she had any inkling of having kept Pat company in bed on a number of solitary winter evenings. She imagines a fetching pink flush on those lovely rounded cheeks.

But Madame Jolie will never know.

She will love Andrea from a distance, unrequitedly.
It is an idea that she is in love with. As ever.

VIII

My books are old-fashioned. They talk of murderers, so are based on the premise that there still exists a respect for life.

An hour's drive from Paris, on the edge of the old forest of Fontainebleau. Gently undulating countryside, winding paths amid the greenery. Barges and riverboats on the mirror-like waters of the canal. The end of summer.

The village, according to the instructions given by the deep husky voice on the phone, is on the Loing canal, a few kilometres from Moret. Having taken a wrong turn a couple of times (no signposting, strictly local traffic), at last the journalist finds it. More a cluster of houses than a real village. Strung out along the main road, the houses are neither old nor modern, moderately large, but lacking in style. Nothing charming about them, nothing picturesque.

It is raining.

The only social centre of any kind in this little hamlet is a modest bar with a tobacco licence, which also operates as a general store and smells of wine and damp sawdust. Behind the counter a woman in her forties is intent on drying glasses. While she drinks a reheated coffee the journalist asks her if the writer frequents her bar.

"Of course, everyone comes here, for the newspaper, cigarettes, the odd grocery."

"So you know her well?"

The tobacconist shrugs her shoulders, guardedly, her black eyes bright and distrustful. "Oh yes, as neighbours, nothing more. I look after her cat when she is away. She's very attached to it, you know."

"What is she like?"

"Reserved. But polite, you know, always says good day, good evening. She keeps herself to herself. There's nothing to tell."

"They say she is brusque, a difficult type, in a word unsociable. Is there no truth in that?"

"I wouldn't know. When she comes here she's always good-humoured, never without a kind word, a smile."

"She lives a very reclusive life? On her own?"

"Oh no," replies the owner. "She has friends, people who come to visit. She often goes travelling. And then others like you, yes, journalists, quite a few of those come here, and not just working for the newspapers, recently" – and here her voice drops into a reverential whisper – "for television as well. I know because, you see, everybody comes to me, for a drink, or to use the phone, or asking for information."

"But in your opinion what kind of person is she?"

"Ah, why so many questions? You don't want to interview me. God forbid!"

"You know your neighbour is a famous writer? Have you read her books?"

"Something of them," says the tobacconist, indicating

with an embarrassed nod a shelf covered with a flower-patterned cloth with a crocheted border, on which stand a few paperbacks. "She gave me a couple herself. But I'm not a great reader. I don't have time, you see."

The rain-lashed streets are deserted. And they don't even have a name. No signpost at the crossroads, no house numbers. She gets lost again despite the tobacconist's directions.

Two figures appear, clutching big black umbrellas, an elderly couple. The journalist asks how to get to Miss Highsmith's house. The two exchange glances, look at her with hostility.

"Miss who?" says the woman.

"Is she the friend of the Poles?" asks the man.

"No, she's a writer. A famous writer."

"Yes, yes, that's her, the friend of the Poles," says the woman. "Just before you come out of the village, turn right, then left."

The house is in an inner courtyard, hidden from anyone hurrying by on the street; it has two floors and is built of yellow stone, like the neighbouring houses, with which it is bound in the village's conspiracy of anonymity. It is that type of building that they call a *pavillon*, a distant relative of the English country cottage: a small rural house with red tiles, behind which the top of a tree can be glimpsed in the walled garden.

The door opens and *she* appears.

The journalist is nervous. The writer has a terrible reputation, they say she is abrasive, moody, an alcoholic, miserly, that she hates women, Jews, the French, the whole world, especially journalists. A witch.

The expression in eyes reduced to two slits behind the smoke that rises from the cigarette held between her lips is surprised and infuriated. For a fraction of a second it is clear that she remembers nothing about their appointment and sees in front of her a nuisance, an intruder in whose face she would gladly shut the door.

"Josiane Clermont," stammers the journalist. "From *L'Express*. We spoke on the phone…"

"Ah," the writer rumbles in that deep throaty voice. "It's you."

"I'm disturbing you," says Josiane Clermont. It is not a question, it is a statement of fact.

For a moment a remarkably large hand covers that totem face. When the hand is lowered, bringing with it the cigarette held between the index finger and the middle finger, the expression is mollified.

"Come in," she says, nodding towards an interior that seems as dark as a cave.

And those two syllables sound as sinister and mysterious as the gloomy den the newspaper reporter is about to enter.

What brings her here is Edith. The name of an invented woman, the protagonist of the writer's most recently published book. All her friends have read it, one of them gave her a copy; eventually, with some scepticism, she too started to read it.

She could not put it down.

The protagonist of *Edith's Diary* is an educated woman who has opinions, although sometimes eccentric ones, about society and politics, and she writes articles vehemently opposed to the war in Vietnam but at the same time she meekly submits, almost with fatalism, to every domestic oppression. Her husband leaves her for a younger woman, her son is an imbecile with sadistic tendencies and financially dependent on her, and furthermore she has to care for a disagreeable old and invalid uncle. Her work as a journalist never takes off and the world around her, which ignores her, seems set on a course of self-destructive madness.

Edith inhabits an imprisoning reality, devoid of hope. So one day, in her diary, she begins to invent another life for herself, a happy one, full of satisfaction. Transforming the dismal and mean-spirited individuals in her daily life, Edith creates the ideal family: a loving husband, a brilliant and affectionate son, a perfect daughter-in-law and adorable grandchildren. The more of an unbearable failure her real life becomes, the more she takes refuge in the other one. The fiction becomes invasive and takes the place of reality.

The result is madness, obviously.

In the end Edith dies, breaking her neck when she falls down the stairs trying to escape being put into psychiatric care.

As she reads, the journalist thinks: this is absurd, impossible, ridiculous.

And then, gradually, as she scans the pages, unable to put the book down: this is how it is. It is true.

An unbearable book. Hateful. Perverse.

Brilliant.

How does this woman, with no children or men in her life, with no family and no roots, dare to put her finger in the wound inflicted on ordinary women, those who try, with such effort, to live a full and normal life?

How does she dare to tell the unutterable forbidden truth? That women lie to themselves, they lie continually. They carry on a pretence of happiness so as not to see the reality of their lives.

(The journalist thinks back on her recent separation and wonders how much longer she would have kept her eyes closed if her husband had not forced her to open them by asking for a divorce so he could marry his young lover.)

It is on account of this book that she is pursuing the writer, she needs to talk to her, and this is not just a work assignment. It is a personal matter.

In the meantime she has also read her other books, all those she could lay her hands on. And interviews, articles. She has found in them, in various forms, the same sideways and disturbing perspective. This woman's mind is a crooked arrow that unfailingly finds the target of human irrationality. For her, mankind is broken in two by a deep and unhealable wound – no illusion of unity and harmony, no comforting ideology or faith. Only her cold gaze on the chaos of desires and impulses.

However, she would never have dreamt of approaching Miss Highsmith the crime writer had it not been for Edith. The journalist is not interested in thrillers or murderers, she is interested in women's lives. Her own. Pat Highsmith's.

She is convinced that the explanation lies there, in lived lives. That she and the writer have so much to say to each other. That she will discover secrets, useful to her and to all other women.

She is motivated by the enthusiasm of the neophyte, by the revolutionary development in the years she is now living through: women have begun to talk to each other, not gossiping or ranting, but really talking, revealing themselves, analysing, baring themselves, looking each other in the face.

That is what she herself intends to do now, here, with this totem-woman who scares her.

She does not really know yet how she will formulate her own questions, and she suspects that what there is to know will not be said or asked but will be found in the interstices of their conversation, in the wrinkles on that Apache-like face.

An open-plan interior occupying almost the whole of the ground floor and looking out on to the garden. A long table, more of a work table than a dining table, on which lie tidy piles of papers, newspapers, magazines and a varied selection of foreign editions of her latest novels. A sitting room area with a leather sofa and armchairs, shiny with use and covered with a couple of brightly coloured Mexican shawls. A simple wooden bookcase – she will later find out the writer made it with her own hands, as well as a couple of shelves and a stool. Woodwork is a hobby of Miss Highsmith. And drawing: among the few decorations on the wall is a sketch of two Siamese cats, angular and disquieting.

On the opposite wall two large swords, which are crossed as if in a duel between invisible enemies. They are Confederate army swords, the writer tells her. A display of Texan parochialism, wonders the journalist? Alongside them, a portrait of her as a young woman: a thin, determined, triangular face, two horizontal slits for eyes, arms held close to her chest as if to protect her secrets.

With eyes half closed, a Siamese cat sleeps on a cushion, watching the intruder.

The first exchanges are awkward and embarassing, as anticipated.

The journalist is anxious to make clear this will not be an interview, that it will be a different kind of relationship. They will get to know each other, unhurriedly, in a personal way. Nothing formal. No tape-recorder, no notebook.

It will be a proper reportage, she already has the title for it: "The most famous hermit in France". "Almost an honorary citizen," she adds with a smile, watching her reaction.

The writer does not say a word. If anything, her diffidence seems to increase.

There follows a very long whole minute's silence.

She had been told the witch had three typical responses: "yes", "no", and "the question is irrelevant". She thought that would not apply to her, that with her it would be different

But conversation, that most civilised of human exchanges, seems light years away from them.

To break the ice she is forced to fall back on questions: "How long have you been in France?"

"About ten years."

"What led you to settle here, what do you like about our country?"

"Uhm, it was a matter of chance. I wanted to get away from England and I happened to come to this area with a friend, I said to myself: why not stay here?"

"Why did you want to get away from England?"

"The English bore me."

"In England, too, you lived in the country, if I am not mistaken?"

"Yes, and life in an English country village is deadly boring."

"Obviously, you prefer living among the French. Do you feel more at home here?"

"No, not at all."

Suddenly the witch becomes talkative. "Your bureaucracy is hellish. Do you know what a foreigner has to go through to live here? You need to apply for a permit for everything. To have a house, to drive a car, everything is damned difficult. Queues, forms, endless waiting, long delays. Not to mention your customs inspectors! They confiscated some cheques I sent to America to pay for some purchases. Have you ever heard of such a thing? An American citizen living in France does not have the right to buy things in her own country? I was treated like a criminal, as if I were trying to steal money from the clutches of your tax authorities. And that's why poor Sammy still doesn't have a cat flap, because I couldn't pay the supplier."

Naturally, she explains, they only make proper cat flaps in America. And that's not all.

"You French," she concludes, eyeing her grimly, "always think everyone is dishonest."

The journalist shivers. It is cold in the room. This is the home of a person who does not allow herself any luxuries, does not pamper herself, is unacquainted with pleasure. Does not love herself.

It is certainly not the moment yet to talk of Edith.

They chat desultorily about her books, the films based on them (the writer hates them all without exception).

"Your protagonists are all men and all killers," says the journalist.

The writer corrects her: "That's not correct, some are victims, they are the least successful."

(Rethink, after every oblique reply, rethink the entire strategy.)

"What is the significance of this attraction towards crime, this patent amorality of the characters?"

The writer gives a brief sigh before replying – she has done this hundreds of times before, and will do so again today.

"I'm a crime writer, I write about crime."

...

"It's a job like any other."

...

"Anyone who commits a crime is an unstable individual."

...

"No one who is happy with their sex life becomes a killer."

...

"Maybe sex is a purified form of violence."

...

"Sex is normal, murder isn't."

...

Brief sentences punctuated with silences, nothing that she has not already said to someone else, that has not already been written in some other magazine.

Since she cannot take another moment of this, the writer leaps to her feet, brings a bottle of whisky out of a cupboard, pours herself a generous measure, hestitates a moment before offering it to her.

The journalist politely refuses.

She does not insist. She avidly takes a few sips, the relief is almost instantaneous.

Slowly, painfully, the journalist regains her presence of mind. The writer's voice, alternating between English and French spoken with a strong American accent, now sounds to her like that of a shy and scrupulous young girl determined to do her duty even though she has no desire to. Suddenly she feels almost sorry for her.

How could she have seemed so formidable?

She observes her. She looks like a pageboy sculpted in wood, one of those crude but poignant statues sometimes found in country churches. Her hands – huge, out of proportion with her slight body – are now stroking the cat, now resting on her angular knees. Her gestures, the thinness of her shoulders, her figure, her swinging foot in a slightly worn black moccasin – these are all very masculine but at the same time fragile. Indefinable. If the person sitting in front of her were a man, she would say he was feminine.

(Obviously she is a lesbian, everyone knows it, it is one of those things you hear on the grapevine, but you cannot write it in a newspaper. This is the strange thing: the journalist feels the same with her as she does with a man, the same constraint, rage, desire to please, a tension snaking through her body which makes her acutely conscious of how she modulates her voice, how she sits on the uncomfortable sofa…)

However, the writer is indisputably a woman. And despite the wrinkles and puffiness and signs of ageing, there is an essential youthfulness about her that is touching. That way of impatiently pushing back her hair from her forehead, like a nervous young girl. And a certain hesitation in speaking, suggestive of an adolescent reserve.

"Why this house?" this journalist asks her on impulse. (Why not a more beautiful place, a more comfortable and luxurious house?) "It's as though you are not so much seeking solitude as camouflaging yourself among people, trying to be just like anyone else in a small French village."

And unexpectedly Miss Highsmith fully agrees, yes, what she wants is indeed a small community in which she can live an ordinary, routine, even boring life. Boredom is good for writing: no distractions, few enticements to take you from your work. And if the people here do not know her, do not read her books, so much the better: it means she does not have to waste time on literary small talk, which she hates, or take part in pointless and irritating social events. A writer needs a place where nothing happens. A small village is the ideal compromise, because you cannot live in the wilderness, you need to have someone to buy milk from, to exchange a few words with every now and then.

Well now, she has found a chink of humanity in that fierce misanthropy. The picture has changed: no longer the hermit (think of another title?) avoiding all contact, but the writer immersed in her own nightmarish inner world who takes refuge in the midst of a peaceful, sleepy, provincial community. Who finds warmth in an unpretentious Madame Jolie, with her Gitanes and her glasses of *rouge*, in order to endure and in some way compensate for the cold and mighty power of imagination that animates her. The journalist holds on to this new image of the writer and reminds herself of a fundamental rule of her profession: you cannot do a good interview unless you like the person you are interviewing.

Now she is talking about Tom Ripley, informing her with satisfaction that he actually lives nearby, at Villeperce.

"But who is the real Tom Ripley?" asks the journalist, fascinated and vaguely alarmed by the tone in which the author refers to him (as if he were a real person, of flesh and blood, who might at any moment ring the doorbell).

"C'est une blague," says the writer, *"comment ne pas comprendre que c'est une blague?"*

Her most famous and most original character, a stunt? A successful joke, a childish prank?

On the threshold of a revelation, teetering on the brink of the unknown, the journalist would like to throw herself over the edge but the impatient writer changes the subject. A clear indication of what will be the frustrating pattern of their conversations begins to emerge.

The Auberge des Saules, in Moret, is a village institution of some antiquity, as you can tell from the creaking joists of the worn parquet, the dull bronze chandeliers that sway slightly in draughts coming from the big windows, and the stone fireplace in the far wall that dominates the huge dining room. From the windows you can admire the views immortalised by Sisley, another foreigner who became enamoured of this corner of France. Not far from here, in the Château de By, lived the painter Rosa Bonheur, who dressed as a man and lived her whole life with a woman.

Tourists, middle-aged inhabitants of the village, boatmen from the barges that ply the canals come and eat the Auberge chef's entrecôte and *île flottante*, and local people celebrate weddings and anniversaries here. The restaurant has preserved the respectably countrified atmosphere of this watery region at the confluence of three rivers, the Seine, the Yonne and the Loing.

The journalist takes the trouble to get a table with a view but the writer, deaf to her exclamations of admiration, does not once raise her eyes to look at the willow-covered islets on the shifting mirror-like waters. And even before they start to eat she shows her impatience with the people at the next table, a family with three restless kids who shriek and run around, scraping their chairs on the flooring. With a theatrical gesture she covers her ears.

"Children!" she says grimly. "I can't stand them."

The journalist is sufficiently sophisticated and intrepid not to be shocked.

"I'm not very keen on children either," she confesses with a complicit smile. "Fortunately nowadays a woman can afford to be truthful and not just spout platitudes. Women no longer have to flaunt their maternal instinct so as not to be considered monsters."

The writer stares at her in silence with what appears to be a total lack of interest. Josiane Clermont pursues the dangerous path on which she has set out, which leads via emancipatory developments and female solidarity to the stirring goal of women's liberation.

"Feminists are tilting at windmills," is the sole response from that big sullen mouth.

(Edith takes a step back and disappears behind the dining room curtains.)

"Are you familiar," the journalist hesitantly asks, "with…" and she lists the *de rigueur* names, from Simone de

Beauvoir to Germaine Greer and Kate Millett.

"Nahh," she says with a wave of her hand as if to sweep the crumbs off the table, "I don't need to read that stuff. It's all whining and moaning."

The journalist feels almost relieved. Virgin soil. She smiles. Was she expecting anything different? No. This is no venerable suffragette but an old witch.

The first sips of Burgundy instil her with courage, almost euphoria. She is across the threshold into the den. Come on, now, she needs to move forward.

They are served their first course. They talk about food, something that never fails to please readers.

"What are your favourite dishes?"

She likes fish, she is not very interested in meat, although raw veal (yuck!) has worked wonders for her congenital anaemia on more than one occasion. French cuisine is over-rated – too fussy, too rich for her. She likes to cook but doesn't do it often, for herself she makes do with quick meals that don't take time away from writing. Once in a while, however, she likes to spoil Sammy, who is mad keen on rabbit casserole.

"Lucky cat," remarks the journalist. Earlier, at the house, when she was left on her own for a few minutes, she had taken a glance at the kitchen and even ventured to look in the larder: it certainly was no chef's dream kitchen, perhaps every now and again the writer cooked herself a plate of spaghetti or a hamburger but from what the journalist could see she lived mainly on cornflakes, tinned beans and beer. Above all, beer, judging by the empty bottles beside the fridge.

No, she is not a great eater, she is saying, evidently bored, she allows herself only one proper meal a day. It's better to keep in trim, it's healthier, more efficient, she continues in that deep husky voice, puffing smoke. She has a horror of obesity.

The journalist, who in recent months has put on several kilos because of the stress of her divorce and the disruption in her life, feels a rush of deep hatred towards her. Is she malicious or does she simply not care whether she hurts other people?

She changes the subject: "Have you by any chance some Polish friends here in the village?"

"Yes, indeed, Solomon and Sarah, two fine people, they live in that dilapidated house just outside the village. They work as farm labourers."

"Farm labourers? And what do you talk to them about?

"The weather, their work in the fields," she says, blowing out a column of smoke through her nose. "About the past. They've had a damned interesting life, those two. A hard life. They escaped both the Russians and the Nazis. An odyssey. Here, they're still regarded as foreigners, after thirty years. Dirt poor, but they get by in a dignified way. They recently bought Charlie, a horse destined for the slaughterhouse, you know, one of those injured racehorses. A splendid beast, highly intelligent. Sol is sure that he will recover and will still be able to make himself useful in the fields."

She contributes (here she lowers her voice confidentially) to Charlie's upkeep and often takes him some treat, carrots, sugar lumps.

Animals, of course. Like many misanthropes, Pat Highsmith communicates better with beasts than with humans. Also because animals do not understand what she says.

"The neighbours, on the other hand, are a pain," the writer

goes on. "They're Italian, a big family who live in the house next door. The Italians are the living example of the harm caused by the Catholic position on birth control; the obstinacy of the Pope on this issue is scandalous. If he could become pregnant, abortion would have been a sacrament by now!"

It is obvious this is an issue she is passionate about. "There are too many of us in this world," she proclaims, brandishing her fork, "women are forced to have too many children. It's the fault of the Vatican, which uses its great influence to prohibit the use of the pill to the poorest populations, who can't even afford to have children! The United States ought to bomb the Holy See instead of picking on Vietnamese or Korean peasants and all those other poor people we have wiped out in recent years! That's what I wrote to the *New York Times* but they haven't published it."

The journalist listens with a certain alarm, hoping that people at the neighbouring tables cannot hear.

"One day," the writer goes on, "the neighbours' kids were standing there, admiring Sammy, and they asked me: doesn't she ever have kittens? And I replied: She's a Siamese cat, children, not an Italian!"

And for the first time she laughs: a surprising laugh, the hearty guffaw of a cowboy in a saloon.

The journalist is torn between (involuntary) laughter and consternation.

"Well," the writer concludes, blowing smoke into her face, "she's also been neutered, of course. Sammy, that is."

To the waiter who suggests a cognac she responds with a curt no. "I can have one of those at home," she mumbles in English.

When the bill arrives, the journalist takes it decisively, explaining the meal is being paid for by the newspaper.

The writer grunts as she gets to her feet. "If I'd known that, I'd have had that cognac."

That went well, thinks the journalist on her way back to Paris. She is exhausted, she has drunk too much, her thoughts are muddled. She feels a mixture of euphoria, annoyance and confusion: so many times she had used the wrong words, got the tone wrong... but it went well, she says to herself again. At the end of their meeting the writer accepted her proposal: they will see each other again in a few weeks' time, Josiane will stay in her house for three days, she will write a long article about her. How the famous writer spends her days, inside the crime queen's private world, and so on.

"Arhh!" roared the writer with resignation.

And then: "Call me Pat."

With a sense of gratitude that surprises her (a schoolgirl getting an award), the journalist shakes her hand: "OK, Pat, but only if you call me Josie!"

"OK," mumbles Pat, hurriedly freeing her hand.

It will be a good piece, they have promised her six pages.

Three days in an ill-heated country house in autumn. She sleeps fully dressed because the blankets on her bed are inadequate but she dare not ask for more.

She goes and has breakfast by herself at Madame Jolie's café-tabac. Pat gets up late, bad-tempered, as if the new day were an insult, she has a bottle of beer for breakfast and does not become human until she has been out in the garden and downed a couple of cups of coffee. But Josie has chosen to ignore this because she cannot tell her readers and she does not yet know how to deal with it herself.

All her plans are going up in smoke.

Along the canal that runs past the boundary wall is a path lined with autumn-gilded trees, just wide enough for two friends to be able to stroll along side by side, an invitation to quiet intimate walks.

Pat hums and haws, looks at her askance, is evasive. When pressed, she blurts out: she hates going for a walk!

Shopping, for which she had such high hopes (two women in the shops together), turns out to be a disaster. No sooner do they get to the grocer's in Nemours than Pat remembers that she has left her shopping list at home and goes wandering round the shelves looking like a whipped dog. Hurriedly and furiously, without paying the least attention, she grabs a couple of tins of soup, some discounted fruit juice, a bottle of milk. In the United States, she grumbles, there are milk deliveries to people's houses early in the morning, it's a lot more practical than having to travel miles to get it for yourself.

Josiane restrains herself with difficulty from asking why she did not stay in the United States if she liked it so much.

It is no better in the butcher's. Three hundred grams of liver for Sammy, six eggs, and out again before you know it because she can't stand the smell of meat and blood.

Having seen a delicatessen with some tempting cheeses on display, the journalist suggests dropping in there in search of local specialities. Pat looks at her as if she were mad, then with an air of dejection heads towards the shop in question. Where she buys a miniscule slice of brie and a goat's cheese wrapped in vine leaves that she obviously does not want but gets in order to please her.

With clothing, things go even worse, if that were possible. Not only does the writer have no intention of trying on a blouse that the journalist thinks would really suit her but she shies away in horror from stopping and exchanging comments in front of shop windows. French fashion is too fussy for her. She prefers plainer things. She orders almost all of her clothes from Brooks Brothers in New York, a menswear store that sends her trouser suits in her size. Other things she buys, if not in the USA, in London, or Munich, or Berlin, cities where she quite often goes for work.

In view of the shopping fiasco, the journalist dismisses the idea of suggesting they cook together. A real pity to lose the writer in her kitchen but deep down she already knew it was not going to happen. In the meantime, since the idea of sharing a tin of soup and a tiny goat's cheese depresses her, she suggests having lunch in a bistro with tables outside, beneath a line of linden trees. The weather has turned fine again, with the autumn sun warming the straw-bottomed chairs. Pat immediately agrees, now it is tacitly understood the newspaper is paying. She smokes, drinks draught beer, picks at her entrecôte (more than once regretting that Sammy is not there to share it with her), makes a vulgar and offensive joke about the French that shocks Josiane and makes her laugh in spite of herself. (Or is it the wine?) And finally the miracle happens: in front of a glass of brandy, Pat starts reminiscing about her early travels in Europe when, not yet into her thirties, she saw for the first time London, Paris, Venice, Naples, and that charming village by the sea, south of Naples, Positano…

Josiane, who has barely touched any food but has drunk two glasses of red wine, observes her with fascination. The witch turning into a seductress. The successful writer. Tapping her cigarette on the packet before putting it between her lips. Her wrinkled face relaxing into a smile. A rule breaker. Outside the norm. What kind of attraction does this woman exert over her? How will it change her life?

"What did you come to Europe in search of?" she murmurs.

Pat takes her time before replying, her gaze unfocused, lost in memory, the sun playing on her eyebrows, reducing her pupils to two shining black dots. How similar she looks, at this moment, to the angular Siamese cats in the drawing on the wall. Just like them, she looks delicate and at the same time sly, distant and *other*, not human.

The journalist pictures the images in the file on her desk at the newspaper, the photos of Pat Highsmith as a young woman. What happened to that twenty-year-old with the camelia-like complexion and the luminous gaze beneath the untameable flop of hair? What remains of the well-groomed jaunty thirty-year-old, with the slanting eyes of a Native American and lips enhanced with expertly applied lipstick?

If beauty is a capital asset for a woman, she must have spent hers without stinting or thinking of the future. Has that made her more free? Happier? Is she still desirable? Why does this besieging of her, in order to conquer her, and find out her secrets, so strangely and disconcertingly resemble an erotic desire?

"The truth, probably," Pat finally mumbles.

Josiane takes a while to grasp that she is replying to her question: What did you come to Europe in search of?

"But have you been happy here? Are you happy now?"

Pat stares at her with hostility, perhaps simply in disappointment. She grabs the red-and-white chequered napkin and brandishing it as though to give added force to her statement, she says: "Happiness is vastly overrated."

And she gets to her feet. The meal is over.

The moment has passed. Josiane's life has not changed.

Pat replies dutifully to her questions but she does not bother to hide the fact that they bore her and that for her they are a painful necessity, like having a tooth extracted.

What is more, Josiane has the impression that Pat sometimes really does not understand. That she has difficulty in translating the questions into her mother tongue, the one in which she thinks. A mysterious language.

"The most famous hermit in France" includes four photos of Pat: in the garden, with her cat Sammy, at her typewriter, and in her armchair, the latter being a formal portrait, in which she is wearing a geometrically patterned jumper, a silver and lapis lazuli necklace (a souvenir of Mexico), and she is smiling benevolently, with her mouth closed. The photographer was clever enough to catch a spark of genuine human warmth in her eyes.

The text conveys the impression that the novel writer is a wise and witty woman, who is moderately eccentric and lives according to unusual but rational principles.

The writer of the article seems to know her, and to admire her, like any successful person, but without any misgiving. One might think of imitating her, of following her advice (write every day, live your life with moderation).

THE PRICE OF DREAMS

The journalist flicks through her article (not the six pages she had been promised but in fact seven!) and she does not know whether to regard it as a joke, like Tom Ripley, or an emulation of Edith's diary. A success in any case.

Not only have none of her questions been answered but they have all been rigorously expunged from the text, first of all by her and then, whatever was left of them, by the editor.

Her questions: waste product. They remain in her mind, they keep her company in her new apartment overlooking the rooftops of Paris – romantic and impractical, all that she can afford after her separation. Soon, she hopes, she will get a pay rise. In the evening, before her sleeping pill takes effect, when the disappointments, the mistakes, the lost opportunties in her love life and in her career, and the countless humiliations, great and small, of the day that has just ended are whirling in her mind, she wonders about things such as: how does a woman who is so thoroughly unpleasant come to be admired and even loved – by her readers, by the friends that, as she has seen for herself, she is surrounded by? It's a goal that usually only a man can attain. But let us take this further: how does a writer remain so true to her vision, to her almost pathological nonconformity, yet at the same time make sufficient compromises with public taste to assure her success?

The key, obviously, is to be found in work. Constant work, and about this the witch does not lie – indeed, she almost never lies, she just keeps things to herself, omits to mention them – and she does not mince words: perseverance, effort, ambition. Just like Josiane herself. Among the poor justifications for leaving her cited by her husband: for you, the newspaper comes before me.

But is the admiration of friends and readers enough of a reward for a career? Happiness is vastly overrated, she thinks, tossing in bed, waiting for sleep, as for a cold and faithless lover who will not be home before dawn.

During the following months Pat agrees to see her again, several times.

Long conversatons, little gifts (books, flowers), a few lunches together.

Every so often, usually when she is having her third glass, Pat becomes talkative, even confiding. These are only brief moments, glimpses of intimacy, immediately suspended.

Underneath that rough and abrasive exterior, Josiane realises with amazement, Pat is defenceless. Like a young girl: unsure of herself, vulnerable, incapable of adapting to adult strategies of survival.

Obviously Pat is a little infatuated with her. When they are together, the erotic element is always there, for Josiane mostly in a negative way (she is certain that she does *not* want a relationship with the writer) but also increasingly in the form of a protective tenderness on her part. After a while she categorises their relationship as a sublimated love. Her recent feminist experience tells her this situation is more common among women than people think.

Her analyst (since her promotion she has embarked on Freudian therapy) has advised her to reflect on what she sees of herself in Pat.

She knows: there is in every woman a witch, a recluse, a murderer.

An intractable dangerous side but also a resource.

A bomb that could create a new opening in her life.

Or explode in her hands.

But of course Josiane is above all an ambitious journalist and Pat is above all a celebrity.

The notes pile up on the journalist's desk.

Incomplete, contradictory, often discouraging responses that need contextualising and organising.

The Americans have lost sight of the truth.

Europe has always inspired me. Foreign countries stimulate the imagination.

America is a country that has lost its ideals. Any remaining illusions regarding democracy have finally crumbled thanks to the criminal policy of supporting Israel, a state founded on a religious principle and on the oppression of the inhabitants of Palestine. And this is now much more obvious since Begin and his rightwing fanatics won the election. Do you know how much Israel costs the United States? How many millions of dollars a day?

Who is Edith? I could have been her if I had got married. Preparing breakfast every morning, then lunch, then dinner. Looking after the children. Scrubbing the floor. Ugh. Unless I had married a rich man, I would have been in the position of a servant, carving out a bit of time to write between one load of laundry and the next. I would have gone mad.

Yes, I considered it once. About the age of twenty-eight, twenty-nine. But fortunately I realised in time that it would have been a disaster. I'm not cut out for marriage. We would both have been terribly unhappy. He wasn't rich, he was a writer. We remained friends.

Edith's son is a nonentity, a moron, a bit of a sadist. He might be dangerous if he weren't a coward. Capable of killing, in certain circumstances. Well, what should a mother do if she realises she has a son like that? She cannot but be aware of it. Can we blame her if in her diary she invents a different reality? A parallel life? We all need to dream, it is the only way to continue to hope...

Edith is an American citizen who is profoundly disillusioned with America. And she writes. Like me, ha, ha! The difference is that I am not married and I have no children.

I write in my bedroom because writing and sleeping are two kindred activities. They both require you to free yourself of conscious thought. And then having a bed nearby is convenient, if I want to take a nap while I'm working I don't have to move somewhere else. A nap is often helpful. You fall asleep with a problem, you wake up with a solution. Your brain works for you while you sleep.

Reality and truth are not the same thing. They are two different, sometimes irreconcilable things.

What do I read before I go to sleep? The dictionary. It is the only book that does not tell lies.

I have never been discriminated against as a woman. In my profession the fact of being a man or a woman makes no difference at all.

No, no, I have nothing to say to young women, I cannot be anybody's ideal. No life can be taken as a model, least of all mine...

Young women have no need of me, they are stronger, bolder, more free... what would they want with a wreck like me? Ha, ha!

I could never be a criminal. I am too respectful of the law. Whenever I pass a policeman I always feel guilty, I think that he is coming to arrest me, even though I haven't done anything. That's why criminals fascinate me. They are free. They defy fear. They are creative. They know no boundaries.

Love passes, work remains.

…I don't think my love life is of any interest to readers…

Yes, I've lived with a person, three or four times. Never for long. The life of a couple is not for me. I have to feel free.

Yes, they were women.

Yes.

Her honesty is admirable. She could have used one of the other two replies – "no" or "the question is irrelevant". Instead, with obvious vexation, she said "yes".

But what are women to Pat Highsmith?

When she is not in love, what feelings do they arouse in her?

She can't bear them. She prefers men, they are more lucid, more humorous. They know how to play. They don't have all those stupid hang-ups about sex.

The female body, she blurts out one day, offends her, disgusts her, it's dirty. It disturbs her to talk about her bodily functions. Feminist discussions about menstruation and child-birth: yuck! Please! And she covers her face with those huge hands that look like those of a strangler.

A little later, the same day, she shows her a photograph of a fair-haired girl, "my young friend in Berlin". What is the expression on her face? Pride, melancholy, nostalgia?

Blind adoration?

She puts it away again as if it were a sacred object.

She has grown fond of her. Sometimes she imagines they are joined in the same type of ambiguous relationship that exists between her characters, two men locked in an intense struggle that usually ends only with the death of one of them. But it will be different with them because they are two women.

Things are improving for Josiane Clermont. She has found herself a bigger and less inconvenient apartment, an ardent and amusing young lover. She has lost weight. She has almost stopped taking sleeping pills.

She will not kill Pat Highsmith. She will introduce her to the world, it will be a birth rather than a death. She will create for her a mirror in which the old witch will see an image of herself that is more real than reality, and she will be pleased, she will be touched, she will say, "thank you".

She will save Pat Highsmith from her own contradictions, she will highlight the best in her, make her presentable, likeable – without betraying her.

Josiane Clermont the journalist has an ambitious project in mind: she will become Pat Highsmith's biographer.

Despite the horror with which the subject she has chosen for herself regards everything that is public, despite Pat's profound mistrust of journalists and her total allegiance to a private life – Josiane is convinced she will be able to do this. She is counting on the fact that her friend the writer, the brilliant witch, now trusts her. She likes her. She is a bit infatuated with her. After all, theirs is a loving friendship.

She makes the mistake of telling the person concerned.

Pat makes an abrupt volte-face and disappears.
They will never see each other again.

October 1978, Fromoncourt

Dear Josiane,

I am sorry for having abruptly broken off our conversation yesterday but your suggestion of becoming my biographer is disturbing and creates a sense of alarm in me.

I thought I had been clear: I do not feel any need of a biography – far from it, I only want to be left in peace.

Times have changed, you tell me. People are interested in the private lives of writers. Especially women writers. Female creativity (an expression that makes me shudder) and the need to provide women with positive role models blah blah blah. Well, let me say that I have no desire to measure how times have changed in relation to me and, as I have already said, I am particularly unwilling to be a role model of any description.

You tell me that you came into my house as a friend, not as a journalist – that is completely untrue. Perhaps, if we had met at the grocer's or in the dentist's waiting room, if we had met in completely private circumstances, without either of us knowing who the other was, discussing the price of milk or the state of our molars – we might possibly have become friends.

But you came to interview me for that damned article. Friendship is something else, it cannot grow on those foundations.

I think it would be better if we did not see each other for a while. Good luck in your career.

P.H.

March 1979, Fromoncourt

Madame Clermont,

I have already told you that owing to my commitments I cannot see you.

Thank you for the roses you sent me – you should not have bothered, three dozen are really too many, I do not even have a vase to put them in, so I had to leave them out in the garden in a bucket, and as it rained last night they are now ruined.

Yours,

P.H.

April 1980, Fromoncourt

Madame,

I was not at home when you called but even if I had been I would not have answered the doorbell.

I repeat, I do not want any biography, my life is my own affair.

I advise you not to pursue this and I warn you that I have discouraged all my friends from having anything to do with you. None of them will give you an interview after my death. You will get nothing out of them and if you insist on publishing a biography of me, my executor will take you to court.

Biographers may feed on my corpse like jackals if they wish – after I am dead I will not feel any pain. But as long as I am alive I intend to keep them at bay.

Yours,

P.H.

IX

If you feel the world does not make any sense,
you will see that it makes a little more sense
after a drink or two. (Three could be too many.)

For some time now death has been a constant thought.

Not that she did not think about it before but when she was younger it was mostly a dramatic idea (dying, killing, an explosion of ecstasy or desperation, all things that afford a certain satisfaction to the ego) whereas now it is a slight persistent pain like that of a toothache kept under control with analgesics, which reminds you that inside you something is wearing out and deteriorating incessantly.

A sense of mortality that intensified during the months when she waited in vain for Andrea, when the garden of the house at Fromoncourt, with the espaliered pear trees and the clematis (which did not take, it was not the right kind of soil) and the maple tree at the far end of the lawn, conveyed a cold and in some ways comforting message of extraneousness. That place, which she had worked on with her own two hands, had a life of its own that was indifferent to hers and would continue beyond hers.

The idea of one's own impermanence has some

advantages: no one is obliged to carry this terrible weight of being oneself for an infinite period of time, there is an end to us all. And so much the better.

Death also has a practical implication, it is called one's estate.

And Pat's estate is divided into two, with not a very clear distinction between them, as with everything else in her life. The division goes down to the roots but does not cut right through them, the way a reluctant surgeon might use his scalpel to separate organs that are fundamentally interconnected: on the one hand there is her public writing, with the income that derives from it (the money she has put aside and the money yet to come for as long as the books are in print), and on the other hand there are her private papers. A cupboard full of documents in which she keeps notebooks, files, papers, albums, her lifeblood, essential to her being. This ectoplasm of writing can and must survive, at least for a while, even after the rest of her is dead. It is the only kind of immortality she can conceive of. But how to guarantee the best chance of survival for her written remains?

To whom should she leave her money and her papers? A thought that torments her to the extent that makes the other, that of death, seem almost attractive. And along with her estate, there is another insoluble and rankling cause of anxiety: taxes.

The avid French have set their sights on her money, and having subjected her to a bureaucratic nightmare before granting her the right to reside on their sacred soil, now, on the grounds that she has established her residency here, they are insisting that all her earnings be channelled into France and that she pay taxes to the French government on her total income.

No use telling them she already pays taxes in America. No use even resigning herself to double taxation, after which she would be left with only about twenty per cent of her earnings. They will not capitulate, they want to be the only collectors of her taxes! Which is impossible: the USA will never renounce their right to tax an American citizen, not to mention the UK, where her main publisher is located, and therefore her bank. That is where the royalties from all over the world come, and inflexible phlegmatic Great Britain not only claims its share but hangs on to the loot for months and months, oblivious of fluctuations in exchange rates and of the negligible detail that she, the humble scribbler who has earned that money through her daily labours, might have urgent need of a new car but cannot afford it until Her Britannic Majesty coughs up.

Yet France insists, threatens inspections and sequestrations. However, the thing that frightens her most is not so much that they might fleece her (they are already doing so) but that if all her income is channelled to French soil they would prevent her from exporting it. Which means that she would not be able to travel, or that she would have to go with limited funds, reduced to begging from the banks and the French tax authorities in order to have a small portion of her hard-earned cash!

The only way to work off the rage these thoughts arouse in her is to do some energetic gardening, raking dead leaves or moving wheelbarrow-loads of earth.

The irony of the situation is that she, who cannot bear being tied down, either emotionally or in any other way, should now find herself in the same situation as a several-times divorced husband who has to pay alimony to his exes, a bevy of avid harpies eager to take every penny off him. America is asserting its rights as first wife, England, after a boring and rain-soaked period of living together for just two or three years, does not want to be outdone, and France, with whom she thought she could have a pleasant easy-going liaison between two worldly individuals, is actually trying to impose marriage on her – an indissoluble marriage, seeing as they are Catholic here – that would bind her hand and foot and turn her into a wretched husband, kept on a leash.

A nightmare.

She is becoming impatient with *la douce France*. She considers returning to America, even if only notionally, and of asking her friend and correspondent Constant if she can give her address as her place of residence, so as to re-establish herself as a US citizen in all respects. At the same time she could sell this house and move to another, less greedy country, perhaps Germany, or Switzerland, famously more welcoming and less of a police state with regard to other people's money. But this idea saddens her because actually despite its flaws she loves this house, and because buying a house is easy but selling one is diabolically difficult. She has already bought and sold half a dozen before now, and she knows what she is talking about.

France, with its *douceur*, its panache, its elegance – is cruel.

One day in the village she sees a cat with a docked tail. She curses the unknown sadist who mutilated it. A few days later she sees it again, the docked tail is even shorter, almost non-existent. She starts ranting in the street. The mad old American woman.

Her friendship with Solomon and Sarah is broken off for

ever. Charlie the horse has disappeared, they tell her he was ill, that they had to call the vet, but she finds out – word always gets around in a village – that they have sold him to the butcher in a neighbouring village.

She telephones all the butchers in the area but to no avail. Too many days have gone by, Charlie is already dead by now.

And she gave those two money to take care of him! Scum, lacking in any moral principle, like all the French, all the Poles, all the Jews – and many other categories of people.

Poor Charlie.

It is winter when she returns from one of her work trips and Madame Jolie tells her that her cat is dead. Just like that. Sam is lying in the garage, wrapped up in a box. She looks as if she is sleeping. She has been dead perhaps less than a day.

Madame Jolie says she is very sorry. She looks at her with those big round Betty Boop eyes of hers, her hands clasped on her clean apron.

"I don't understand," says Pat. "I don't understand."

Madame Jolie spreads her arms in a gesture of impotence and looks away. She will never talk, even if she knew something. The damned treacherous French. And damned Europeans.

She is almost certain it was the Italian family who poisoned the cat. Or perhaps some other neighbour ran over it with the car and does not want to confess. Beneath its fur the little body, stiff with cold and rigor mortis, seems intact, no sign of injury apart from a little bloodied foam that has now dried around its mouth.

That night she does not sleep. She stares at the wall and thinks of Sam, her Sammy.

Lucy settled in Ticino a while ago now and does nothing but sing the praises of Switzerland to her, as a country incomparably more civilised than France or Italy.

Efficient and decisive as ever, Lucy finds a house for sale that would be ideal for her, and Pat, who trusts blindly in her business acumen, immediately takes her at her word. It is in a place called Aurigeno and it is a rural building perched on a mountainside on the outskirts of the village, not far from a little square with a tinkling fountain. At first sight the stone walls give a sense of protection, of insulation from the outside.

Only with the arrival of winter, when she has already been living in the house for months, does she become aware of another intrinsic feature of those walls: they let in the damp and the freezing cold.

To heat even one room decently requires a good deal of wood, and in January enough snow falls to keep her housebound. She cannot go anywhere because the car will not start, it is frozen. And the steep cobblestone roads are covered with sheets of ice that put her at risk of breaking a bone every time she has to go out to buy milk or cigarettes.

The valley is narrow, from November to March the sun sinks behind the peaks in the early afternoon, leaving the village immersed in early twilight.

It is not surprising that the inhabitants of that corner of Ticino should be almost all recluses and eccentrics, often heavy drinkers, like the fellow who makes artisanal grappas that burn a hole in your stomach – but are not bad actually, considering how little they cost.

Could Lucy have suggested that house to her – dark,

damp, inconvenient – driven by an unconscious punitive attitude towards her? That would be typical of Lucy.

She looks for another house, ends up buying a piece of land with permission to build, in Tegna, a village a few kilometres from Locarno. It is a sunny plot on the plain, from which you look across the broad valley floor. She starts designing her new house, which will be her last. She has spent her life between walls built by others, adapting; it is time she made her mark on the space in which she is to live.

Pat's last house will be an impenetrable fortress, without windows on the outside, just narrow vents, as in an old castle keep, like her eyes. The whole thing closed in on itself, sunshine and fresh air entering from the inside, with french windows opening onto the garden, and beyond the garden, just green expanse and trees, preferably with a stream, as in Fromoncourt. The stream does not have to be visible, in fact it would be better if it were hidden behind a wall or a hedge, it would be enough to know it was there, to sense the presence – not so near as to be threatening but not too far away either – of the dark waters that have always been seductive and frightening to her, like the thought of ultimate nothingness.

Over there, in the distance, a view of the green mountains of Val Maggia and Centovalli.

Inhospitable, defensive, bunker-like, closed in on itself. A house intended to keep out humanity. Precisely. The house of someone who does not want to be seen or to look out, only inwards.

A prison? If it is the prison of the self, there is a way out – upwards.

Her body, this ill-treated creature. This carthorse, once a fleet-footed thoroughbred, is now weak and drags its feet ever more wearily under the lash of mortality.

She has never pampered it. When she was young she starved it, kept it up all night, wore it out with smoking and drinking and exhausting love affairs. Sex, a brief consolation between one anguished pursuit and another. Like resting on the grass during a forced march.

She was beautiful then, as shown in the pictures her photographer friend took of her during those distant years in New York. They were both promiscuous, he was homosexual and she was attracted to him, she has always liked gay men, she feels free when she is with them. Talking with men, there are none of the constraints inseparable from women's talk, and there is no obligation to be nice, elegant, subdued and polite. You can joke without being punished for it. Gay men don't like women? Well, so much the better. Heteros don't like them either. They can't stand them, unless they are in love with them, and even then there is only one they are in love with, for an uncertain period of time.

She was beautiful and she was not ashamed of posing nude for her photographer friend – for the very reason that he was a gay man, whereas she would have been ashamed in front of a woman.

How many photographers did she pose for? Dressed, but without ever trying to hide the truth about her ageing body. Over time, with the passing years, it would be better to hide it, not even to have a body in fact – to be one of her characters, living only in the imagination.

Her Tom, who never falls ill or ages, remains young and agile, whilst she has been flirting with death for some time. Death is heavy-handed, you need a considerable sense of humour to appreciate its jokes.

One day, as she is reading a tax file sent to her by the perfidious French thirsting for her blood, a red torrent suddenly starts pouring from her nose and there is no way of stopping it. She is hospitalised, which is a bore.

This is followed by various ailments, flu, colds, nausea, two cancers, one of them lung cancer, malign (the other is benign, thank heavens for small mercies). The blood of life is thinning inside her, as in the normal way of things, and it is being replaced with a dark cold liquid, like the Loing canal and the little stream that runs past her last house in Tegna.

At this rate she will die before her mother.

It began with the fire. Already senile and forgetful, Mary went out of the house leaving a lighted cigarette on a dresser. Everything went up in flames, the walls, the piles of old newspapers, the dirty laundry, the dirty dishes, the mouldy food in the broken refrigerator, the cigarette butts, the mouse droppings and a few typescripts that Pat had so often intended to retrieve but had never done so. No use asking the old hellcat to send them to her, for years she has made it a point of honour to be disobliging and annoying.

In dismay, Pat leaves for America, where she regards with a certain regret the fact that Mary did not go up in flames along with the house. There is no alternative but to put her into a home.

Increasingly confused and unable to look after herself, Mary is fine in the old people's home. The Texan cousin tells

Pat in a letter that the old lady is eating and drinking with appetite and has a good rosy complexion. Except at mealtimes when she is firmly settled in a chair, she goes around disturbing the other inmates and stealing their dentures. To keep her clean an incredible number of nappies are used, eight a day. For which Pat pays extra.

Pat does not once go to visit her.

In time, Mary is confined to her bed. She cannot speak, she cannot move, all she does is open her mouth to swallow the food that a nurse introduces between her shrivelled lips. What thoughts go through her mind as she is moved about in the home, from bed to armchair, like a rag doll, without recognising anybody? Will she think the nurse who feeds her and wipes her chin is her daughter? Who knows what it would be like, living like that, in a completely vegetative manner, sleeping and waking, breathing and eating, defecating and – that's all? Is that woman, now reduced to a digestive tract contained within flaccid flesh, still her mother? Thought-provoking questions, which she will one day write a story about, but in practical terms it is clear how things will go: Mary will live till the age of two hundred, draining what is left in her bank account.

Pat writes a story in which a nasty old woman, Naomi, who makes everyone who has ever known her unhappy, outlives her son Stevey – who dies at the age of seventy-four. The forgetful and toothless old woman, no longer nasty, just stubbornly alive, carries on for decades, centuries perhaps – until no one around her is able to work out her age or envisage her death.

Is the original harpy, her mother, immortal?

No, Mary, too, finally passes away, at the grand old age of ninety-five.

Pat, however, as anticipated in her story, "No End in Sight", will die aged seventy-four, the same age as her alter ego, poor Stevey.

To while away the time, she draws up a list of people she has known who have committed suicide.

It is incredible how many there are, within a single lifetime, her lifetime. A small constellation of fallen stars.

The first was Allela, in New York, in the 1940s. She was young, intelligent, full of sensitivity and talent, an extraordinary woman. She was penniless and often on Sundays she would paint portraits of passers-by in Central Park, but it was just a way of paying the rent, in reality she knew she was talented, she knew that she could become a very good artist indeed. She believed in what she was doing.

They had a brief intermittent love affair, of the kind common among *les girls*, they had not seen each for a few months, and Allela was having an affair that according to friends was not going well, when one day she was told that Allela was in hospital, dying, that she had drunk a bottle of acid. The worst thing was that death did not come immediately, Allela had regained consciousness and regretted her gesture and wanted to continue living, continue painting. She died after two weeks of dreadful suffering. Pat was very upset by it: was it her fault? When a person with whom you have shared a part of your life commits suicide, is it not partly your fault? Could you not have loved her better, understood her more? Allela always said they were too similar to be together – two artists, both of them proud and difficult, their happiness the result of a complicated alchemy, quite out of the ordinary. And she died, after having written to her in a letter that Pat rereads in tears: "We have time, Pat, we have so much time." She is left with a portrait by her, which she has always taken with her on all her wanderings and which has hung on the walls of her houses all over the world. A young Pat with a triangular face, with the oblique straight line of her hair cutting across her forehead. Her arms are folded and clasping her shoulders, broad and sculpted in an austere men's jacket. With her head lowered, a serious almost sullen gaze, her mouth closed, she challenges the world. It is a prophetic portrait that resembles not so much the beautiful elusive young girl of those years as the future Pat, the wilfully private and enigmatic woman armed with ambition. Allela's gift has become a talisman, a part of herself outside her mortal body, like writing.

Allela's death was a terrible mistake. She was not one of those weak women who occasionally appear in Pat's stories, the romantic type, incapable of getting her hands dirty with real life, the type of girl her ex fiancé Ned would probably have liked. Allela was tough, like Pat, and in time would have learned the wiles and tricks of the trade that are indispensable for living as Pat has lived, improbably, walking on air, on thin ice, without support or tangible evidence of anything.

And then there was Kathleen Senn, the woman from Bloomingdale's, without whom her many-titled novel – *Tantalus*, *The Price of Salt*, *Carol* – would not have existed. An imaginary febrile love on the threshold of a new life, her life as a writer. That murderous thrill she felt when she spied on her from the garden.

Elisabeth, the wife of her English publisher, with whom she lived a brief Mediterranean idyll, during her first trip to Europe, and from whom she waited for a letter in vain, the whole of the interminable autumn that followed.

Elisabeth killed herself in 1960, while Pat was travelling around the Greek islands. She committed suicide with barbiturates. They had not seen each other for years and Pat has no idea what motive she had for wanting to die, unless it was her failure to reconcile the various and too incompatible parts of her life. As a young woman Elisabeth had been a Ziegfeld dancer in America; then a respectable doctor in London, as well as the wife of a man she did not love but could not bring herself to leave.

She cut out the reports of Elisabeth's death and stuck them in her diary. She seemed not to feel anything. She was so depressed after the debacle of living with Rose in America and the loss of Ellie (or rather the dream of Ellie), and so sure that her life had no sense or purpose, that neither grief nor astonishment were able to breach her indifference. Yet, even in deep depression, she was certain that she would never commit suicide.

And then, much more recently, her friend the writer Arthur Koestler. He was ill and he killed himself so as not to let death win, but he did not go alone – he took with him his third wife, who was much younger than he was, and in good health. A double suicide, but with a single motive, and that was his. Pat holds a posthumous grudge against him. What right had he to convince his wife to die too? One ought to have the courage to face death alone. To take someone with you is violence, murder. The story of Koestler is yet another proof of the feeble-mindedness of women. And of how much violence and injustice there is in the life of a couple.

Shortly after that, her English friend Julian, the one who lent her the flat in London for those six unforgettable days with Andrea. An overdose. Julian was probably depressed because his career was not going well, after a successful start he was sidelined, not getting any recognition. How many times had she hit the blank wall of failure, the wall that seems to exist in the eyes of others, who do not see you, do not hear you, the others who by not uttering your name seem to deny you life.

But that is false, life is elsewhere, pleasure, joy are elsewhere: in the solitary activity of writing.

That is why she has not committed suicide and never will. Unless her lifestyle can be considered suicidal, as it consists of rejecting every stupid rule for keeping you alive at all costs: doing sport, not drinking, not smoking…

To hell with the glib wisdom of keeping you alive at all costs.

If that is suicide, she would recommend it to anybody.

From Pat's correspondence

December '77, Fromoncourt

Dear Constant,

You're right: it is my duty to make a serious and prudent will. I owe it to myself and to my work. My mother is still alive and there is the remote possibility (God help us!) that she might awaken from her senile lethargy and assert some claim in the event of my death.

Everything needs to be laid down in advance, nothing left to chance. My writing is all I have to leave to the world and at the same time it is my self as well, what will survive of me – if it does survive. For how long and in what way, I am not to know. After my death it will not be my concern, but as long as I am alive I want to put things in order.

This explains my delay in sending you the copy of the will. I feel I ought to make further refinements to some details.

Love Pat

March '78, Fromoncourt

Dear Constant,

As regards the will, I think it would help for you to have another person with whom to share the responsibility for my papers. I am referring to Martin Myers, of whom I have spoken to you many times. You have never met each other in person but you will certainly get on, Martin is cultured, sensitive, witty, he is very practical and a real friend. Martin is a very highly regarded academic; he has been living in France for years, in Saint-Paul de Vence. He has a wonderful villa with a garden where yours truly has spent some happy times staying with him and his partner, Geoff, a musician. I think it would be a relief for you to be able to count on Martin in the event of my death.

What do you say? Of course this does not mean that I do not trust you, and it does not detract in any way from your role, you would still be the one dealing with my notes and all the most important writings, he would mostly take care of my more private papers, which are of interest only to those directly concerned, and ultimately therefore to very few people.

While we are already on the subject, we had better confront once and for all *the* thorny issue: it is no secret that

I am queer to the core, anyone who wants to know, knows, or will find out if they take the trouble to investigate, and let them, I have nothing against that. If people are going to talk about me, they will also have to talk about the people who have been important in my life, and certain names are bound to be mentioned. Although there have been very few women with whom I have lived – just Lucy and Rose (my relationship with Catherine in England cannot technically be called a cohabitation). I certainly do not intend to flaunt this aspect of my life but it does exist, and I do not even want to deny it. On matters of this kind Martin could be of great help to you.

Sometimes I wonder, what is the point of worrying so much about what will remain of me. When I am no longer here, what does it matter whether everything goes to hell or not? And these papers, that have been following me from one house to another, from one continent to another, who can they possibly be of use to?

But on the other hand I tell myself that it is in these papers, published or otherwise, that the meaning of my work lies, the only thing of mine that I feel is worth saving, and towards which I feel an obligation. It is my way of fantasising about immortality. I do not have a god to cling to – not that I have ever felt the need of one – and I do not believe in reincarnation, so all my hopes are placed in what I will have managed to create in my one and only life.

Besides, I know that Graham Greene has bequeathed all his documents to an American university in exchange for a load of money. If he has done it, why not me?

If I could pull off a coup like that, naturally you, together with Martin, would retain a discretionary power on the use of the papers, while the university would relieve you of the burden of finding somewhere to place them.

Let me know how you are, and tell me what you think of my proposal.

> Looking forward to hearing from you,
>
> Pat

20 March 1978, Fromoncourt

Dear Martin,

I wrote to Constant a few days ago, explaining the idea I mentioned to you in my last letter. I am ever more convinced that I would like to see certain things entrusted to you. Constant is a dear friend, a good-hearted soul, but there are aspects of me and my life that I would prefer to know were in your hands because you are able to understand them better than she does.

As you know, Constant is a freelance journalist, she is widowed and has a daughter (my godchild – sometimes I tell her I am her wicked godmother, ha ha) who has not yet "found herself" and seems to me well on the way to spending the rest of her life unemployed, financially supported by her mother. I really do not know how women deal with the everlasting crisis that children represent! The only thing that makes me moderate my judgement with regard to that terrible creature, my mother, is the thought that she also had me to contend with, which certainly was not easy. My mother should not have had children – I ruined her life, and she mine. But at least I did not live off her.

Constant is intelligent, energetic and practical; I do not know what I would do without her in America. We met at Barnard, ages ago; she is one of the few women with whom

I have kept up an entirely "pure" friendship, that is to say uncontaminated by other issues. Thank goodness.

She knows everything about me. That is because I have never hidden anything from her, although I have often spoken to her obliquely, without going into details. Constant is not the type to be shocked, but she is rather attached to convention and respectability. How can I put my private papers in her hands? She would feel obliged to defend my reputation and would probably burn the lot.

So, dear Martin, I really would feel much better if I knew that you were the custodian of some, the most intimate, of my papers.

I do not want my writings to do anyone any harm, nor do I intend to divulge anyone else's business – but it is very possible that after my death someone may want to write something about me, and so the problem will arise. And even though I do not wish to speak of certain things while I am alive, when I am dead it is bound to become known that I was queer through and through. However painful the subject might be, it will need to be confronted, simply because *it is true*; not to mention the fact that my example might contribute to helping someone else in my situation, which I would not mind.

Love

Pat

Switzerland, 198…

Dear Constant,

I am in fairly good health, although the cough still bothers me. In the end not having a single tooth of your own left in your mouth is not so bad, at least they do not cause you any pain. And how are you? I hope you have got over your ailments from last winter.

How is your daughter getting on? Has she finally found a job? And that young fellow she was seeing recently, has she managed to scare him off as well, or not? Don't worry too much about her, I keep telling you, her problem is that she ought to be more independent at her age (and lose forty pounds or so, if she wants to find a boyfriend).

I am writing to tell you that with regards to my estate, I have finally reached a decision, I will leave all the money to Yaddo, the writers' retreat where I was invited in '48. That is where I wrote part of my first book, and I still recall with pleasure the calm, the quiet, the evening drinks with the other writers. I want my money to be of assistance to those young people who, like me at that time, need help and encouragement to write.

My friends, you included, are more or less my age – if I left them money they would not even be able to enjoy it any more, and it would only end up in the hands of their children, something that frankly makes no sense, and which I would prefer to avoid. I hope you agree.

Look forward to hearing from you. Take care.

Love

Pat

Fortunately, there is no shortage of work, far from it; Pat cannot satisfy the many requests. If she were faster, if she could write more spontaneously, at a brisk pace, and produce a couple of books a year, she could get them published. With a certain degree of envy she thinks of those writers who churn out one, two novels a year... unfortunately it is now too late to change her method: a first draft, a completely rewritten second draft, and finally yet another revision. Now that everyone is asking her for something, anything, she has to recognise with regret that she is unable to dispense with her meticulousness – or is it more accurate to call it slowness?

In any case, work is more than ever her only distraction.

Writing is a joy that comes at a high price. Often she makes slow progress with her novels, and then she does writing chores, she devotes herself to reviews and articles just as a housewife would work her way through a pile of shirts to wash and iron. Grumbling. Just as well, little jobs keep her occupied, she cannot stand idleness. On the other hand, all these articles are a tremendous nuisance that prevent her from concentrating on more serious ideas, and perhaps that is exactly why progress with the novels is slow.

As ever, and more than ever, she is dissatisfied with herself. What has she achieved in life? Yes, agreed, there are those books neatly arranged on the shelves and displayed on the table in the sitting room, piles of various editions of her books – French, German, Swedish, Dutch, Italian, Spanish, Japanese, and even American (ha ha!) – but what is the point of them all if one is not writing? What is the measure of success, or rather... of art?

Someone might be able to answer this question, but certainly not her. She has always know that she and Art, with a capital

A, have very little to say to each other. She is a craftsman, or a commercial artist like her mother, who did fashion design for advertising, and like many of her characters. She produces entertainment, that is what she is paid for.

Beauty and perfection are the dream that is always pursued but never attained. There is also art with a small a, and that too is a matter of striving, not of achievement.

Perhaps something of her will be remembered, people will say: "Highsmith? Ah yes, the one who created Ripley."

Then that too will be forgotten.

And what does it matter anyway? When she is no longer here, nothing will matter to her any more, and this too affords her some consolation.

Her satisfaction is momentary, the price of living is dissatisfaction.

How do people get by if they don't write? (Or paint, or compose music, or practise some other form of creativeness or, to spell it out, liberate themselves?)

However much one might try to make life interesting, it sometimes becomes boring, *intolerably* boring, and then she invents another story, thereby saving herself from boredom, she escapes from that horrible thing that is the self, with its anxieties and vanities, and finds a perfect solution – a crime, an escape, a stroke of luck, something that rarely happens in life – everyone should do the same!

Write, sculpt, draw, get to work!

But do not delude yourself, it takes effort, inspiration does not come on demand, it comes when you are exhausted having wasted the day in fruitless endeavours, when your lover leaves you, or when you have to have your last remaining teeth extracted – it comes and saves you when you are assailed with human tribulations, and that is when you must recognise it and grab it at once.

This is what she would like to say to humanity, to that section of humanity that interests her, the one that is full of energy and capable of nurturing hope – the young.

There remains work, there remain dreams. In the evening after she has filled her cat Charlotte's bowl, she lies on the bed and summons up her dreams.

Then three girls rise out of the darkness in the room, slender as young tree trunks, as lithe as spirals of smoke. They dance for her, in the air, within reach and intangible.

They have the faces of Andrea, of Liz, of Valérie, of a young woman encountered a few days earlier on the street, in the supermarket, or glimpsed one foggy Ticinese winter's evening. How can anyone be unhappy as long as there are beautiful girls in the world?

And meanwhile people across the world continue to kill each other, to destroy forests, the Pope carries on exhorting the masses to procreate, until the time comes when human beings, having multiplied to excess like locusts, devour the whole planet and that's the end of it. And her country continues to support Israel and to finance the extermination of the Palestinians.

She suddenly gets up, grabbing hold of the *International Herald Tribune*, her usual source of information about the shambles in the world, and brandishing it like a stick.

Something needs to be done. She will do it, and do it right now.

She put a sheet of recycled paper in the typewriter and throws herself into the task.

To the Representative for Texas in the US Congress, Washington DC

Dear Sir,

I am an American citizen resident in Italy but I follow with close attention what goes on in my country and its foreign policy. I have read that you voted against the proposal to reduce the budget for US financial support of foreign states, Israel in particular – I am writing to inform you that I do not intend to vote for you in the next elections.

It is absolutely shameful to spend American tax payers' money – and I know what I am talking about, as someone resident abroad I continue to pay my taxes to the USA, and they are not inconsiderable, I assure you – to finance a state committing daily atrocities against a civilian population and infringing their most basic human rights. A state that is secular only in appeerence but in reality led by religious fanatics. What are we the taxpayers of the USA doing, financing holy wars? Sponsoring the murderous activities of modern crusades? As if it were not high time we liberated ourselves from religion, in all its stupid and oppressive forms!

But I was forgetting: it seems that Americans, too, are subject to epidemics of religious stupidity that increasingly infects the ignorant, and the contagion is spread by television, which allows hysterical preachers to put on performances that would be laughable if they were not so horrendous and depressing.

You should know that I am not the only one who thinks this. Many Americans abroad share my opinion: no more financing of Israel, and with the money saved we could invest in culture: universities, libraries, scholarships, all things needed to defend us against the barbaric imbecility threatening to overwhelm us.

Think again!

Yours

Laura F Smith

She rereads the letter to herself, corrects a few words, retypes it making two carbon copies, remembering just in time that Laura F Smith has already written before, not to this member of Congress but to another, from Switzerland however, whereas this letter is from someone resident in Italy. She replaces the signature of Laura F Smith with that of Marjorie Rossi Clark, a perfect name for an American woman who has decided to settle in Italy.

Tomorrow she will ask a friend who has to go to Chiasso to post it from there.

You should know that I am not the only one who thinks this: how true! The same sentiments and opinions have already been expressed by Ned Fenton of Louisville, now resident in Fontainebleau, Anna Linscombe, who lives in Ticino, Joan L Patrick who posts her letters in the post office also used by Pat's publisher in Zurich, and dozens of others. An ever growing band of indignant Americans. We'll show them, ha ha! At least they should know what we think of them!

As happens increasingly often, the laughter turns into a coughing fit.

There is no reply to her letters. They seem to disappear into the void, like the one sent to Anita Bryant years ago. But writing them is a way of letting off steam, it is fun – and the only thing an old woman like her can do.

She writes much less these days in her black notebooks, the notes are briefer, and written at greater intervals.

But she never tires of rereading them. She finds her past self, of a few or many years ago, penetrating or obscure, joyful or unhappy, and that past self always arouses in her a certain irritated tenderness; and most of all she finds ideas, unresolved complexities to work on. Bones to chew, as Lucy describes them. An image that does not displease her: a determined old dog that will dig up buried bones and conscientiously gnaw away at them. She makes notes in the margins of her notebooks. She comments on the truth about life – in so far as it is possible to get close to the truth when you are alive – and finds that it changes over the years, as your point of view changes. However, the past is never completely left behind, nor is it very far away: her more or less aged self now converses with her youth.

The young Pat is still alive within her, although her voice is becoming ever more distant.

It is in order to preserve it that one day, a day very close to the end, she thinks of entrusting it to women who are unknown to her and whom she has never wanted to know but with whom, perhaps, the young Pat might find some common ground.

From PH's papers

20 September 1994, New York

Dear Pat,

I have to admit to being surprised. You ask me for the address of the Lesbian Herstory Archives in New York, and you will find it written below. You tell me you would like to bequeath to this institution your diaries – in which I imagine you write of people and situations that have most compromised and damaged your personal life and your talent as a writer.

Allow me to say that the idea of putting the most delicate aspects of your private life in the hands of hysterical radical feminist lesbians (Herstory! what are they trying to do, change the language we speak? Ridiculous!) seems regrettable...

There are other gay organisations whose addresses I am sending you. Recently I saw an exhibition on "the gay experience" at a library in New York, which was a combination of aggression and self-commiseration. Not very pleasant.

It is none of my business but I feel bound to tell you: if you accept being labelled a "lesbian writer", the meaning of your work will be entirely distorted. Is that what you want? Is that what you intend to leave to posterity?

Do you want your face displayed on Gay Pride banners?

In the small circle of artists and oddballs that you frequent they all know that you are queer – but do you want the whole world to know?

Do you want to put yourself on the same level as Jeanette Winterson, Rita Mae Brown, Adrienne Rich, Audre Lorde and people of that kind?

It would be better to burn those diaries – if you want to be awarded the Nobel Prize one day. You never know... or at least keep them well wrapped up and locked away in some state archive, where one day perhaps, in many years' time, some scholar will take the trouble to study the connections between your private life and your writing.

With love

Constant

Pat will not contact the Lesbian Herstory Archives in New York. And she will not write back to Constant, her faithful friend who seems here to be laying claim to her role as epistolary wife – and what American wife is not ambitious and if necessary tyrannical when it comes to her husband's career?

Her strength is failing. She is ill, eats very little, weighs very little. Within four and a half months she will be dead.

For the first time in her life she allows herself to be looked after by someone who lives in the house with her, a carer. A man. He prepares meals for her, he does the shopping. Friends who are worried about her have practically imposed him on her. He is a kind man who has decided to quit secular life and enter the religious life, and perhaps Pat serves as an introduction to exercising compassion and detachment. The future recluse lives with the seasoned recluse in the fortress house, each respecting the other's space, silences and moods.

Towards the end of the year, the last trip, to Paris, for both pleasure and work, accompanied by a young gay friend. In the photograph in which she appears with her friend and the actress Jeanne Moreau, her face is long and thin, triangular as in the portrait Allela painted of her so many years before. But the lips are not tight with the determination of one confronting the future in a combative way; they are relaxed, pendulous, the unfocused eyes look towards approaching death. Pat is defenceless, overcome with bewilderment like every living creature facing the end. But she does not put up any resistance, she does not fight against it.

Before dying, she will in a furious rush finalise the much deferred arrangement: the sale of her private papers to a state archive, the Schweizerische Literaturarchiv in Berne, where they will be looked after by courteous but firm librarians, like nurses of terminal patients.

X

I am beginning this book with the greatest piece of wisdom that I possess: the certainty that there are no rules.

Writing and life intertwine and continually contaminate each other. This happens in subterranean regions where profound transformations take place. One of these, of vital importance to Pat Highsmith, occurs gradually in the last years of her life, and it concerns the image of a young woman.

That represents her youth, it is herself mirrored in the eyes of the ideal lover, it is the beloved, one and all.

It is Andrea Stern, the girl in Berlin. The golden girl. Beautiful, intelligent, full of talent. Courageous, determined. She will be successful. A shining star casting light even from afar.

But even stars may die.

Andrea loses her light. As the years pass, her work as a fashion designer does not take off. Her relationship with Dora von G has ended a while ago now. Pat has received a long and unexpected letter full of grievances. Andrea feels abandoned and exploited: she and Dora have made films together and now Dora claims to be the sole director! And the apartment they shared, who gets that and who has to leave? The young woman has consulted a lawyer, and Pat reflects on the burden of living together and on its aftermath, and she wonders whether Dora finally had enough of her companion's much vaunted freedom, or maybe it would be more accurate to call it promiscuity. Does Andrea still boast of making love in nightclub toilets? Does she still claim the right to pick up lovers and jobs and then drop them without paying any penalty?

Pat and Andrea see each other only rarely, commitments allowing, meeting up for a few hours or a few days at intervals of months or years. Pat wonders if she has misjudged the girl. Was what seemed like self-confidence perhaps partly arrogance? Was the frank and fearless defence of her freedom in reality indifference to the feelings of others?

But what she cannot forgive, what she cannot accept is the gradual and apparently irreversible transformation of Andrea. The bright and very beautiful girl full of energy has turned into an apathetic, depressed, overweight woman in her thirties with no plans for the future.

She learns with horror that Andrea does not earn her own keep: Nanny Germany pays her unemployment benefit while she spends her time watching tv, doodling and burning Indian incense.

Perhaps it is just a growing pain, with Berlin going through a difficult period in the years before reunification... but Pat has no patience with such excuses, she does not know how to be idle (she, the creator of the man of leisure par excellence, Tom Ripley) and she abhors dependency.

Her golden girl – the brilliant image that has kept her company through horrible suffering in the wake of love – has metamorphosed into a failure, a woman without hope. Her idol has been destroyed.

It is with clear-eyed cynicism, with a cold and subtle fury that one day, listening to Cole Porter singing "Use Your Imagination", she thinks of using her imagination to exact her revenge.

Ten years have passed since, first in Berlin and then in London, Andrea's kisses filled her with terror.

(From notebook number 43, 1987-90, undated)
  Keim for a story

A woman, disappointed in the man she loved, who has betrayed her ideal, kills him.

He was young, brilliant, full of courage and dreams. Then he let himself go, became fat and lazy. The woman has put up with other disappointments, other betrayals, but this – this she does not tolerate.

At the place where they have arranged to meet – a little square facing the river, a few hundred metres from the station – Eve waited, looking around.

It was pouring with rain and the square was almost deserted. The few passers-by hurried along beneath umbrellas. There had been an unusual amount of rain for the time of year, and that morning as she was getting ready to leave, Eve had heard on the radio of severe weather conditions and of schools closing.

Eve was sorry she had come. Perhaps for nothing. It would be typical of him to change his mind without telling her. Eve felt irritation but above all – she realised – a sense of relief. Just as she was about to head back to the station, she saw a shabby figure, all wrapped up, coming towards her. Her first instinct was to quicken her pace, as if to avoid an importunate beggar. But something made her stop.

"Hi," said the man catching up with her. He wore a none too clean beige raincoat and was waving a battered umbrella. He had on his feet gym shoes that had once been white and he carried over his shoulder a shapeless bulging grey-green canvas bag. In that pudgy face, with a disfiguring boil on the chin, the eyes were dull and anxious. But what produced in Eve an obscure, almost undiluted alarm was his hair, which she remembered as being blond: a spiky dishevelled fuzz of a reddish tint. She knew that it was fashionable among certain groups of young people to dye their hair unlikely colours, but in his case it seemed deliberately intended as an uglification and rejection of himself. She hastily lowered her eyes and noticed, above the collar of his raincoat, the edge of a green and purple scarf. She had given it to him years ago, during a trip to London, which was perhaps when she had most loved him.

So he had come, thought Eve, as a wave of shock and embarrassment slowly spread through her.

And her very next thought was that the situation had worsened more than she might have guessed from his letters, she thought he was short of money again and was about to ask her for something, and she hated the idea.

They stared at each other for a few moments in silence. It seemed that neither of them could find anything to say. Eve could not express what she was thinking. The man appeared indifferent, listless.

She suggested going to a cafe. She tried to speak in a practical and assured tone of voice, and even to smile, something that cost her a great effort.

But there was no such place in the little square, and so they followed the road that ran alongside the canal. As they walked they exchanged a few trite remarks. He barely said anything at all and spoke with no feeling whatsoever, and after a few minutes she began to find the situation intolerable.

There was very little traffic in that neighbourhood. The hotels and holiday homes along the river, which at that point broadened into a little lake, were mostly still closed up, and they had a desolate air about them. The whole town was ghostly, the rare passers-by rushing off as if they were being chased. It was midday but the sky was so dark it might have been evening.

A taxi appeared at the corner of the street.

"Let's take it," she said.

"To go where?" he replied, with a sardonic lack of enthusiasm. His voice was like an echo, a pale shadow of what his voice used to be.

The taxi overtook them and disappeared.

Eve felt as if she had lost her only opportunity to turn back and save herself. She moved away, slightly quickening her pace, as if to distance herself from him, so as not to be seen in his company. But there was no one to see them.

The rain became less violent and slowly eased until it almost stopped, but the sky remained solidly overcast.

Now he was telling her a complicated and boring story of resentment and betrayal and of wrongs he had suffered. Someone – the woman with whom he was living when she first met him – had behaved badly towards him, she had stolen his ideas, used him and dumped him; someone else – Eve did not know who, and did not care to know – had taken advantage of him; others had let him down. Friends betrayed him, people disgusted him.

Eve was not listening.

She knew it all from his letters and from previous conversations. He did not have a job and more importantly he had no enthusiasm or ambition or ideals any more. He had stopped fighting, just given up, and was leading a completely passive existence.

He had recently left the place where he had been living, he told her, a disused factory in West Berlin transformed into a commune, which a few years ago had been a socialist paradise on earth and now, can you believe it, turned out to be a cruel disappointment, a bastion of authoritarianism and repression where, among other things, they tried to make him work shifts in the canteen, a job far beneath his talents. So he was now homeless; all his worldly belongings were in the battered shoulder bag he was carrying and in a suitcase in left luggage at the station. He did not yet know where he would go, maybe Munich, or Hamburg; he knew people in both cities.

Or perhaps he would go to India next year. A country that still had a spiritual dimension.

Eve gritted her teeth, not knowing whether it was more the word "spiritual" that caused her to do so or the phoney tone of voice in which it was said.

She thought he was one of many drifters who had shown promise when young, a promise never realised, and who had ended up being supported by some relative, or on state benefits.

Or who had become a tramp, one of those unidentifiable creatures of no specific gender who wander the streets of the city, both visible and invisible at the same time, living their lives in a parallel world that never intersects with that of so-called normal people.

No, Eve suddenly said to herself with a tremor of anger. He was not only that. He was not just one of many. He was the man she had loved.

And look at him now, she thought, clenching her fists.

Overweight, out of condition, with threadbare cuffs. And his hair! She had mistaken him for a tramp, and he had been such a dandy.

They had reached the last of the houses. There was a bend in the road, turning away from the river. A path continued along the riverbank and without consulting her he followed it.

Eve trailed after him reluctantly. With every step there grew inside her a cold anger towards this man who was unaware of her emotions – rage and resentment, and yes, a sense of having suffered an injustice – or even of the discomfort he was inflicting on her, making her walk through the mud and keeping her out in the cold on that stormy day.

The man stopped in front of a bench facing the river, which at that point was narrow and deep, and being in flood, it was exceptionally swollen. The water, flowing furiously and throwing up grey spray, came over the banks and lapped the bright green meadow. Here and there, big, uprooted, slowly floating tree trunks created moving dams around which the current swirled and roared: disparate objects (Eve saw a dustbin, a red ball, a rubber boot) were carried along rapidly, bouncing on the water and sometimes getting caught in the branches.

He threw his bag and his umbrella on the bench and lit a cigarette. It was not raining any more. In the meantime, he said without looking her in the face – in the past his gaze had been clear and direct – he had thought he might stay with her for a while, in her house.

Eve was a writer, and she lived alone in a little mountain village, about an hour by train from Zurich, where she had a small house with room for a guest.

Eve stared at him.

He was serious. He had no idea.

Or he was simply too lazy, too selfish and too short of resources to ask himself what her feelings might be – and perhaps even his own, if he had any. Eve considered the prospect of finding herself confronted for days and weeks with his face, his body, his gestures, which were all the more unbearable for being the distorted echo of what she had once loved.

"Don't you like my hair?" he asked her tauntingly.

"It doesn't matter what I like," said Eve in a neutral tone of voice.

He seemed to be searching for a response but he soon gave up with a shrug of his shoulders. He reminded her that she had invited him in the past.

It was true. She had invited him, years ago, and he had never come. He had too many commitments then. He never found the time.

There was a period when the idea of having him near her, under the same roof, would have made her deliriously happy.

"You cannot come and stay," she said in a hoarse voice. "It's not possible."

And mentally she added: "I would end up killing you."

He assumed a childish, wounded expression. (Another betrayal, another disillusion to add to the list.)

She sensed that he would not insist. She could get rid of him, very soon. She would accompany him to the station, give him a bit of money, as on other occasions. He would disappear again for months – if she was lucky, for years.

But this thought did not calm her. She was aware of her breathing being laboured.

Now he had his back to her and was standing at the edge of the river, on a boulder half under water.

Eve gazed at the stocky, slightly hunched figure, with the belt of his raincoat tightened round him. And in his place she saw the slender silhouette of a fair-haired young man in a white dinner jacket, with a fresh silk shirt and a gold chain on his chest. He had a face of perfect beauty, with bright mysterious green eyes, a clear confident voice. It was him, ten years ago. A youth everyone fell in love with, men and women, a young actor full of talent and ambition, who was to achieve great things. The incarnation of hope, of an ideal.

She had loved him humbly, from a distance, with gratitude, willing to share him with others, accepting that she was not the only one or the most important to him. In the early years this love had caused her intense suffering but also sustained and inspired her. She had never asked anything of him.

Except one thing.

To remain true to himself, to the exultant young man with the radiant future. The ideal who had entered her life and her books, illuminating them.

The golden boy he had destroyed, turning him into something grotesque.

The man threw the cigarette butt into the river roiling at his feet.

This gesture was like a signal to Eve.

Everything happened with the greatest rapidity and ease. Eve was at his back in an instant and pushed him with all her might, stopping just in time to save herself from falling into the turbulent waters after him.

He went under without a cry, the sound of his fall drowned by the thundering river. The beige raincoat whirled round for a few moments like a dead leaf caught in the wind, and then was swallowed up by the murky current. Eve thought she heard a brief sound, something between a scream and a whimper, that was immediately extinguished by the thud of one tree trunk crashing into another in the middle of the river.

She remained standing on the boulder, trembling, her muscles painfully tensed.

There was no trace of what had happened. She thought perhaps she had only imagined it all: their meeting, her feelings, his gesture, they were a complete fabrication, the fruit of her imagination. Then a patch of green and purple – the scarf – appeared for a moment a few metres downstream and at once disappeared.

In a flash Eve's mind became crystal clear. She did not regret what she had done nor feel any remorse. She had to get away from there, to get back home as quickly as possible.

She picked up the bag left on the bench. It was not too heavy. There was no reason to take the broken old umbrella with her, so she flung it into the river, which took care of making it disappear instantly.

She walked back to the station, choosing the emptiest roads. It seemed a much shorter distance going back. She felt a contained euphoria, a sense of liberation and fulfilment. She would like to have had a drink and a couple of inviting places caught her eye but it was better not to.

As she had thought, the receipt was in the outside pocket of the bag. At left luggage they immediately handed over the suitcase to her.

It would be unwise to leave it there. Sooner or later an unclaimed suitcase would attract attention, it would be opened in an attempt to identify its owner. Better to take it with her, along with the bag, and to get rid of both calmly, so that no one would ever find them.

She wondered if the chilly-mannered inattentive clerk would remember her. It was unlikely.

The first train that would take her home was about to leave, she was just in time to board it.

This story – featuring a woman killer, a rarity in the works of Patricia Highsmith – was never to be written.

Journalists have asked her so many times whether, having committed so many imaginary crimes, she has ever wanted to commit a real one.

What a stupid question! Of course she has. Like anyone else.

Pat Highsmith is first and foremost a writer. In other words her every vital function is linked to writing. And emerges from that which comes before writing, the deep black water of dreams, sleep and the unconscious.

Ever Present Subject.

Pat carries with her throughout her life the recurring idea of writing about that which cannot be spoken of. Not only her homosexuality but also her multiple love affairs and the need not to renounce any of them. Today, perhaps, it would be called her polyamory; in any case, her horror of monogamy as a lie and a betrayal of the truth – that is, eternal and ubiquitous desire.

Not to talk about women (except to kill them). Not to talk about herself. These are the rules for survival as an author.

But in her notebooks there is the regermination of the seed of a *Novel in the First Person*, which in the early Sixties develops into a leggy plant, incapable of growing to maturity. Her protagonist is a married woman who has a relationship with another woman, and an on-going affair with a younger one. The narrative is in the form of a long letter in which the woman relates her past (an unconventional mother whom she loved and who died prematurely, a great love affair with another woman, to which family and social pressures put an end) and explains her reasons for choosing not to be monogamous.

In the life of every writer there are seeds that do not come to fruition, plants that wither before growing or are killed off by the cold season. Novels that are never written, or only partly, that we will never read.

But the life of every writer is a long struggle, almost a battle, to get the most unlikely seeds to germinate. A battle, often lost, to extend the boundaries of the sayable.

It is during the Seventies that Western women change the world, or to put it more modestly the world of women changes, and the boundaries of the prohibited become more shifting, less hard-and-fast.

Pat Highsmith might not have noticed were it not for the girls she meets. The young women of the Seventies – Toinette, Andrea, Valérie and others – are different from those of preceding decades, and for a few years Andrea Stern is representative of them, a synthesis of them all, as Carol contained within herself all the beautiful, impulsive and courageous women of post-war New York.

The young women of the Seventies embody hope, redemption. They are not afraid, they are not ashamed, they are splendidly free and sure of themselves (at least that is how Pat sees them).

But are they really? How solid, how real, is their freedom?

How broad and powerful are their wings?

They are no longer wings of stone like those of Nike – but perhaps the wings of a moth, flying rapidly and crazily round a light (sex, desire), at risk of getting burnt? Or of being crushed in a brutal collision with the world.

New York, in the Eighties.

Elsie is twenty, she is beautiful, full of life and of hope. She is a cauldron of energy, and has the scent of a promise as yet undisclosed, everyone would like to be near her and drink in her heady presence. The girl comes from a small provincial town, she is unfamiliar with the reality of the metropolis, with its hidden dangers. She thinks she is free, she believes that everything that was forbidden in the narrow-minded small-town world she comes from is possible in a big city like New York: to be anti-comformist, a rebel, to love anyone she wants to, to go where she pleases, at any hour of the day or night...

Elsie is naive, she underestimates danger, she is unaware of her own fragility and mortality – like most young people.

Right from the outset, Pat knows that something is bound to happen to Elsie, she pictures her lying on the ground on a New York street, her blonde hair red with blood...

The novel is called *Found in the Street*, because it begins with a wallet stuffed with dollar bills that is lost and found on a New York street. It is an old fantasy of hers, of Pat's (but who has not dreamt at least once of such a thing?) that of finding something of value in the street and returning it to its rightful owner. A gesture of uncalculating honesty that has an obsessive element to it – but is not honesty perhaps obsessive? When Ralph returns the wallet to its owner, Jack, he feels like a hero – more than that, a saviour. As ever, when a person does someone a good turn, he wants something in exchange, he wants too much...

Ralph is a middle-aged night security guard who because he has so much contact with the more brutal and violent side of the city has developed a kind of atheistic fundamentalism, he sees evil and corruption everywhere. He is by nature a stalker, like so many of her characters, one of those men motivated by the strange desire to spy on and shadow the object of their love or their hatred. He is also a misanthropic doomsayer, like Pat, and his author has an amusing time describing his manias and obsessions, capturing a reflection of herself in the distorting mirror of the character created by her.

Jack, the owner of the wallet, who now despite himself has a connection with Ralph he did not want and does not like, is a young, educated and sophisticated urban professional, a gentle dreamer with a beautiful wife with whom he is in love and a lovely child.

Jack and Ralph are not so much opposites as two faces of the same man, there runs between them the ineliminable split, the divide without which we cannot live: between fragile private happiness and the violence of the external world, between idealism and prejudice, hope and hatred. Between the dreams of youth and the cynicism of old age.

And Elsie is another found treasure, like the wallet – but much more precious and vulnerable. A treasure that no one can keep or return. Or save.

Jack and Ralph both love Elsie, in divergent ways. Ralph wants to rescue her from her life of perdition, Jack wants to help her to be free.

But it is with Natalia, Jack's beautiful wife, that Elsie goes to bed, and she does so off-stage, as it were – eros remains hidden, what really matters, the burning nub of the story, is left out of the narrative, barely acknowledged, invisible – it is mentioned to us, but not shown…

A strange fantastical three-way pursuit takes place on the streets of New York: swift-footed Elsie, fired by the incandescent energy of youth, races towards her goal, dreaming Jack follows her, Ralph tries to stop her amid apocalyptic mutterings… until the day when Elsie is found dead in the street.

Who killed her?

Readers suspect Ralph, Jack is convinced of his guilt. The two confront each other, come to blows.

(Again two men fighting over the body of a dead woman, that little Miss Know-it-all, Violet, would say.)

But it was not Ralph.

This time the killer is a woman, Fran, a character who makes a few fleeting appearances before the crime, generating around her a sense of revulsion and alarm. Fran is butch, a masculine woman and not at all attractive, she has a terrible reputation and she is a drug-dealer. A lesbian, as Pat's mother, Mary, probably imagined lesbians: contemptible misfits, ugly, scruffy and dangerous. No one loves her (and how could they?) and this fills her with even more hatred and envy.

She is Pat's worst nightmare, her own image seen in the most distorting, most unacceptable of mirrors.

Fran is another face of that same spectre that thirty-five years earlier terrorised Therese in *The Price of Salt*, a female spectre that appeared to her in the guise of an elderly colleague, a worn-out wreck, a symbol of the failure, poverty and loneliness to which women for whom a comforting heterosexuality is alien are doomed. And then there was the image of Carol, the radiant goddess who turns into a ferocious harpy.

Love affairs between women do not last, because inherent within them is the embryo of betrayal and desertion. The other face of this forbidden love is hatred, self-contempt and contempt of your partner. This is what the world with obsessive repetition keeps telling the young Pat, who blocks her ears, but how can she not hear?

Years have gone by, the world has changed. Is it now possible to live your sexual life freely, as Elsie does, without fear of the consequences of transgressing? Is it possible to defy convention and not pay the price?

Can you be true to yourself and follow without a care wherever desire leads, fly without crashing into any obstacle?

Live in the light without being at the mercy of the shadows?

Elsie's trajectory provides an unequivocal answer: no.

Simply claiming the right to be yourself, without taking account of the world's hostility, is naive and dangerous. A politically misguided and immature move.

After so many years' struggle the spectres still triumph.

At twenty-five, twenty-seven years of age, Pat writes down in those black notebooks her tormented reflections on the Ever Present Subject. Phrases that are like crossed swords: the homosexual, she writes, will always be weak, no matter how strong, because doomed to hide their most intimate feelings. And a little further on: the homosexual is superior to the ordinary man because the conditions of his existence compel him to be in continuous creative tension, and to live in the white heat in which artists – or outlaws – are forged.

Where is the truth? In which of the two antagonists looking each other in the face, each denying the other?

Who is Andrea? Is she the much loved Elsie or the despicable Fran? Or both?

Love, love that makes you forget everything, that effaces reality, that ravishes the mind with an enchanting dream until nothing else counts but the presence of the beloved, or the thought of her, which ennobles everything and makes it resplendent... love that effaces time. Love with its sleepless nights, as in Moscow, when no one ever goes to bed, and Prince Myshkin goes visiting everyone in the small hours, and it is still almost light because it is summer, and they have those long conversations seated on benches in the garden. Love that creates divine idiots. Love that creates artists.

It is this that Elsie provokes in everyone who meets her, this is her power. She rekindles youth in those around her, she ignites dreams in minds clouded by reality… Elsie is one of those only half-understood dreams from which Pat awakes in a daze, torn between overwhelming nostalgia, desire, fear and an anguished, forbidding question that forces her to revisit her old and never forgotten sense of guilt.

"But do you treat women well?" wonderful easy-going Liz asks her one night. Liz questions her with a sad, solemn look, and Pat wakes up with a start, finding herself in the dock. No, she does not treat them well. She is constantly killing them off.

Even the golden girls, the dream girls like Elsie.

She begins to suspect there is something wrong with her dreams. Or with the dreamer.

And what if it were time, at the age of seventy, to make her peace with reality?

To lay down arms, as with the swords on her wall: after the death of her mother they are no longer crossed in combat, but aligned in parallel, in non-aggression.

In December 1994, at the age of seventy-three, and a couple of months before she died, the writer Patricia Highsmith declares in an interview with the Swiss magazine *Du*:

"I thought that men were more active, better at defending themselves physically. I also used to think that women were not motivated enough. Today I see things differently. Yes, today woman behave in a very different way compared with the days when I was at college. When I was young, most women wanted to get married, and when you get married, my generation thought, you must obey your husband and forget about having a job, it would have been too difficult. Today it is different, and that is certainly a good thing."

In Zurich one day, a couple of years earlier, a gay friend and his partner take Pat out to lunch at a restaurant on the river. The place is all dark wood, an old chalet with low ceilings, and the atmosphere is informal and welcoming. Pat is cheerful and enjoying herself, with gay men you can tell dirty jokes that would scandalise the ladies. On a table there are some books and magazines. Pat is intrigued by an issue with a semi-naked man on the cover, she flicks through it. She notes with interest and curiosity the photos of muscular males dressed only in certain leather accessories.

"Are there publications like this for women?" she asks.

"I don't know, I don't think so," replies her friend.

His partner says yes, there probably are a few magazines, if Pat wants he will get hold of some for her.

"Oh, don't bother," says Pat. She is not really interested in seeing nude women with whips and gags. Apart from making jokes, she is puritanical when it comes to sex and women.

"Oh look!" she exclaims. "There is something about this place in it! This very place!"

The two explain that it is a gay guide to Europe, gay discotheques and dark rooms, but also bars and restaurants. A capital G beside the name of a place indicates that it is exclusively gay, a lower case g means the clientele is mixed, gay and non-gay.

This is a small epiphany for Pat, who had in mind a novel

in which a young gay man is assassinated and the police suspect his friends; now she sees the scenario change before her. Places like this exist, where two young gay men and an old witch like her can drink beer and eat *würstel* and potato salad and feel at home among cordial, friendly people, without having to hide or lower their voices. And there are guides to such places – which are to be found everywhere, in all major European cities.

The world has truly changed. It is time for dreams to change too.

At the heart of the story there is a girl, Luisa, who resembles the Therese of long ago who was in love with Carol, but she is less naive because she has been treated much worse by reality. Abandoned by her mother, Therese was raised by nuns in a convent, whereas Luisa has run away from a mother who does not love her and a stepfather who abuses her, she has been homeless and has been living on the street. And then she is "adopted" by a dress designer in her fifties who keeps her prisoner, like a princess locked in a castle and doomed to languish without love.

The dress designer Renate is a perfect harridan, with a club foot, a tyrannical nature and a pathological hatred of homosexuals. She is the last harpy Miss Highsmith has the pleasure of killing off in her long career as a witch-hunter. Renate will remove herself from the scene – not without a little help from Luisa and her friends – by falling down the stairs, as happens to women who prepare their own demise (see Edith), having for too long cultivated an obsession with death. And she will bequeath to her ward and victim everything she possesses: her house, money, business, social respectability. And the possibility of choosing whom to love, the handsome Teddie or the cheerful and lively Dorrie.

The principal architect of Luisa's liberation is Rickie, the male protagonist. Rickie is a middle-aged gay man who works as a commercial artist (like Pat's mother, Mary) and resembles his creator Miss Highsmith: he is an artistic craftsman and a dreamer, a mild-mannered individual unable to assert himself with others but with a capacity for immediately making friends, he likes to joke and drink, he carries within him the sadness of lost youth and a need for idealised love. But he does not have Pat's temper, her idiosyncracies, her moods; he is good-natured and easy-going. And in the end he gracefully comes to terms with reality, accepting a relationship with a policeman in his thirties, not too handsome, not too young and, what is more, married – instead of the twenty-year-old he is in love with, with no hope of his love ever being reciprocated.

The title, *Small g – a summer idyll*, is true to its contents; it is a story that might almost be described as pastel-tinted (were it not that it begins with a brutal murder committed in the course of a robbery and ends with the dramatic death of a witch), because the characters are supportive of each other, they form alliances, they have fun together and help each other. They do not betray each other. They openly form a community and their relationships are ones that last – exactly what they could not do in the Forties and Fifties.

Many critics do not like the book. It is an incoherent book, they say, saccharine, without bite. They miss the old, cruel and obsessive Highsmith whose every line keeps us reading with bated breath while her heroes venture ever further down tortuous paths, following irresistible and dangerous impulses...

Her style is ever more careless, they say. That may be true. Pat is old, older than her years, and alcohol has for too long been exercising on her its effectiveness as a disinhibitor of the imagination. Alcohol, the magic telescope that shortens the distance between the real and the imaginary. But alcohol takes its toll. It burns the synapses. It flattens the writer's style. Style, which the old witch has never cared a damn about.

However, the novel sells well – and fast, because the death of the author is excellent publicity.

For many this is obviously a fantasy.

A politically incorrect fairy-tale – as fairy-tales generally are – in which the good guys, who are all queer, dispense their own justice and then dance happily on the harridan's grave. And there are no golden boys or golden girls any more, only young men and women of flesh and blood, fragile and resplendent, approached by their author with reverential awe, with adolescent shyness. She does not want to define them, she does not want to put them in a cage, because in the end they must be free to make the two most important choices in life: who they love and what work they do.

The harridan Renate tumbles down the stairs and breaks her neck because she is in a state of shock: she has seen two young women, Luisa and Dorrie, in bed together. If her mother, Mary, had seen her in bed with a woman, would she also have taken a tumble?

Chewing on a light cigarette (her concession to lung cancer), Pat sniggers with amusement, but with a touch of bitterness. Should she have tried it? Stopped hiding, stopped denying, confronted her mother with the irrefutable evidence?

But it was not the right time for it then. Now is the time.

Obviously the wicked witch who dies is also herself, Pat knows this. It is her mother emerging inside her, the hateful inevitable double. This is the abrasive, ill-mannered Pat, the misogynistic, anti-semitic, cantankerous and mean Pat, who spits blood, grumbles, and hates everyone. The Pat who keeps imprisoned in her shrivelled body the young woman of the past, like a princess locked up in the castle dungeons – occasionally a momentary glimpse of her can be caught in her eyes, and then at once she disappears again.

This is the last book, another would not be possible, seeing as the author's death is recorded in its pages.

For twenty years and more Pat has been writing and rewriting her will.

Although she started well in advance, death is catching up with her. Documents for so long left incomplete, decisions brooded on and not taken, are all finalised in furious haste at the last minute with the help of friends.

But her real testament is her last novel. That, she managed to finish, despite her declining strength. For months she lives on transfusions rather than food, her body is reduced to a fragile skeleton weighing nothing.

It is winter, the start of 1995. The last winter.

The last words of her last novel – the English edition will come out one month after her death, whereas the Americans have not yet accepted it (true to form, ha ha!) – refer to Rickie, her alter ego, and this is what they say: "The funny thing was, Rickie in a quiet way felt happy."

A man is dying. His dog follows him to the grave.
His cat, however, leaves him, so making death easier for him.
(Last *Keim* for a story)

What a mystery the body is. That cumbersome mass that contains life, that *is* life. What an effort some of those murders cost her, the first Ripley murder, when Tom kills Dickie in a boat, hitting him with an oar, repeatedly, using the edge of the oar and bringing it down on him like a hatchet, then jabbing it into his ribs like a bayonet, and Dickie's body, still alive during the brief eternity of the crime, resisting the slaughter with all his might.

The struggle between life and death, with gritted teeth, sweating, heart beating wildly, blood frozen with anguish.

Much better the rapid murders, almost pure emanations of thought: a pistol shot or the expert stab of a knife, and it is all over. Better still when the victim gets rid of himself or herself, as in the later books, by drowning or falling down the stairs.

In death as in love what counts is the idea.

But now that death for her is no longer an idea, now that it is right on top of her, has got inside her – her body, which has stopped putting up any resistance, has now become more substantial and in its opacity more present.

She has always taken a utilitarian view of the casing of flesh that contains her thoughts, as men usually do. The body is the container of desires, the dark mass in which the brain vicariously indulges its lusts and its anxieties. By turns a silent servant, an instrument, a burden, an obstacle, a faithful companion, boring and limited.

Now that the last lover is clasping her in the most intimate of embraces, Pat becomes aware of *being* a body, she realises that her thoughts follow the rhythm of her arduous breathing, that the life remaining to her is darkness, weight – yes, weight, her thin arms and legs lie on the mattress like stones – and this weakened skeletal body needing help is *her*. She is this.

She surrenders herself. She has no other choice. She accepts it.

She thinks of her mother. The archetypal witch, the prima donna she has loved and hated. She thinks of her mother's mindless death, of the years that she outlived herself, a blinded body bereft of thought, manipulated by strangers. Luckily, the same fate will not befall her daughter.

She thinks of her tidy monastic home. Of the cat Charlotte, independent and feral, not affectionate like poor Sammy, and so much the better. Vivien, her American friend, will take care of Charlotte, the cat will be fine in her little house with a garden, she will soon adapt.

She does not think about the cupboard full of papers, because a merciful pain throughout her body but in her legs especially prevents her from doing so. Whatever becomes of the black notebooks, the letters, the sheets of paper, the photographs and the countless mementoes of her life , they no longer belong to her, what is much more hers now is the pain in her legs that makes her moan quietly, like a wounded beast.

The nurse asks if she can do anything for her before she goes. Her shift is about to end.

"Yes," says Pat. "You could massage my legs. They hurt."

The girl sits down beside the bed and lifts the bedclothes, running her cool fingers across the patient's dry and fragile skin.

There is almost nothing left on these delicate bones, thinks the girl, who is accustomed to the spectacle of death but nevertheless is surprised by the feel of these shrunken filament-thin muscles.

The patient's head falls back on the pillow. She closes her eyes.

How many years without being caressed?

This is pleasure, this surrender to caressing hands, being just a body, sinking into a dark tranquillity. And in turn absorbing the girl's youthfulness, her warmth, her unknown life. Losing herself.

How often has she longed to die, in such moments?

And to think that it is so simple. A hospital bed, a dying woman, a nurse.

Death is simple, like a well-written page. It comes naturally, at the right moment, it does not need endless rewriting.

Friends telephone, asking for news of her. She replies or has someone else reply that she is better, it is nothing, tomorrow she will be having some tests done and they will be sending her home.

Towards evening Vivien calls, and offers to come and spend the night with her.

In a firm voice she says she doesn't want anyone, there is

no need. Everything is fine. Tomorrow.

When they asked her about dates for the presentation of her book, which will be coming out in a few weeks' time, she did not want to fix anything. She has always been reluctant to make commitments she could not be sure of keeping.

But to friends, she says: "Tomorrow."

Tomorrow is a word the living always believe.

At six thirty the following day the nurse comes in, pushing her trolley, just as she did the previous morning.

The patient is lying on her back, asleep. The thin face on the pillow is grey, one hand, large and as dry as a leaf, lies on the bedcover.

The girl looks at her. She holds her breath, approaches, touches her forehead.

It is still warm. It must have happened only a few minutes ago.

She thought she was asleep because her eyes are closed.

The girl does not wonder whether the patient in those last moments thought of Carol of long ago, or of Andrea, or of easy-going Liz – or of her, Maria, who was the last to caress her. She cannot wonder about this because she knows nothing of the life that has just ended, but she does know – she is a nurse – that the old lady died a peaceful death, in her sleep, perhaps even dreaming.

*Friends are life's most precious gifts. And the most
delightful thing is to break down barriers – of which
I possess a somewhat higher quantity than normal.*

Interview with Vivien D, 2008

Yes, she could be unpleasant. Say terrible things about anybody, whatever category of person they were. It was her way
of letting off steam. Sometimes when she had been drinking
she could be very obnoxious. But on the whole they were
superficial outbursts, and I paid no attention to them. Pat was
like that, a pressure cooker.

A loner, anti-social? That is an allegation to be taken
with a pinch of salt. She was not a socialite. She hated public
events, parties – they say that when she was young she went
to them often, I find that hard to believe, maybe she went in
order to drink. She preferred to be with one person at a time,
she liked company for short spells. But here she immediately
made friends, and she saw them regularly.

Even in her friendships she was unpredictable: I never
knew who she might take an interest in. Lots of people asked
to be introduced to her but I didn't know whether she would
like that person or whether she would take against them. And
those who knew her sometimes distanced themselves from her
because she wasn't *nice* – she was not what you would call a
respectable person.

She was interesting, fascinating, amusing – but not respectable.

She was strange. Once, in a shop, someone stopped her and said to her: "Miss Highsmith, I adore your books!" She was appalled and leapt backwards as if she had been assaulted.

She didn't like to be touched, kissed on the cheek. She had a strong sense of physical boundaries.

Social contact of the kind that we take for granted was difficult for her, she endured it, she felt out of her element, it was painful to her. She was hypersensitive, she hated crowds, music that was too loud.

Obviously a lot of people didn't like her.

Her life centred on work. Once someone, a young man, wrote to her something along the lines of: Do you think I could become a writer? And she said: But how can you ask such a question? If you can imagine not writing, then you are not a writer.

I think she only found peace in writing.

We never talked about her homosexuality. I didn't even know about it until – at a certain point, during the years when she was already living in Ticino, it became socially acceptable to be lesbian, and so you could mention it... but I didn't know anything about that lover of hers, Andrea, I only found out one evening, maybe two weeks before her death, when she told me she wanted to destroy certain documents. They were in a brown file. She asked me to carry it into the kitchen, because she didn't have the strength any more to carry even that light weight. She was very weak. We threw the file into the trash.

She was not romantic, no. She did not burn it, she threw it into the trash. The result is the same in the end.

I didn't particularly like her books. I've no interest in murder. But I do like her stories, they're amusing, refreshing. *Little Tales of Misogyny*, for example: she takes the essence of something, and expands it, exaggerates it: it's very amusing.

She didn't have a television but she would listen to the radio every evening, and she read the newspapers. We talked about politics, books, films. We went to the cinema.

I had two small children and I was working but we used to see each other regularly. She gave me her things to read when they were finished but I'm not a critic, I didn't make critical comments. My role in her life was – one of kindness, calmness, support perhaps.

What interested me was her vision of life: she saw things, she saw them differently, in an unusual way, and as a result you, too, saw more clearly. After talking to her it was more difficult to take refuge in platitudes, the way people usually do.

Talking to her was like cleaning your glasses. Afterward you saw more clearly.

Ticino is a small place, claustrophobic, you have to be careful what you say because everybody knows each other: but with her you could talk in the certainty that she wouldn't go round repeating what you had said.

She was kind, in her own way. Yes, Pat was kind. A gentle person.

She wasn't interested in my family life. She would ask: "How's the family?" And I would say: "Fine." And that was the end of it. And I was happy with that. But I liked going to visit her, her house was for me an oasis of calm. She knew how to listen. She knew how to laugh. It was lovely, sitting there chatting to her about what was going on in the world, drinking my tea while she drank her whisky.

Towards the end, she was just skin and bone but she managed to remain independent, in her own home, until a few days before she died. She died with grace, without fear, strangely she wasn't even depressed.

All she said was, it was difficult for her to confront the unknown.

I enjoyed her company. Even now, after all these years, I miss her.

Author's Note

Biographies are like maps of cities: they show the main streets and the crossroads, they name the squares and the alleyways. They can be very precise and accurate and extremely useful. But they do not usually tell you why you should go to that particular city, or in search of what, and where you might perhaps find what you go looking for.

These things, I believe, only stories will tell you. And stories are, necessarily, fiction – that is to say, narrative, myth, imagination, perspective… they are subjective, not objective. If they were objective they would not be stories, and they would not tell of questions, passions, mysteries, nothing of what makes a good story.

That is why this book is not a biography of Patricia Highsmith, although it contains many elements drawn from her documented life, and on the whole it remains faithful to those documents. But there are also invented things, and obviously interpretation and perspective are paramount. Some names are real, others not. Dates reflect actual chronology quite faithfully. The diary extracts and all those parts in which my character "Pat Highsmith" expresses herself in the first person are plausible. The epigraphs at the head of each chapter are almost all verbatim quotations.

I have read all the novels and stories by and about

Highsmith, two weighty official biographies, and some unofficial ones, all the critical commentaries I could find, a plethora of articles and news items. I have consulted her work notebooks and personal diaries held by the Schweizerische Literaturarchiv in Bern.

Then I tried to forget the homework I had done so diligently, I closed my eyes and I reinvented "my" Patricia Highsmith.

Acknowledgements

As ever my thanks go to my agent Rita Vivian for her support, her equanimity and her capability. Thank you, Rita.

And thanks to Marilena Rossi for her warm encouragement and friendship, and to Alessandra Maffiolini, who has edited the pages of this book with enthusiasm, care and a light hand.

Dedalus Celebrating Women's Literature
2018–2028

In 2018 Dedalus began celebrating the centenary of women getting the vote in the UK with a programme of women's fiction. In 1918, Parliament passed an act granting the vote to women over the age of 30 who were householders, the wives of householders, occupiers of property with an annual rent of £5 or graduates of British universities. About 8.4 million women gained the vote. It was a big step forward but it was not until the Equal Franchise Act of 1928 that women over 21 were able to vote and women finally achieved the same voting rights as men. This act increased the number of women eligible to vote to 15 million. Dedalus' aim is to publish 6 titles each year, most of which will be translations from other European languages, for the next 10 years as we commemorate this important milestone.

Titles published so far:

The Prepper Room by Karen Duve
Take Six: Six Portuguese Women Writers edited by Margaret Jull Costa
Slav Sisters: The Dedalus Book of Russian Women's Literature edited by Natasha Perova
Baltic Belles: The Dedalus Book of Estonian Women's Literature edited by Elle-Mari Talivee
The Madwoman of Serrano by Dina Salústio
Cleopatra goes to Prison by Claudia Durastanti
The Price of Dreams by Margherita Giacobino